Dear, Brother,

STEVEN DAVIS

Dedication

To the Brothers – Thomas, John, and Joseph

To Zoe and Owen, who provided illustrations for this book to help explain the story of their great-great-great grandfather, Joseph McGonagle.

To be at 'Home, Sweet Home' once more,
　　To gather with those most dear.
To bear the 'Battle Cry of Freedom',
　　To ensure nothing more to fear.

　　　　-Steven Davis

To the Reader:

The letters and memorabilia used in this book have been stored in several old cigar boxes and handed down through several generations in my wife's family. These items are over 170 years old. It is a family story. It is America's story. Throughout the book are letters, photographs, documents, and family memorabilia used to tell a story about three brothers, Thomas, John, and Joseph McGonagle, Union soldiers from Ohio engaged in the Civil War.

There are drawings made by my grandchildren, who are direct relatives of Joseph McGonagle. Sheet music, poems, and illustrations from the Civil War era are woven into the story. Each is identified with a number that corresponds to a guide, named 'Chapter Notes', in the back of the book, to provide more detailed information and documentation.

The McGonagle brothers are gathered around a campfire on a cold, windy night in December of 1862. It is the eve of the Battle of Stones River, near Murfreesboro, Tennessee. Join them as they sing 'Home, Sweet Home' and 'Battle Cry of Freedom'. Hear them reminisce about piano music their sister Nancy played. Learn their thoughts about the Confederacy. Listen as they discuss, laugh, and argue, as only brothers are apt to do, about family, Scottish ancestry, and American history. Recall family letters with them, discover their family heritage, and share long-held family lore and secrets.

There is a guide at the back of the book, named 'Civil War Era Slang' that explains slang words and expressions used during the Civil War. I hope you enjoy Dear Brother as much as long sweetening on a sheet iron cracker.

HOME SWEET HOME

SONG. COMPOSED BY H.R.BISHOP. 3½.

INSTRUMENTAL ARRANGEMENTS.

WESTERN, OR EASY TRANSCRIPTION.

RIMBAULT, EASY.

LAST, BRILLIANT VARIATIONS.

Philadelphia F.A.NORTH&Co. 1308 Chestnut St.

Washington D.C. W.G. Metzerott & Co. San Francisco M. Gray. Detroit J.P. Weiss

Chapter 1

Thomas, John, and Joseph listened as one of the regimental bands for the Union Army of the Cumberland stretched out the last chord into the frigid night. The song was a familiar Scottish song for the three McGonagle brothers. "Home Sweet Home". The brothers listened as the last note from a piccolo played. The sound, played by the 5th Pennsylvania Infantry, Company A, faded into the distant Tennessee valley.

"Home! Home!
There's no place like home.
There's no place like home!"

The brothers studied each other's eyes. Faint smiles crept across their tired, weathered faces. Their silhouettes flickered against the large rocks as the campfire flames would rise and fall on the whims of the raw December wind. Thomas McGonagle, the oldest of the brothers, poked the embers of the fire to keep it going, each jab sending up sparks of red ash into the air. John broke a few branches on his knee and placed the cedar limbs on the fire. Joseph, the youngest brother, tugged at the quilt he had draped around his shoulders to chase away the Tennessee winter. The quilt helped to chase away the cold that eased deep into his bones.

"Hearing our Union regimental bands play 'Home Sweet Home' makes me feel fit as a fiddle," Joseph said.

"Aye, laddie. Nothing like thoughts of home to make you smile," Thomas said.

"Isn't 'Home Sweet Home' a Scottish melody?" Joseph asked.

"Of course. Anyway, our family claims it's Scottish. The words are actually from "The Maid of Milan", an opera written by an American poet - John Payne. The music was composed by Henry Bishop from England. Our mother always said Henry Bishop got his inspiration to write such a beautiful song after a trip to Edinburgh," John said.

"That doesn't surprise me. I can imagine our mother saying something like that," Joseph said.

"Aye, laddie. 'Scotland is my country, the land that begat me. These windy spaces are surely my own. And those who here toil, in the sweat of their faces, are flesh of my flesh and bone of my bone'," Thomas said.

"That's a verse from a poem titled 'Scotland' if I'm not mistaken," John said.

"Aye. Written by Sir Alexander Gray," Thomas said.

"You know what does surprise me though?" Joseph asked John.

"What?"

"Whenever Thomas talks like that," Joseph kidded.

Thomas smiled at his two brothers. The wind carried the last notes of the 5th Pennsylvania into the surrounding trees. Joseph suddenly stood up and looked out into the darkness. He was surprised to hear the 'Home Sweet Home' melody begin to play again. He was confused. The song was being played on the other side of the river. Joseph turned to ask his brothers what was happening. Then he realized the music wasn't being played by a Union band now. It was the same song being played by a Confederate band that had camped on the other side of the river.

As soon as the Pennsylvania musicians stopped playing, the Confederate 28th Alabama regimental band started to play 'Home Sweet Home'.

"Jumping Jehoshaphat!"

"That surprises me too Joseph. I've never heard of a Confederate band playing the same song in answer to a Union band," Thomas said.

"Guess those johnny rebs miss being home as much as we do," John said.

The McGonagle brothers listened and were surprised again when a Union band began to play 'Home Sweet Home' just as the music from the Alabama Confederate band faded. The sentimental song of "Home

Sweet Home" continued to play alternately from the Union camp and the Confederate camp, back and forth. The enemies were separated by only a few hundred yards. It was a river, Stones River, that separated the Union Army from the Confederate Army.

Most regiments, whether they wore the blue uniforms of the North or the gray uniforms of the South had their own regimental bands. Each Army enjoyed playing 'Home Sweet Home'. Neither side wanted to stop playing. The North had favorite songs, like 'Hail Columbia'. The South had favorites also, like 'Dixie' or 'Maryland, My Maryland'. 'Home Sweet Home', however, was a song that belonged to both sides. The words and the music to the song were meaningful whether you wore blue or gray. A Union Army band tried to perform the rendition better than the Confederate band that played next. Another Confederate band would then try to play their version better than the Federal band.

Thomas winked at Joseph. The brothers exchanged smiles as they listened, each having thoughts of the Ohio home and farm they had left a few months ago. The sounds of the night mixed with the different musical instruments. A trumpet, drum, flute, guitar, or piccolo ebbed and flowed with the wind, trees, and the river. The sounds swelled and waved like wheat that rippled in a prairie wind. It was common for a Union band or a Confederate band to play music in the evening for their soldiers. Tonight, however, was unusual. The music became a contest between the Union and Confederate regimental bands. 'Home Sweet Home' meant as much to a Yankee Blue from Ohio as it did to a Johnny Reb from Georgia.

Both the Union and Confederate Armies prepared for a potential battle that might take place sometime the following day. They set up tents, scouted the area for any food they could forage, and scraped the mud off their boots. They attempted to dry out some clothes, which was difficult when it continued to rain into the evening.

Before the music contest of playing 'Home Sweet Home' began, the Union regimental bands initially had played some of their patriotic music. The Army of the Cumberland had just marched sixteen miles from Murfreesboro through the cold and rain of a Tennessee winter. And mud. Deep mud. The Army stopped just short of crossing over

Stones River. As they settled in for the night, the Union band of the 22nd Indiana played a favorite song of the North – 'Yankee Doodle'. As the 22nd Indiana began to play 'Yankee Doodle' a second time, the 79th Illinois and 15th Wisconsin bands joined in. The song was repeated several more times. A final rousing version played as other regimental bands from Ohio, Minnesota, and Michigan joined in.

Thomas McGonagle liked 'Yankee Doodle'. He didn't know all the words. He quietly sang the first verse.

"Yankee Doodle went to town, riding on a pony," Thomas began. Then he kind of stumbled around the words until the song ended with the last verse. He knew the last line and sang it loudly at the end of each verse. As the song played, he sang each last line even louder.

"Mind the music and the step and with the girls be handy," Thomas sang.

"Jumping Jehoshaphat! I've never heard you sing so loud. Watch out or you'll be recruited to head up the choir of the entire Army of the Cumberland," John kidded.

1.3

"That was special, especially when all of the regimental bands joined in. I wonder how those rebs across the river liked hearing 'Yankee Doodle'?" Joseph asked.

"I doubt any of them were singing any louder than Thomas," John said.

"That reminds me. I've been thinking about asking you something," Joseph said.

"Oh, that's not surprising," Thomas said.

"Not surprising at all," John said.

"Why is our Army called the Army of the Cumberland? Isn't there a Cumberland somewhere in Scotland? And Pennsylvania? Does it have something to do with the Cumberland Gap? Or Cumberland, Ohio?" Joseph asked.

"Whoa there, laddie. You're getting your Cumberland's all mixed up," John said.

"Aye. You never fail to amaze me with your questions Joseph," Thomas said.

"Well, there's a Cumberland in Scotland, Pennsylvania, and Ohio and we are all a part of the Army of the Cumberland, smack dap in the middle of Tennessee. All those Cumberland's makes me wish for some bromine and seltzer right now for the headache it gives me. Why wouldn't I be confused?" Joseph asked.

BROMO-SELTZER CURES ALL HEADACHES. TRIAL SIZE, 10 CTS.
1.4

"Okay. We'll help untangle all the Cumberland's for you Joseph. When the North first formed an Army at the start of the war, one of the armies was called the Army of The Ohio, with soldiers from Ohio, Illinois, and Indiana. After several consolidations with other states, the name changed to the Army of the Cumberland, which combined many armies from the different states," Thomas explained.

"Now the Cumberland that's talked about in Scotland is named after a historic county in Northwest England. The Scottish counties of Dumfriesshire and Roxburghshire form the northern boundary of England. When emigrants from Scotland settled in Pennsylvania, they named their new-found land New Cumberland. This was a tribute to the old country," John said.

"You can thank Daniel Boone for discovering the Cumberland Gap. The trail is a twenty-mile route through the Appalachian Mountains where Kentucky, Virginia, and Tennessee intersect. It's the only way to travel west for hundreds of miles around there," Thomas said.

"Didn't you travel through the Cumberland Gap once?" John asked Thomas.

"Aye, laddie. It's a beautiful part of the country. Beautiful trees, towering hills. A lot of travelers have come through that pass. Most

1.5

even escaped the Indians. It's the ideal spot for a massacre, you know. There is just no getting around having to go through the Cumberland Gap. Abraham Lincoln's parents and grandparents traveled through the Gap," Thomas said. Joseph straightened his back and thought about questioning Thomas to see if the remark about Abraham Lincoln was true. He could tell though that Thomas wasn't just making that up. He decided to stay quiet for a moment.

Thomas and John paused to let Joseph think about the different Cumberland's they had discussed. John pointed to the quilt that Joseph had around his shoulders.

"Think of all the Cumberland names just like blocks on this quilt. They're separate but they all fit together," John said.

"You're thinking about New Cumberland, Ohio because we have an uncle that lived there. You know, Uncle McCaslin," Thomas said.

"Aye, laddie. With a name like McCaslin McGonagle, you couldn't be anymore Scottish if you tried," John said.

"I remember now. We met him a few times. I have this memory of a summer day long ago when father read us a letter he received from his brother, McCaslin, who lived in New Cumberland, Ohio," Joseph said.

"That's right. The letter began 'Dear Brother'," John said.

New Cumberland August 15th 1851

Dear Brother Inasmuch as I have an oppor
tunity of sending you a line by hand. I have
Concluded (notwithstanding I have written some three
letters heretofor all of which remain unanswered) to de
vote a few moments in again addressing a few lines to
you. I am happy to say to you that we are all
tolerably well at present. Some of our children of
whom we have 5 – 4 Boys & 1 girl) have been quite
ill. for some time past but are now about well.
I am still working at my trade. doing all I can to
make a decent livelihood which indeed is about as
much as I can do as as there are two other shops in
this place besides mine. I have had no correspon=
dence since last spring with any of our brethren
but have lately heard from Alexander by a man here
who saw him working on the road he sent me word
that they were well. I also occasionally hear from
Thomas & Joseph. at last accounts they were well. I rec'd
a letter from Cousin Ellen McGonagle youngest daugh
ter of Unkle John. who informs me of the health of
our friends in Clarion County. We of this part
of the Country have Just about got done harvest a
most abundant Crop of Wheat & Oats and the
Corn looks also remarkably Promising at present
As Mr West is about ready to Start I will have
to close my hasty scroll by again renewing my
request for you to drop me a few lines
        Yours Affectionately &
            in much haste
R. McGonagle   M. McGonagle

New Cumberland   August 15th   1851

Dear Brother, In as much as I have an opportunity of sending
you a line by hand, I have concluded, not withstanding, I have
written some three letters, here to for all of which remain unanswered, to devote a few moments in again addressing that we are all
tolerably well at present. Some of our children of whom we have 5 -
4 boys & 1 girl - have been quite ill for some time past but are now
about well. I am still working at my trade, doing all I can to make
a decent livelihood, which indeed is about as much as I can do as
there are two other shops in this place besides mine. I have had no
correspondence last spring with any of our brethren but have lately
heard from Alexander by a man here who saw him working on
the road. He sent me word that they were well. I also occasionally
hear from Thomas & Joseph, at last accounts they were well. I rec.
a letter from cousin Ellen McGonagle, youngest daughter of Uncle John, who informed me of the health of our friends in Clarion
County. We of this part of this country have just about got done
harvest, a most abundant crop of wheat & oats and the corn looks
also reasonably promising at present. As our rest is about ready
to start, I will have to close my hasty scroll by again renewing my
request for you to drop me a few lines.

R. McGonagle   Yours affectionally &
                                      in much haste,
                                      M. McGonagle

"That letter is what got you thinking about New Cumberland little brother. The letter was sent to our father, Robert McGonagle. It mentions several of our father's brothers. There were seven brothers all together. Our father, Robert was the oldest. Then Alexander, Thomas, John, James, and Joseph. The youngest brother was McCaslin. Uncle McCaslin was a cabinet maker and had a shop in his town. The letter reminds me that it's time for me to share and pass on some family stories to you. For one thing, our father named us after the names of his brothers, right in order: Thomas, John, and Joseph. And Joseph, you got your middle name, Alexander from another brother. When the bands have stopped playing 'Yankee Doodle', you're going to get a family history lesson, Joseph," Thomas said.

Thomas stood up from the large rock he was sitting on and stretched. He could tell that things were wrapping up and this was the last time that a Union band would play 'Yankee Doodle' for tonight. He repeated the words to the last verse of the song.

"Mind the music and the steps and with the girls be handy."

The last note of "Yankee Doodle" from the Union regimental bands faded. Thomas cleared his throat. Just as he started to speak, the Confederate 19th South Carolina and the regimental band started to play "Dixie".

"Well, Beat the Dutch! Those darned Johnny Rebs are going to answer back with a song of their own. Our family discussion is going to have to wait until this battle of the bands is over," Thomas said.

The three brothers listened to the first few lines of the song.

> *"I wish I was in the land of cotton,*
> *Old times there are not forgotten;*
> *Look away! Look away! Look away! Dixie Land."*

Then they busied themselves with the campfire and were quiet as they made their spot a little more comfortable for the night ahead. They each gathered branches and were placing them on their fire as the Confederate band ended 'Dixie'.

> *"Away, away, away down south in Dixie,*
> *Away, away, away down south in Dixie."*

Not to be outdone by the bluecoats, the bands from the 38th Mississippi, 15th Texas, 22nd Kentucky, and 27th Arkansas joined the 19th South Carolina, as they played "Dixie" several times.

While 'Yankee Doodle" played, the McGonagle brothers participated in the song. Joseph sang some of the verses. Thomas sang loudly and enjoyed being a conductor, with wide sweeps of his arms. John held a branch that he tapped against his leg in rhythm to the song. Now that the Confederate bands played 'Dixie', the McGonagle brothers were not so attentive to the music. John gathered more branches for the campfire, Thomas rearranged and packed his haversack so it would be ready for whatever tomorrow would bring. Joseph used a nail to pry mud off his boots. The brothers listened as 'Dixie' played. They tolerated the rebel music but were uninterested and continued to busy themselves with other things.

For a Confederate band to counter with their own song was unusual. Particularly on a cold night when both the Northern Army and Southern Army gathered on opposite sides of a river, in anticipation of a battle the next day. The soldiers expected that the music for the night was finished.

The 22nd Indiana regimental band decided they couldn't allow "Dixie' to be the last song their fellow 'Billy Yanks' heard before they settled down for the night. 'Hail Columbia' was their selection. After the first few verses, several Federal bands joined in. As 'Hail Columbia' progressed, the song built up more and more to a crescendo. The regimental bands played a rousing rendition. It was a battle of the bands. The challenge was on.

"Hail Columbia, happy land! Hail, ye heroes, heaven-born band,
　Who fought and bled in freedom's cause.
Firm, united let us be, rallying round our liberty,
　As a band of brothers joined, Peace and safety we shall find."

The patriotic songs played by the North stirred such strong feelings that Joseph felt like he could march into battle at this very moment. Thomas, John, and the other soldiers of the Army of the Cumberland felt the same immense pride from the music and it motivated them to their very core. The soldiers in the gray uniforms were likewise stirred deep within their souls. The Confederate soldiers knew they would be replaying 'Dixie' and the 'Bonnie Blue Flag' in their heads as they fought hard to force the 'Yankee Doodles' from Tennessee.

The Confederate bands answered the band challenge. As "Hail Columbia" stopped, some of the Southern bands answered. Their selection was the dynamic Confederate song 'Bonnie Blue Flag'.'

"Jumping Jehoshaphat! Those rebs are going to play again. Have you ever heard of anything like this happening before, Thomas?" Joseph asked.

"If I had to guess, I would say that it's the opening of the ball," Thomas said.

"This is the start of the battle?"

"Well, kind of. It's a battle alright," Thomas said.

"Oh, you mean a music battle?" Joseph asked.

"Aye, laddie."

1.10

"We are a band of brothers and native to the soil
Fighting for our liberty with treasure, blood, and toil
And when our rights were threatened, the cry rose near and far
Hurrah for the Bonnie Blue Flag that bears a single star!"

1.11

"Hurrah! Hurrah!
For Southern rights, hurrah
Hurrah for the Bonnie Blue Flag
that bears a single star."

"Then here's to our Confederacy, strong we are and brave,
Like patriots of old we'll fight, our heritage to save;
And rather than submit to shame, to die we would prefer,
So cheer for the Bonnie Blue Flag that bears a single star."

"Hurrah! Hurrah!
For Southern rights, hurrah!
Hurrah for the Bonnie Blue Flag
that bears a single star."

As the final 'Hurrah' of the 'Bonnie Blue Flag' vibrated into the surrounding Tennessee valleys, a freezing mist was finding its way into the camps. The Union bands were quiet and didn't resume playing. A stillness hushed over the Armies camped by Stones River. There were no more Northern retorts of one of their rousing marches. The battle of the Union and Confederate bands appeared to be over, each side had enjoyed their band competition. The soldiers, on both sides of the river, all had thoughts of now settling in for the night, having some coffee, finding something to eat, organizing for the next day, and getting some sleep.

"You know, the blue flag with the white star was one of the first Confederate flag designs. You still see it but also you see a lot of the 'stars and bars flag' they use now," John said.

"What does that single white star on their blue flag mean?" Joseph asked.

"Well, supposedly the Confederacy has said the white star represents purity," John said.

"Beat the Dutch! I bet they mean white purity! That's enough to make me want to go to blue mass," Joseph said.

"The blue color on the flag is supposed to represent truth," John said.

"I don't like anything about that flag and I really don't like that they use the word bonnie and call it the Bonnie Blue Flag," Joseph said.

"I agree with you on that. I never could figure out why they had to use bonnie, a Scottish word, to describe their flag," Thomas said.

"A man by the name of McCarthy wrote the song and he was Irish. He could have used the Irish word for beautiful, which is alainn. Instead, he used the Scottish word for beautiful, which is bonnie," John said.

"The 'Alainn Blue Flag' just doesn't roll off the tongue like 'Bonnie Blue Flag'," Joseph said.

Thomas and John decided to not add anything else to their conversation about the Confederate flags. They knew Joseph would inevitably ask another question. Sure enough. Joseph started to ask another question, then stopped. It usually took something like an earthquake or a runaway team of Percherons to stop Joseph from asking questions. His mouth dropped open in astonishment. The unexplainable, remarkable music softly reverberated through the trees. Soldiers, no matter what they were doing, stopped to listen. The song stopped Joseph from asking his question.

This was an unusual, unplanned experience that had not taken place previously during the weary war. Joseph recognized the familiar music as soon as the 49th Ohio regimental band started to play 'Home Sweet Home'.

"Home Sweet Home"

"Mid pleasures and palaces though we may roam,
Be it ever so humble, there's no place like home.
A charm from the skies seems to hallow us there
Which seek thro' the world, is never met elsewhere.
Home! Home!
There's no place like home.
There's no place like home!"

"An exile from home splendor dazzles in vain
Oh, give me my lowly thatched cottage again
The birds singing gaily that came at my call
And gave me the peace of mind dearer than all.
Home! Home!
There's no place like home.
There's no place like home!"
1.12

'Home Sweet Home' was a Northern sentimental favorite. This was a mournful melody, unlike the rousing, cheering songs of 'Yankee Doodle' and 'Hail Columbia'. It was sad, gentle, tender. Many a toughened veteran felt a lump in his throat as the lonesome melody played. As the last note from the 49th Ohio sounded into the mist of the dark night, the 6th Kentucky Confederate band played again their wistful version of 'Home Sweet Home'. At the conclusion of their song, the 10th Indiana Union band played 'Home Sweet Home', followed by the 33rd Tennessee, then the 15th Wisconsin, then the 19th South Carolina. The music continued with only a single Union band or Confederate band playing the same song, back and forth, back and forth.

Stones River burbled over the rocks and at times seemed to join in the chorus of 'Home Sweet Home'. Thomas McGonagle felt the powerful emotion and melancholy of the song as it was played back and forth from Billy Yank to Johnny Reb. John crouched to rearrange branches in the campfire, the cedar logs crackled as they shifted. A hoot owl called. The wind swayed cedar tree branches as they creaked in protest. The bitter Tennessee wind came in different directions. The McGonagle brothers listened to different instruments as each regimental band played the melody. Army veterans slapped tears away as they cascaded down a tired face. The McGonagle brothers commented that 'Home Sweet Home' felt very close when a Union band played. Home felt far away when a Confederate band played. The song played by the Union 42nd Ohio faded as the Confederate 12th Virginia began their rendition of 'Home Sweet Home' from the other side of Stones River.

At times, the Union soldiers would sing along, their mournful voices matched in turn by the Confederate soldiers as their thoughts all focused on family – mother, father, a sister. Sometimes different regiments joined in to sing the words to 'Home Sweet Home'. Other times, just a single band played the long, slow melody. The verses triggered different memories of home. Each soldier, whether their uniform was blue or gray, felt impassioned as they thought of homes that were so far away. A home in Ohio or Arkansas, where they were loved, where they listened and enjoyed songs as a dear sister or a mother played the piano.

Before the McGonagle brothers joined the Army, they enjoyed sitting on the porch of their farmhouse as their sister Nancy played songs on the family piano. After a long day of work on the farm, each brother enjoyed listening to a variety of piano music. They yelled out favorites that they particularly wanted to hear. This frequently caused wrestling, when one brother felt cheated over the selected piano choices. Then, the concurrent scolding from their mother.

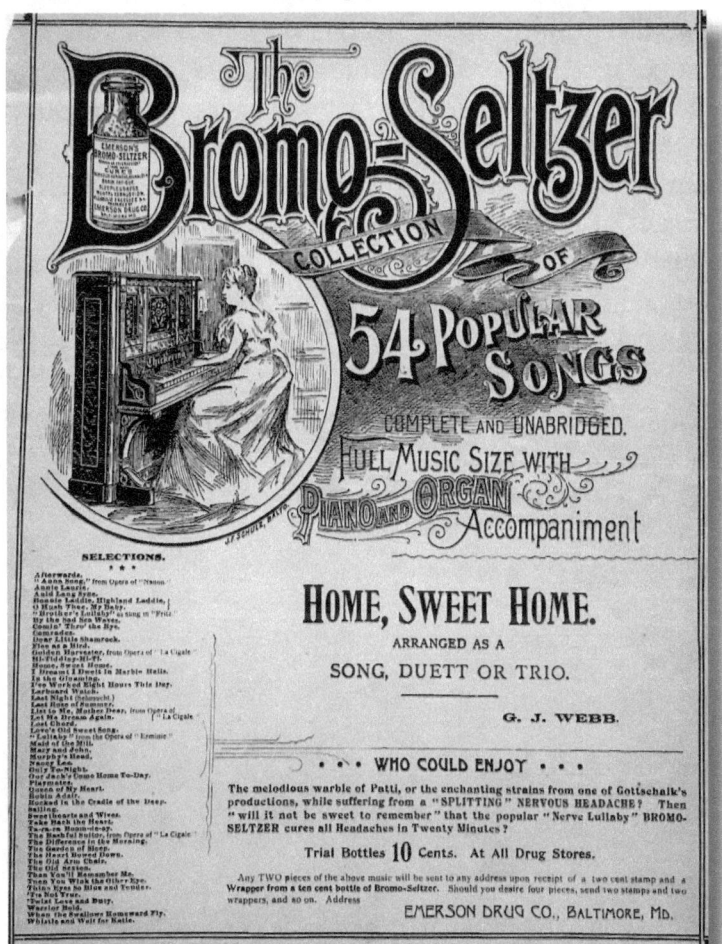

1.13

Thomas, John, and Joseph McGonagle each thought about their Ohio home and family as they listened to 'Home Sweet Home'. Before the war brought them to Tennessee the brothers listened to piano songs in the evening after a hard day of farm work. Their mother rocked in her favorite chair and hummed along with the songs. Their father built the rocking chair from the oak trees on their land. It had taken him most of one winter to finish it. The brothers watched their mother in the evening twilight as she concentrated on the border of a quilt.

The last notes of 'Home Sweet Home' faded into the night air from a trumpet of an Alabama Confederate regiment. An Indiana Union band began the song just as the Alabama trumpet's sounds lingered.

Every soldier, Union or Confederate, faced the same thought and the same dilemma. They didn't want to continue to brush away tears or feel the lump in their throat as they listened to the song over and over. However, they didn't want the song to stop being played either. The beautiful melodies being played on the frigid December night forced images of family and home to the forefront of their thoughts. A home that was far away, A 'Home Sweet Home' they realized they may never see again and, in some ways, made it difficult to listen to as it played back and forth. However, at the same time, they did not want the memories that 'Home Sweet Home' provided to stop either.

Some of those memories reminded them of what they were fighting for.

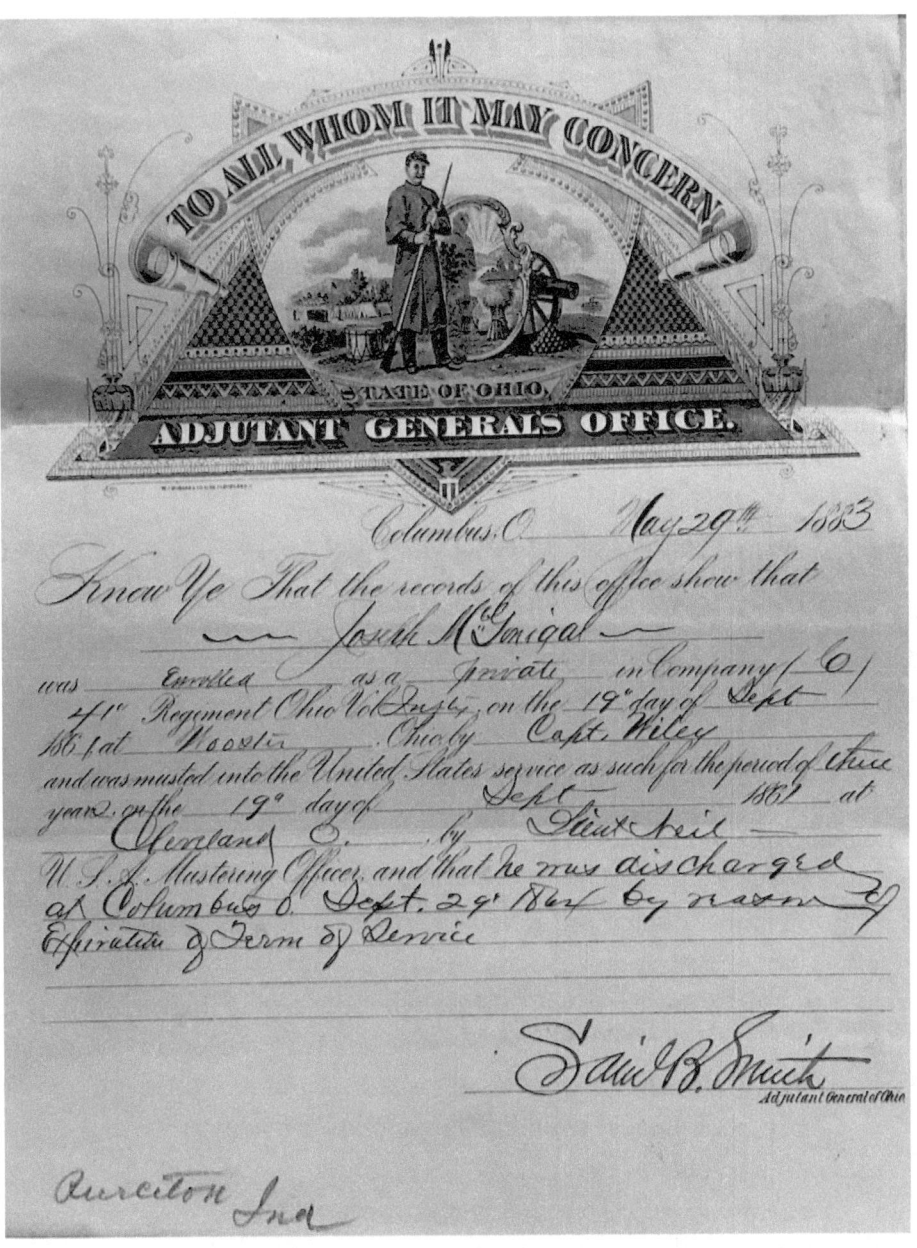

TO ALL WHOM IT MAY CONCERN

STATE OF OHIO,
ADJUTANT GENERALS OFFICE.

Columbus, O.   May 29th 1883

Know Ye That the records of this office show that
Josiah McGonigal
was Enrolled as a Private in Company (C)
41st Regiment Ohio Vol Infty on the 19th day of Sept
1861 at Wooster Ohio by Capt. Wiley
and was mustered into the United States service as such for the period of three
years on the 19th day of Sept 1861 at
Cleveland O. by Lieut Neil
U.S.A. Mustering Officer, and that he was discharged
at Columbus O. Sept. 29th 1864 by reason of
Expiration of Term of Service

Saml. B. Smith
Adjutant General of Ohio

Bureton Ind

Chapter 2

Thomas McGonagle poked the fire with a large branch and pointed the stick at his bothers like a conductor's baton. He started to sing the words to the song as the Indiana regimental band began to play again. He waved the baton as if he were conducting the New York Symphony and motioned to his brothers to join him. John rubbed his three-day growth of beard, started to sing, then gently elbowed Joseph to join.

"Home! Home! There's no place like home.
There's no place like home."

"Oh laddies, your Scottish ancestors would have been mighty proud to hear you sing like that," Thomas said as he continued to wave his baton.

"Yes, indeed Thomas. Nancy would have been amazed that all three of us were singing together. She always coaxed and coaxed us to come in from the porch and sing while she played the piano," John reminisced.

"I remember Nancy pretended to be mad when we wouldn't sing along," Joseph said.

"She even went three whole days without playing one time when you wouldn't sing along with us Thomas," Joseph added. He stood up and poked at the campfire.

"That wasn't me that wouldn't sing along," Thomas protested.

"That was John, as I recollect."

"Not by a jug full, Thomas. That was you. Don't go accusing me of such a dastardly deed of refusing to sing. Joseph and I both went in the house about the fourth- time Nancy threatened to stop playing but you teased her by not coming in the house," John said.

"And who made you the conductor anyway Thomas? Give me that

branch so I can add it to the other ones in this fire."

"Have you ever heard of a band contest like that taking place as both sides prepare for a battle?" Joseph asked.

"No, that was unique. It just happened without being planned," John said.

"By the way, I'm still sticking by our story that you were the one that wouldn't sing when Nancy wanted us to. John's got it right, dear brother," Joseph said to Thomas.

Joseph stood up stretched the quilt out with both arms, then sat back down on the large rock and wrapped the quilt tighter around his shoulders. He placed his hand up to his left ear and strained to hear if 'Home Sweet Home' started to play again. Joseph tilted his head in the opposite direction but heard no more songs being played. He believed the music contest had concluded. He could hear the wind more now as it whistled through the brush.

"I was just about to give you a turn to stay warm with this quilt, Thomas until you got your facts mixed up about who was singing or not," Joseph said as he tried hard to suppress a smile.

"Okay, okay. I'll acknowledge the corn. But I can think of a lot of other things the both of you did to tease Nancy," Thomas kidded.

"Well, since you have admitted that you were the one who refused to sing, you can have the quilt for a spell," Joseph said as he handed the quilt to Thomas.

"Thanks, Joseph," Thomas said.

Thomas stood up, then swung the quilt over his head and around his shoulders.

"But let's not forget I'm not the only one in this group that teased Nancy about her piano playing. I remember one summer day when one of you hid her sheet music in the barn," Thomas said.

Thomas slanted his head towards the ground as if this would help him remember.

"That was you, wasn't it Joseph?" Thomas said.

"Uh—," Joseph looked up at the dark sky.

Thomas and John looked at each other with knowing smiles, then watched as Joseph squirmed.

2.1

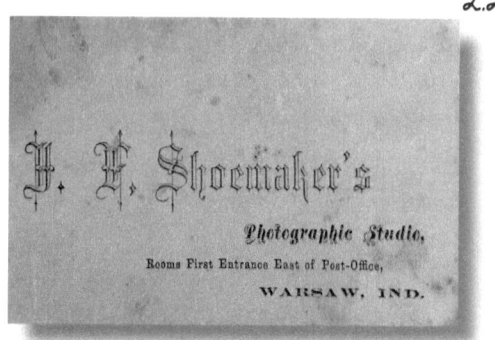

2.2

"Yeah, I guess I'll own up to that little trick," Joseph confessed.

"I can tell you, I never did that again. Nancy was so mad when she found that sheet music tucked under her horse blanket in the barn that she wouldn't talk to me for a week. The worse part was that she wouldn't play my favorite songs for a week either."

"I remember, laddie," John said slowly.

"She really made you toe the mark."

"Your favorites Joseph, like 'Beautiful Dreamer' and those Scottish ballads you like so much, like, 'Mary Bell' wasn't played on that piano for a while. You just had to dream about hearing them in your sleep, beautiful dreamer that you are," Thomas teased.

Joseph learned growing up that John and Thomas could tease him mercilessly, like teasing him that he enjoyed singing 'Beautiful Dreamer'. It wasn't the manliest song ever written but he liked it. The more they teased him, the more he protested. The more things they would say, the more he defended his actions and the deeper the hole he dug for himself. This invariably set him up for more teasing. It had taken him several years to finally do what his mother had advised him. She used to tell Joseph 'when life gives you lemons, make orange juice'. When Joseph first heard this advice, he dismissed it as a Quaker platitude that didn't apply to him at all. Over the years though, he realized what his mother meant. Just do the best with what you have and when things aren't going your way, just change directions. Joseph used this advice on many occasions, one being able to redirect teasing from his older brothers. Instead of setting himself up for another humbug, he stood up and walked over to the campfire. The verses of 'Beautiful Dreamer' silently played in his head.

2.3

"Beautiful dreamer, wake unto me, starlight,
    And dewdrops are awaiting thee."
"Sounds of the rude world, heard in the day,
    Led by the moonlight, have all passed away."

Joseph rubbed his hands over the campfire as a gust of wind caught his coat. He had enjoyed the regimental bands playing 'Home Sweet Home'. He even knew which band was playing, without even looking, because the sounds were so distinctive. The 42nd Ohio band had a tambourine. The 14th Pennsylvania had an Appalachian dulcimer. Joseph recognized the different instruments that each regimental band played. The 12th Illinois, one of the few Scottish regiments, had five bagpipes. Joseph shook his head in disbelief at this very strange moment in time. The wind cascaded the sounds of water over rocks. He looked at the darkness across Stones River. It was difficult to believe there were 20,000 Confederate troops just over there. He knew they were close because when they would play their Confederate music, he could judge how far away they were.

Joseph hadn't realized until tonight that Johnny Rebs claimed 'Home Sweet Home' as their song as much as the Union soldiers. Guess I'll keep that thought to myself or it will add to the list of things that Thomas and John could tell me that I don't know about. He did like talking to his brothers though. War is such an ugly part of life. Having older brothers to give me advice is a big advantage. At least most of the time. Joseph was thankful they guided him on the right path. He was anxious about the next few days. Would there be a battle? Or would one side choose to fight in another place, on another day? Uncertainty stirred within him.

"Ah, Joseph laddie," John said in his best Gaelic voice.

John stood beside Joseph at the campfire. They were both quiet. The campfire flickered with the wind, the embers glowed, then faded again. Joseph hadn't thought about his favorite Scottish ballad for a while until John mentioned it. Joseph liked 'Mary Bell' particularly well because he could always sing the verses in the most Scottish brogue that he could imitate. Joseph was aware of the irony that he enjoyed 'Mary Bell' so much. Thomas had explained the history behind the ballad to him several times. An Irishman fell in love with a Scottish lass. Their love was not to be because it violated the Statutes of Kilkenny. A marriage between a man of Norman blood and a woman of Gaelic ancestry was forbidden. Joseph reminded Thomas that statutes that existed a hundred years ago were not valid now. He pledged that he would marry anyone he wanted, whether she be Irish, Scottish, English, or Welsh.

2.4

"*Mary Bell, sweet Mary Bell, with dimpled cheeks, where fairies dwell.*

Indeed, we love thee. Oh! How well. Mary Bell, sweet Mary Bell." **2.5**

Joseph's favorite Irish ballad was 'Molly Bawn', which he also sang in his Scottish brogue, instead of his Irish brogue. Joseph was glad that John had mentioned it. Now he could go over the verses in his head and imagine a beautiful lassie by his side, instead of imaging what was on the other side of Stones River.

"*Oh, Molly Bawn, why leave me pining, all lonely waiting here for you,*

While the stars are brightly shining because they've nothing else to do." **2.6**

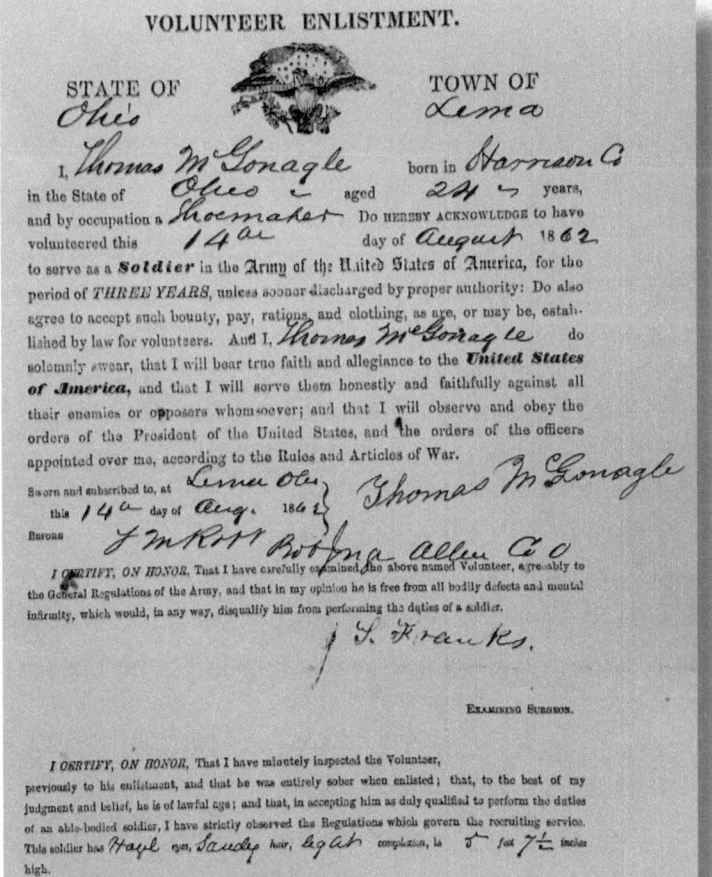

2.7

Chapter 3

DECLARATION OF RECRUIT.

I, *Thomas McGonagle,* desiring to VOLUNTEER as a Soldier in the Army of the United States, for the term of THREE YEARS, Do declare, That I am 24 years and months of age; that I have never been discharged from the United States service on account of disability or by sentence of a court-martial, or by order before the expiration of a term of enlistment; and I know of no impediment to my serving honestly and faithfully as a soldier for three years.

GIVEN at *Lerna Ohio*

The *14th* day of *August 1862*

Thomas McGonagle

Witness:

3.1

Joseph and John were quiet. They both turned around at the same time, to warm their backs by the campfire. Brothers often do the same things at the same time. Neither one of them was aware that they both turned at the same time. But Thomas knew. He watched them as they turned in unison and smiled. Joseph noticed Thomas smiling broadly and wondered what prompted a smile. Before he completed that thought, some of the verses to 'Molly Bawn' replayed in his head again. Oh, Molly Bawn, why leave me pining. It reminded him of some of the other ballads that he enjoyed so much.

"Well John, Nancy got back at you for not singing. She refused to play your favorite Scottish ballad, "Let Us Haste to Kelvin Grove'," Joseph said.

"Speaking of Nancy, I sent her a letter yesterday," John said.

"Where did you find a three-cent stamp to put on the envelope?" Joseph asked.

"Didn't put a stamp on it. The post office will still mail a soldier's letter without any postage, you know."

"Nice of Uncle Sam to pay for mailing your letter," Joseph said.

"The U.S. government won't pay for it. They will just let a soldier mail it without a stamp."

"Then who pays for it?"

"The recipient, whoever you mail the letter to, has to pay for it."

"What? I didn't know that. When they have to pay for the letter, it must be about as welcome as having to go to robber's row," Joseph said.

"I hope Nancy doesn't perceive getting a postage due letter as another one of the many tricks I've played on her over the years," John said.

"Is a Copperhead a no-good skunk? Oh no, she wouldn't think that at all," Thomas kidded.

"Three-cents can add up if you send her a lot of letters."

"It's even worse if you send a letter way out west to Oregon. Then it costs you ten cents," Thomas said.

"Nancy is in Allen County in Ohio now, right?" asked Joseph

"Yep. In Lima, in Allen County. Her husband, George Porter is in the Union Army too. You know, 'Let Us Haste to Kelvin Grove' is a great Scottish ballad that Nancy enjoyed playing. Especially when the three of us would all sing 'Bonnie Lassie O' as loud as we could. When we really got going I think they could hear us from Wayne County to Allen County. Or maybe as far away as Meigs County," John said.

"Meigs County?" asked Joseph.

"Aye. It's down south, on the Ohio River."

> *"Let us haste to Kelvin grove, bonnie Lassie O.*
> *Thro' its mazes let us rove, bonnie Lassie O.*
> *Where the Rose in all its pride*
> *Paints the hollow dingle side,*
> *Where the midnight fairies glide, bonnie Lassie O."* 3.2

John was now the brother in deep thought. Why did he mention Meigs County? What caused that particular county to pop into his thoughts? Then he remembered.

John had spoken to Ambrose, a soldier he had recently met. The McGonagle brothers belonged to the 41st Ohio Infantry. Ambrose Bierce enlisted in the 9th Regiment, Indiana. Both their regiments were under command of Colonel William Babcock Hazen and both regiments had marched together a few days ago when they left Murfreesboro. John was reminded, when the 9th Indiana played 'Home Sweet Home', of one of the strange things that can happen in life, even during the heat of battle. John and Ambrose had fought side by side at the Battle of Shiloh in April of 1862. They both had taken cover behind a fallen wagon when the shooting started. Between firing at the Confederates and reloading, they discovered they both had grown up in Ohio. While discussing the things they had in common, Ambrose told John that he wrote short stories and poems. When there was a lull in the fighting, John asked Ambrose if he would recite one of his poems. He remembered the words. The poem was called 'Corporal'.

> *"Corporal"*
> *Fiercely the battle raged and, sad to tell,*
> *Our corporal heroically fell!*
> *Fame from her height looked down upon the brawl*
> *And said: "He hadn't very far to fall."* 3.3

"I think one of your favorites is 'Coming Thro' the Rye'. Right, John?" Joseph asked.

John was lost in thought, recollecting about the poem, and Shiloh. It took several moments before he realized Joseph had yet another question and mentioned his name. As he considered an answer, he was thankful to get the prophetic lines of 'Corporal' out of his mind. Prophetic because he had seen a boy, no more than thirteen years old, that lay on the battlefield when the fighting at the Battle of Shiloh was finished. John had heard the slang expression 'somebody's darling' before and didn't know what it meant. He now realized what it referred to. That brave 'somebody's darling' didn't have far to fall. John took a deep breath and shook his head to chase away the image.

"That's right. I always liked 'Coming Thro' the Rye' and 'Mary of Argle," John said.

"And we all know mother's favorite song. We've heard it over and over tonight."

"Home Sweet Home," the three brothers all quietly said together.

3.4

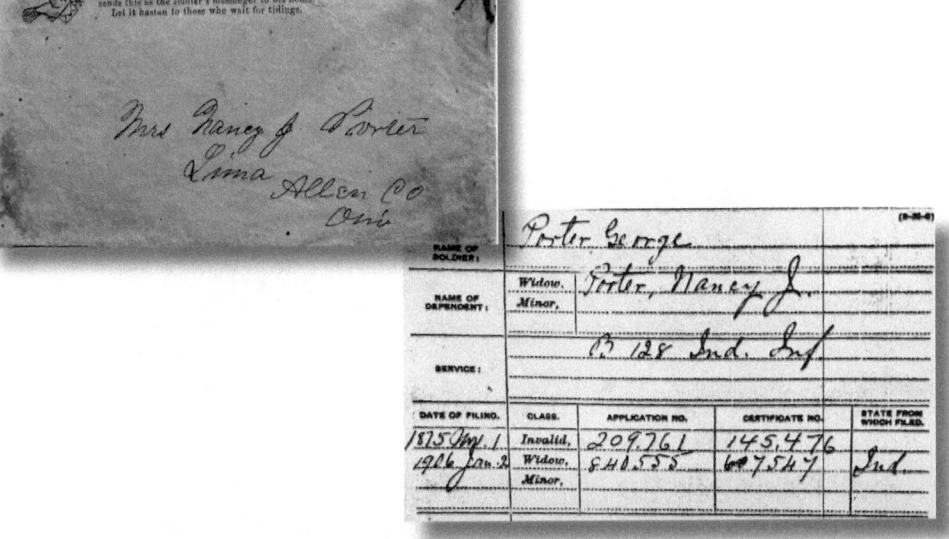

3.5 The McGonagle brothers smiled at the memory of home. Hearing both Union and Confederate bands playing the same song back and forth was unheard of. Not a soldier in camp could recall this happening before. The Civil War had raged for over a year now. To consider the same song being played by regimental bands, where one band wore the blue uniform and the other band the gray, on a battlefield was unprecedented. It was particularly meaningful to the McGonagle brothers because it was their mother's favorite song.

"Be it ever so humble, there's no place like "Home, Sweet Home," Thomas said.

Chapter 4

The McGonagle brothers each reflected about their Ohio home, their mother, and how much she enjoyed 'Home Sweet Home'. Thomas looked more closely at the quilt his mother had made for the three of them. He admired the quality of the work on the hand-stitched quilt that enveloped his shoulders. Isabella McGonagle was well-known for her talent in their community and surrounding counties for making beautiful quilts. Thomas admired his mother for her many talents, an expert quilter just one among many.

"You know, I think about home and I think about Ohio all the time," said John.

"We haven't talked about home as much as we have tonight. It seems like a long time since we left Ohio and marched off to war," Thomas said.

"I thought I was the only one that missed my home and family," Joseph said.

"You're not the only one. All three of us miss being home. I think hearing 'Home Sweet Home' takes us all back in time. We remember how much home means to us," Thomas said.

"Look at this quilt. This isn't just any old quilt. Mother made it, just for us."

Thomas turned a corner of the quilt back to look at the other side. Their mother had sown her initials there. Thomas realized that the colors, pattern, and hand stitching of the quilt around his shoulders were so 'Isabella Lisle McGonagle'. If a hundred quilts were hanging on a clothesline, he could easily pick which quilt his mother had made. She was just that good. Many a mother made quilts for her family but the McGonagle brother's mother had extraordinary talent. She not only made them for warmth but each quilt she made had a meaning. Isabella McGonagle's quilts were admired by anyone that knew anything about quilting.

"Mother finished this quilt just before we decided to fight in this war. Because I was the oldest, she took me aside and told me she made it just for us. She wanted us to take turns sharing it. Giving us this quilt was her way of doing what she could to help us make it through this war," Thomas said.

Thomas rubbed his fingers over the initials his mother had stitched into the quilt. He added up the months the brothers had been in the Army. He figured it was just about half of a year now. The brothers passed a lot of time talking. Or arguing. Sometimes they argued loudly. Brothers could have discussions for long periods, all in full agreement, whether it was music or politics. Then one brother would criticize another brother. Maybe Thomas commented about the lack of effort Joseph displayed as they all unloaded a wagon of hay into the barn. Joseph, of course, answered back with a few choice words.

Then, it was off to the 'Camptown Races', as their father liked to say.

The Scottish blood in them could boil over and one brother would have a 'knock-down-drag-out' with one of the other brothers. Then the next day, two of the brothers were known to have a 'Scotland chat' with a neighbor that caused a problem with the other brother. It was a McGonagle brother thing.

"John – do you remember when Joseph got into that row with the big Irishman by the name of O'Connor?" Thomas laughed.

"Aye. Ole Joseph would punch him, then he'd say 'bet my money on the McGonagle nag' and punch him again. Pretty soon, he'd say, 'somebody's gonna need a rag'. Then Joseph would punch him again," John said.

"He'd say his words to the tune of 'Camptown Races," Thomas laughed.

"And what did he say when O'Connor gave up the fight?" John asked.

"Do dah! Do dah!" Thomas and John both sang together.

"The Camptown ladies sing this song. Doo-dah, Doo-dah.
*   The Camptown racetrack's five miles long. Oh, de doo-da day.*
Going to run all night. Going to run all day.
*   I bet my money on the bob-tailed nag. Somebody bet on the*
gray." 4.2

Thomas chuckled to himself. He had discussed a lot of subjects with his brothers but he couldn't recall ever having discussed quilts with them before. He also realized that now all the brothers were talking quietly. Talking quietly was unusual for the McGonagle brothers, to say the least. However, now they were discussing quilts instead of rifles or baseball. Baseball certainly was a recent topic to discuss. Or argue about the rules of baseball. The brothers had watched their first game in the spring. Thomas knew the quiet talk was because none of them wanted the other soldiers in their company to start teasing them about their discussion about quilts.

Thomas could just imagine one of the sergeants saying something like, "Okay girls, time to skedaddle and put your quilt away for the night."

A comment such as that might certainly incite all the McGonagle brothers to the 'Camptown Races'.

Thomas stood up, rearranged the quilt around his body, then sat back down on a large rock. Joseph walked away from the campfire and sat next to him. John used the toe of his boot to arrange a few branches in the fire and then joined them.

"Our Mother and the mothers of all the soldiers have a tough row to hoe too. They worry constantly about how we're doing and pray against hearing about the death of a son," Joseph said.

"And more and more sons are killed the longer this war goes on," John said.

"She sure did a good job with this quilt. I think it's the best one she ever made. At first, I thought it was crazy to take turns carrying a quilt all across the country. Mother, as usual, was right. She knew this would be something that we could all use," John said.

"Thank goodness, she gave us a quilt. There is some poor sap in

Company C whose mother gave him an umbrella as he marched off to war," Thomas laughed.

"Umbrella? Oh, that's about as useful as a hole in a canteen."

"Mother made this quilt with a lot of consideration. It's not too heavy or too big to pack in our bread bags," John said.

"What pattern is this quilt anyway?" Joseph wondered.

"You mean you don't know? You must have had your head in a feed sack all these years," Thomas said.

"Joseph must have decided to absquatulate when mother explained about quilt patterns," John kidded.

"I suppose you and Thomas both know what this quilt pattern is," Joseph said.

Joseph looked at John and Thomas for an answer. He hoped one of them would just give him a simple answer but that could be too much to hope for. As the younger brother, he was used to getting a lot of advice. Also, a lot of kidding.

"Sure, I know. My head hasn't been in a feed sack, like someone I know. That quilt pattern is---" John started to say. He stood up, picked up a few branches, and squatted to place them on the fire.

"Let's see – it's called a hummingbird pattern," John said as he winked at Thomas.

"I saw that wink. You must think I'm full of bark juice. This is not a hummingbird quilt pattern. I know what that is because Maggie Lisle showed me a quilt she did once and told me it was a hummingbird pattern," Joseph said.

John and Thomas enjoyed kidding their little brother. As most older brothers do, they had a way of getting Joseph agitated. They could push him into a real conniption. It didn't seem to matter whether they teased him

4.3

about horses, rifles, or lassies. Or even when the subject matter was as varied as quilting.

"If this quilt is a hummingbird pattern, I'll eat my hat and volunteer to be a dog robber," Joseph said as he pointed to the quilt Thomas had around his shoulders.

"Dog robber, eh? If you're detailed from the 41st Ohio to be a cook, I'll eat anything, maybe even some embalmed beef, instead of whatever soup you come up with."

"Hey. I make good soup when I have to. Nobody ever got the Virginia quickstep from something I've made," Joseph said.

"I don't know about the quickstep but you're right about one thing. A hummingbird quilt sounds like something Maggie would make," Thomas said.

"The real truth is that the quilt pattern that mother made for us is called a bear's paw," John said.

"I see. It does look like one big bear's paw. I realize now that mother made some bigger quilts with some smaller bear paws on it," Joseph remembered.

"Aye, laddie. It's a bear's paw. On a cold December night like this, it's mighty welcome," Thomas said as he shifted the quilt around his legs.

Thomas and John looked at each other. Thomas nodded at John and he nodded back. John scratched his beard. Thomas scratched his head. They were both thinking the same thing without a word being spoken. It was a brother thing. John nodded at Thomas. Thomas knew John wanted him to start the story.

"Guess it's time we told little brother the family quilt story," Thomas said.

"What story?" Joseph asked.

Joseph could tell his brothers weren't kidding this time. He just kind of knew when they were saying things to kid him and when they weren't. He knew that Thomas and John were about to tell him a story about his family he was unaware of.

"Well, Joseph, you are the youngest brother, other than Robert who is ten and still back in Ohio. Because you had the reputation that you couldn't keep a secret for longer than seven seconds, the family decided to wait until you were older to be informed of the family secret," John started to explain.

"Guess you're old enough now to discuss this with you, Joseph. Besides, there are not too many people you could tell now that we're somewhere in the middle of Tennessee," Thomas kidded.

"You tell him the story, Thomas. You know it better than I do anyway," John said.

Thomas looked around. There were several other soldiers close by. He took a corner of the quilt in each hand and spread his arms out wide behind his back.

"You sit here on my left Joseph. And you sit here on my right John," Thomas said.

Thomas nodded his head to the left. Joseph sat next to Thomas. Thomas nodded his head to the right. John used a branch to rearrange the logs in the fire, then he sat beside Thomas. Thomas put an arm around each one of their shoulders and held the quilt so it covered all their backs. Thomas cleared his throat. He spoke in a voice that was just above a whisper. He cleared his throat again and began the story.

"I'm going to talk kind of low so no one else hears. This is the story Joseph," Thomas began.

"The pattern on this quilt is called a bear's paw. Mother chose this pattern because it is actually a code that can be interpreted about the quilt," Thomas said.

Thomas paused and could see the puzzled look on Joseph's face. He continued his story.

"The quilt code is a way to communicate with people that don't know you. When a slave, or people that are helping a slave escape, notice a bear's paw quilt hanging nearby to a house, they know that home is a safe place for them. The quilt code could be passed along as a secret without everyone knowing. The bear's paw in the quilt quite often has a black color. Black was also part of the quilt code and people would recognize that home to be a place of refuge," Thomas explained.

"So, not only the bear's paw but also the color was significant," Joseph said.

"That's right. Mother would even place the quilt so that the paws would point people in the right direction. People knew they could follow the footprints of the bear. Just like bears go to water and berries for food, mother provided those that needed help a place to rest, have food, and be cared for before they moved onward," John explained.

"I thought quilts were just used to keep people warm – until now anyway," Joseph said.

"The bear's paw and also the tumbling block pattern is used as a quilt code. Mother had quilts with other patterns but she would put the bear's paw quilt on the clothesline or drape it over a chair on the porch or sometimes she would place it over a window with the bear's paw showing to the outside," Thomas said.

"I thought she covered the quilt over the window just to keep the cold out. However, she was displaying a secret. People that knew how to interpret the code on the quilt also knew the meaning of the quilt. Now I understand the quilt meant that our home was a safe place for them," Joseph said.

"Now you know the whole story," Thomas said.

"Well, it was about time you told me these 'home sweet home' secrets. What other secrets do you have that you haven't told me?" Joseph asked.

"Well, we will see how good you keep this secret and if we can trust you, we might tell you some of the other family secrets," Thomas said and winked at John.

4.4

Chapter 5

Joseph and John stood up so they were no longer surrounded by the quilt that Thomas was holding. Thomas could read the look on Joseph's face. It said either 'I can't believe that I didn't know about the quilt code'. Or 'I can't believe you didn't tell me before'. Thomas slapped Joseph on the back as if to welcome him as a total, complete, family confidant now.

"It's your turn for the quilt John," Thomas said.

Each brother tried to be careful to not extend past his time using the quilt. The three of them could argue and fight about a lot of things and eventually work things out. They could fight over cards, they could argue about who had the best horse. They could argue if one brother wasn't pulling his weight with doing chores. But the changing of the quilt was never something that one brother took advantage of by using it longer than anyone. Or not giving it to another brother when it was time.

"Mother showed her support for us going off to war by making this quilt. She also worked hard to help make a flag for our 41st regiment," Joseph said.

"Mother will also keep those home fires burning too until we all come home."

"Colonel Hazen was certainly appreciative of the ladies in Geauga County and the other Ohio counties for the special care they took in sewing the national flag and our regimental flag," Thomas said.

"It's a special honor that we serve in Company C, the color company of our entire 41st regiment. That honor is definitely something to peacock about," John said.

"You've got that right, John. It is an honor, especially knowing that a color company is selected by the Regimental Commander based on courage and steadiness under fire," Thomas said.

"It's a dangerous honor. Regardless of what happens in a battle, the duty of every soldier is to guard the national flag and the regimental flag. Under no circumstances are we to allow the Confederates to capture either one of those flags," John said.

"Whoever is carrying that flag gives the Confederates something to aim at too. I figured that out when we were in the middle of the Battle of Shiloh. The color sergeant was hit by a bullet and could not continue to hold his flag erect. He was on the ground and struggled to keep the colors from touching the ground. Bullets showered all around him. A swarm of rebels saw a chance to take the flag," Joseph said.

Joseph looked at Thomas in amazement and admiration, as he remembered what happened next. Thomas was about twenty feet away when he saw the flag bearer had been wounded. Thomas yelled to several Union soldiers to help save the colors. The Confederate infantry from the 13th Arkansas tried to get in position to capture the Union flag. The soldiers fired at the Confederate Army of the Mississippi regiment to slow their advance and prevent them from taking the flag away. Thomas ran to the aid of the color sergeant and picked up the flag. With his rifle in one hand and the flag in the other, he secured the colors. Thomas insured the colors did not fall into the enemy's hands.

5.1

"That was an incredibly brave thing to do Thomas. You could have been somebody's darling right then and there. Weren't you concerned one of those bullets had your name on it?" Joseph asked.

"Well, Joseph all I can say is this. It's better to be a lion for a day than a sheep for the rest of your life. When Colonel Hazen accepted the colors, he did say that we would never tarnish the splendor of its purity. When you are in that kind of situation, just charge ahead," Thomas explained.

"Just charge on ahead, eh?" Joseph said.

"Yep, that's all there is to it, Thomas said convincingly.

Chapter 6

The 41st Ohio regiment had marched through a thick Tennessee mist early on the morning of December 30, 1862. It was obvious to the McGonagle brothers that an autumn drought had ruined a lot of the crops in this part of Tennessee. An early winter had blanketed the ground with six inches of snow a few weeks ago. The snow had mostly melted now due to a series of icy rainstorms. The ground was pure mud at times, which made marching difficult. As autumn was now giving way to winter, the soldiers were marching up to sixteen miles a day in driving rainstorms and biting cold. Today had been one of those sixteen mile days. The brothers were glad to get to camp, build a fire to dry their clothes, and warm-up. They took turns placing branches on the fire to keep it going – not too big, they didn't want to attract enemy attention. A cold north wind started to blow, throwing embers into the wind. Stronger bursts caused the flames to spread out and rise. Each of the McGonagle brothers wanted to continue talking for a while. They hoped talking would divert their attention and make the cold more bearable.

"It was also an honor that Company C was asked to come forward to receive the flag when it was presented to us just before we left Camp Wood in Cleveland," Joseph said.

"That's where you almost got thrown out of the Army, Joseph. Before your service even started. What a pie eater you are," John kidded.

"Pie eater! Don't go calling me a pie eater! I'm a soldier now," Joseph objected.

"You are now but you almost weren't then," John said.

"Hey, I didn't know you weren't supposed to move when you're in formation," Joseph said.

"By moving, I suppose you mean you didn't know you're not supposed to wave wildly to the ladies from Wayne County during the flag presentation," John laughed.

"Well, I waved but it wasn't wild. And I won't do that again," Joseph said.

"I do believe the look that Captain Cole gave you could have knocked you into a cocked hat. I swear I could feel the steam coming off of him and the ground shaking," Thomas said.

"I confess the Captain was a little wrathy," Joseph said.

Colonel Hazen was grateful to receive the colors on October 28, 1861. He would be moving his troops on October 29. As he held the national flag in one arm and the 41st Ohio regiment flag in the other, he addressed the crowd that had gathered to see the Union boys before they marched to war.

"I am glad to meet you here today, to thank you for what your county has done for this regiment. She has furnished many men of whom we are all proud, of whom you and the country should be proud. You have come here today to present us the emblem of our country's greatness. We thank you for it, and will never tarnish the splendor of its purity. We are soon to leave you, perhaps some of us not to return. It is probably better that we all should not return. But go where we will, we know your hearts go with us, and such as do return are sure of a hospitable welcome. We will do our duty and may no one disinherit the greeting so dear to the soldier when the battle is over. On behalf of the regiment, I thank you heartily for the happy compliment just paid them and must bid you now adieu."

6.1

Joseph was ready to change the conversation about his lack of soldierly decorum at the ceremony to receive the flags for the regiment. He hurried to change the subject before Thomas could exaggerate another story about him or to give John a chance to call him a pie eater again.

"Hearing this story about our mother using her quilts to support the underground railroad doesn't surprise me. She always helped someone whether she knew them or not. Father was also like that. He was always ready to lend a helping hand to a neighbor or other family member," Joseph said.

"The example that they set for us helped decide to enlist in the Union Army. Here we are somewhere by Murfreesboro, Tennessee ready to fight those rebs so we can hold this country together. And get rid of this slavery problem. In the last two days, we have marched in mud and driving rain. We don't have our fighting orders yet but I'm pretty sure we will fight tomorrow. We'll send old Johnny Reb packing back to the south. I can feel a battle coming, just as certain as you can predict a terrible hail storm when you see dark clouds that boil on the horizon," Thomas said.

6.2

"You are usually right about things like that Thomas. You have some kind of Scottish warrior spirit in you that senses when those dark clouds are gathering and know a battle is soon at hand," John said.

"Were all the Scots warriors?" Joseph asked.

"Almost all. One exception that comes to mind is a Scottish poet," Thomas said.

"Oh, you mean William Shakespeare, right? "Joseph said.

Joseph smiled widely. Thomas gave him a stare that could have melted iron.

"Yes, I know Shakespeare wasn't a Scot. You were probably thinking of your favorite poet, oh, what was his name? I know - William Burn," Joseph said.

That was too much for Thomas. He stopped staring at Joseph, looked at the campfire, and shook his head. Then he looked at John with an expression that said 'help me tell Joseph about the most famous poet from Scotland'. John knew Joseph was having a fine time teasing Thomas but even he wasn't certain how much Joseph knew, so he came to the rescue of Thomas.

"Well, Joseph, you're close. His correct name is Robert Burns and he is known as the national poet of Scotland. You even have some of his poems memorized, right Thomas?" John asked.

"Let's see. I have several favorites. I like one of his poems named 'To a Mouse'," Thomas said.

"Small, sleek, cowering, timorous beast, O, what a panic is in your breast!"

"You amaze me with the stuff you have rolling around in your head, Thomas," Joseph said.

"I just remembered I have a small book of poems in my haversack that has several of Robert Burn's poems in it. I can read the first few verses if you like," Thomas said.

"You're carrying around a book of poetry? I don't believe it. What else have you got in that pack of yours?" John asked.

"Things that would surprise even you, dear brothers. In fact. there is another surprise in here that I will tell you about later," Thomas said.

"I'll read just the first few verses."

> "*To a Mouse*"
> "*Small, sleek, cowering, timorous beast,*
> *O, what a panic is in your breast!*
> *You need not start away so hasty, with hurrying scamper!*
> *I would be loath to run and chase you, with murdering plough.*" 6.3

"What do you think is the meaning of the poem, Thomas? You have probably thought about that since this is a favorite of yours," John asked.

"I think the poem does have a meaning. Neither mice nor men can escape their destiny. The death of the mouse symbolizes the vulnerability we live through and experience every day," Thomas said.

"What do you think the meaning of the poem is John?"

"Well, I think the meaning is summed up by one of the verses that I remember. 'The best-laid plans of mice and men often go astray'," John said.

"What do you think Joseph?" Thomas asked

Thomas and John looked at Joseph and wondered what his explanation would be.

Joseph shrugged his shoulders. He knew poems often had hidden meanings and he liked discussions about different interpretations of the same poem. It was just that he wasn't particularly gifted to determine an interpretation all on his own. Escaping destiny? Plans askew? Maybe it's just a poem about some poor mouse that got his home plowed under by a farmer. That's what he thought but he didn't want his brothers to think he wasn't smart enough to come up with an explanation on his own.

Joseph shrugged his shoulders again.

"Guess I'll have to think about that for a while."

"While you're thinking, I'll read you a line from another Robert Burns poem. You can recite this to a Scottish lassie on your wedding day. The name of this poem is "Red, Red Rose. I'll read you the first few verses," Thomas said.

6.4

"A Red, Red Rose"
"O my Love is like a red, red rose
that's newly sprung in June,
O my Love is like the melody
that's sweetly played in tune."
6.5

"So, what did you think of that poem Joseph?" John asked.

"Well, I think someone that compares a woman to a red rose obviously has to be a poet, probably a Scottish poet. And whoever reads this poem to his bonnie lassie has to be an idiot. A Scottish idiot," Joseph said.

As Joseph gave his philosophical interpretation of the poem, Thomas took a sip of coffee. Just as Joseph ended his summation, before he could swallow his coffee, Thomas snorted and laughed so hard that he blew the coffee out of his mouth. John laughed too, at Joseph's observation of the poem. And seeing Thomas snort his coffee onto the campfire.

This was an opportune time for the changing of the quilt. John handed the quilt to Joseph just as a shear of wind whipped the quilt so hard that he lost his grip on one of the corners. The quilt waved wildly as Joseph struggled to get it in his grasp. He then bundled the quilt into a ball, got a firm grip on each corner, and situated it around his back. Joseph sat down on the large rock by the campfire and partially sat on the quilt to keep it from blowing over Stones River and into the hands of some Johnny Reb.

Chapter 7

"That's enough poetry for you Joseph. What I can tell you about the Scots is simply this. The Scots were great warriors. Our great-grandfather McGonagle was a warrior who fought in a Scottish Highlanders regiment during the Seven Years War. The first name of our grandfather McGonagle was Thomas, and the first name of our great-grandfather McGonagle was also Thomas. Because I share the same first name as those warriors, I have that same fierce warrior deep within me. It's not bragging to say that almost anyone in the county knew they might as well be fighting a bear as getting into it with me," Thomas said.

"Jumping Jehoshaphat! Our family tree has a lot of people named Thomas. Why didn't they throw a Joseph name into the family tree somewhere? With so many Thomas names, it's too hard to keep them straight. I'll have a hard time knowing which Thomas you're telling me about. So, I've got an idea. I'm going to designate great-grandfather Thomas McGonagle as Thomas One and grandfather Thomas as Thomas Two and you are Thomas Three just to keep things straight which Thomas we're talking about," Joseph said.

Joseph pointed a finger at Thomas without letting go of the corner of the quilt.

"You're Thomas Three," Joseph repeated.

"Since you have the same first name as our grandfather's, I expect you can tell me all about the Scottish soldiers and the famous battles," Joseph added.

"Indeed, I can laddie. Great-grandfather Thomas McGonagle – One - was part of the Scottish Black Watch Regiments that fought for Britain. His regiment fought in the Seven Years War," Thomas said.

"Wait a minute. He fought for Britain?" Joseph asked.

"That's right. The family history that is passed down says that great-grandfather grew up in the Scottish Highlands. The Highlands are in the rugged northwestern part of Scotland. An ancient Celtic language was spoken that combined Irish and Scottish languages, The Scottish Gaelic pronunciation for the Scottish Highlands is Gaidheal-tachd – the place of Gaels," John said.

"What? I've never heard that word before. Gaelic? Black Watch? How am I supposed to remember all this? I can't even pronounce the words," Joseph said.

"Well, listen to the rest of our great-grandfather's story. He was born sometime around 1740 and during those times it was hard to survive. Britain had conquered Scotland years before and then recruited Scottish soldiers to fight other battles and wars for them. Thomas McGonagle One was in a Black Watch regiment that agreed they would fight for Britain. The catch was that the Scottish Highlanders weren't told where they would be fighting. At this time, the Seven Years War was taking place between Britain and France and being fought all over the world, including America. His regiment, the 42nd Highlanders, was forced onto a ship that sailed and ended up in a place in Canada called Nova Scotia. From there they fought their way into the Great Lakes territory." John said.

"That's incredible. I never knew any of this. To think that our great-grandfather was fighting over this same country that we're fighting in now - over a hundred years later," Joseph said.

"I assume the Seven Years War lasted seven years, right?" Joseph said.

Before Thomas could answer Joseph's question, Joseph asked another question.

"Did great grandfather McGonagle ever go back to Scotland?" Joseph asked.

"Don't rush the story, Joseph. You're getting ahead of yourself," John said.

"The War was called the Seven Years War in Britain, France, and Europe. This was in the 1756 to 1763 time-period. In America, it's called the French and Indian War," Thomas explained.

"The French and Indian War – I've heard of that," Joseph said.

"Our great grandfather was part of the Black Watch?"

7.1

"The Black Watch was a special regiment of Scottish Highlanders. They get their name from the dark color of their tartan," John said.

"What's a tartan?" Joseph asked.

"Are you sure you've got any Scottish blood in you at all Joseph? The tartan is a special design of a plaid cloth with stripes of different colors. The original role of the regiment was to 'watch' the Highland Country. So that's where the Black Watch name came from," John said.

"To be part of the Black Watch wasn't for just any run of the mill soldier either. You had to be a fierce fighter and to be part of that regiment you had to prove it. I need to tell you Joseph that I was fortunate to be in a position to save the colors of our flag at the Battle of Shiloh. But I wasn't the first in our family history to do that. Our Great Grandfather McGonagle saved the colors of the Black Watch regiment during a very pivotal battle during the French and Indian War," Thomas said.

"That's incredible. You're telling me that our family was saving the colors, going back generations. That warrior blood in you isn't just for fighting. It also propels you to save the flag, if need be," Joseph said.

"Aye, laddie. The warrior skills of the Black Watch were tested more than at any other time when they had to fight against Chief Pontiac," Thomas said.

"Sounds like this is where the Indians in the French and Indian War come in," Joseph said.

"Yes indeed. Just like the Black Watch regiments were known for their fierce fighting abilities, so were the Ottawa Indians under the leadership of Chief Pontiac. Chief Pontiac was head of the Ottawa tribe during the time of the French and Indian War. He had been allied with the French. When France lost the war, Chief Pontiac organized several Indian tribes to keep fighting. They organized to fight their common enemy – the white settlers," John said

"This was a huge alliance of Indian tribes. Ottawa, Ojibwa, Potawatomi, Miami, Kickapoo, Piankeshaw, Seneca, Cayuga,—"

"Cayuga! That's how the county in Ohio that you're from got its name, John," Joseph interrupted.

"Yep, and speaking of Ohio, we need to tell you about the Battle of Bushy Run during the French and Indian War," Thomas said.

"The Battle of Bushy Run? Was Thomas McGonagle One in that battle?" Joseph asked.

"You bet your tartan he was," John said.

"Amazing! Tell me the story."

"Okay, so pay attention, Joseph. This is important to not only our family history but the history of Ohio. Chief Pontiac's rebellion captured Britain's only garrisoned fort in Ohio country – Fort Sandusky. This all led up to one huge battle, pitting the huge alliance of Indians against the American British colonists. The colonies were mostly defended by the Scottish Highlanders and a few native American tribes of the Delaware, Shawnee, and Huron that were on the same side as Britain. This was the Battle of Bushy Run," Thomas said.

"Where is Bushy Run?" Joseph asked.

"Pennsylvania."

"This was a very pivotal battle. Chief Pontiac and his Indians had captured so many British forts that they were a great threat for the British colonists to be able to expand westward into the Ohio territory," John added.

"Who won the Battle of Bushy Run?" Joseph asked.

"Who won?" Thomas looked at Joseph with a disbelieving look.

"Your great-grandfather Thomas McGonagle and the rest of the Black Watch of Scottish Highlanders were victorious, of course. They were Gems of Scotland," Thomas said.

7.2

"They won the Battle of Bushy Run, which was one of the most significant Native American conflicts in history," Thomas said.

"We can be very proud of our Scottish heritage. Yet again," John said.

"The main reason Chief Pontiac was defeated is the same reason that makes the difference in the Civil War battles we fight today, Do you know what that reason was?" Thomas asked.

"I bet I know. They ran out of ammunition," Joseph said.

"Yep. You are as sharp as an Arkansas toothpick, laddie. The Indians no longer had their French allies to support them with ammunition. Chief Pontiac was forced to end the battle and sign an agreement to give up a large portion of the land that they once controlled. The Pontiac War ended with the Proclamation of 1763, which stated that any land west of the Appalachian Mountains belonged to the Indians and the colonists were not to settle there," Thomas said.

"Guess that didn't work out too well for the Indians, did it?" Joseph said.

"No. Not by a jug full. That's a story for another day," John said.

"What happened to great-grandfather McGonagle then?" Joseph asked.

"Remember – the Battle of Bushy Run was in Pennsylvania. The colonists were so appreciative of the Scottish Highlanders for their victory at Bushy Run that they were given an option of a land grant in Pennsylvania instead of a monetary reward. Great-grandfather decided to be awarded some land and then returned to Scotland. He married, had a family but never returned to Pennsylvania as he had planned. He died in Scotland and his estate went to our grandfather, Thomas McGonagle Two," Thomas explained.

"So, Grandfather McGonagle emigrated from Scotland and settled on the land grant in Pennsylvania that was given to his father in consideration of being part of the Black Watch Scottish regiment during the French and Indian War," Joseph said.

"Bully for you, Joseph, You've got all the facts correct. After Thomas McGonagle Two came to America, he married and raised his family, including our father, Robert McGonagle, who was born in Pennsylvania. Thomas McGonagle Two was able to live and farm on the land that was given to Thomas McGonagle One," Thomas said.

"Jumping Jehoshaphat! That was certainly one long journey from Scotland to America, back to Scotland for decades before our family arrived back in Pennsylvania," Joseph said.

"And then we didn't even stay there. You could say our family took our music to the state of Ohio," John added.

A gust of wind suddenly gashed at the McGonagle brothers and the campfire. The force was so strong that Joseph tilted backward. John grabbed at him to keep him from falling over. Joseph regained his balance and walked over to the campfire. He put his hands over the fire to warm them as he looked out towards the darkness across Stones River. Joseph was deep in thought about the family stories Thomas and John had told him. He rubbed his hands over the fire but finally was aware that there wasn't any warmth coming from the campfire. He looked at where the fire had been, then realized that the wind had blown the campfire out. Joseph turned to say something to his brothers, opened his mouth to say something, and then closed it when he realized Thomas and John were both staring at him. They had kind of an astonished look on their faces and Joseph knew they had watched him as he absent-mindedly tried to warm his hands over a nonexistent fire.

"Need a Lucifer to get that fire going again, Joseph?" John asked with a smile.

"You noticed too, eh?" Joseph said.

"Yeah. About 10 minutes before you did," Thomas said with a big smile.

"Okay, okay. I acknowledge the corn. Now, are one of you going to hand me some Lucifer's to get this fire going again or just sit there like a couple of big bugs?" Joseph replied.

Thomas rummaged around in his haversack, then handed Joseph a match. Joseph arranged a few small cedar branches, then took his cap off, squatted next to where he hoped the fire would start again. He struck a match on a rock. He tried to shelter the match with his cap but the wind blew the match out before the fire caught. Jumping, Jabbering Jehoshaphat! He could imagine how he'd be teased even more by his brothers now. Joseph hung his head in resignation for a moment. He waited a few moments to listen to the comments that inevitably would come. Joseph didn't turn around to look at them. Hearing no comments, he just held his arm out until one of the brothers dropped another match in his hand. This time, in addition to his cap, he used his body to shelter the match from the wind. Soon there were a few wisps of flame and he stayed until it was a real campfire again. Thank goodness. He wouldn't have to use the third match to get the fire started again.

"Now, I know why they call them Lucifer's. You just have a devil of a time to get them to start a fire," Joseph said.

Joseph again remembered the words of advice from his mother.

"When life gives you lemons, make orange juice."

Before Thomas or John could tease him about the length of time it took him to get the fire going again, he diverted them by asking another question.

"Do you suppose grandfather carried any bagpipes with him when he left Scotland?" Joseph asked.

Thomas smiled at Joseph's obvious attempt to stop him from commenting on Joseph's fire-making skills. He decided he would let his younger brother off the hook. This time.

"That's a good question Joseph," Thomas said as he watched the relief on Joseph's face.

"Bagpipes were first used in Scotland hundreds of years ago. Ireland started using bagpipes later and are different than the Scottish bagpipes. The Scottish bagpipes have one octave, whereas the Irish bagpipes have two octaves. Which reminds me of another bit of family history. Your great-grandfather, Thomas McGonagle One broke the law," Thomas said.

"I suppose this is another family secret I'll have to keep quiet," Joseph said.

"Well, here is the story. I'll bet you didn't know that bagpipes were banned in Scotland at one time, did you?" Thomas asked.

"Balderdash! Are you bluffing me?"

"No bluff. The Highland bagpipes were banned in Scotland in 1745 when Bonnie Prince Charlie convinced the Highland Scots to go to war against England. The bagpipes were considered an instrument of war by the English government and banned throughout all of Scotland after the Battle of Culloden. Anyone that carried or played bagpipes was punished. The only way bagpipes survived was credited to those who kept them in secret for several years," John said.

"Let me guess. Grandfather McGonagle was one of those that kept the bagpipes hidden so they could later be played without punishment," Joseph said.

"You're as right as a bottle of Dalley's Magical Pain Extractor," Thomas said

 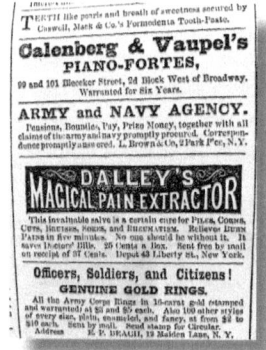

"Where did you hear about this magical pain extractor?" John asked.

"There was an advertisement in 'Harpers Weekly' a few weeks ago."

"I could have used some of that for my toothache two days ago."

"Did you just use some Bromo-Seltzer to get rid of the pain?"

"Couldn't find any, so used a standby. Think it was called 'Ole Red Eye'," John grimaced.

"Who in blarney was this Prince Charlie?" Joseph asked.

"Bonnie Prince Charlie's father, King James of England, was exiled to France because he wasn't doing enough to stop the influence of French Catholicism on the crown. Prince Charlie enticed a group of Scots to join him in a rebellion against England in to retain his father to the crown. Their effort failed and the playing of bagpipes was forbidden," John said.

"Thomas McGonagle One was a Black Watch warrior through and through and refused any order to get rid of his bagpipes. By keeping them hidden, he was one of several Scots that helped ensure the survival of the bagpipe," Thomas said.

"Well, I would say that maybe he broke the law by not obeying an English order regarding the bagpipes. However, if the bagpipes were considered an instrument of war and if he relinquished those, did that mean he would have to give up his sword too?

"I can't imagine any Scottish warrior doing that," Joseph said.

"Well, I'm proud of you Joseph. You grasped this part of our family history so well that I could say 'I love nae a laddie but ane'," John said.

"Great use of a Scottish ballad in a sentence, John," Thomas said.

"I just think that if you give up your bagpipes, you are also giving up music. When you think about it, music has meant so much to our family. We have just been talking about our favorite Scottish ballads that Nancy played on the piano for us. That is an important part of our lives. You don't just give that up," Joseph said.

"You have grasped the essence of why Grandfather McGonagle broke the law. Sometimes, it may be the law but that doesn't make it right." John said.

7.5

"Did you ever read 'The Merchant of Venice' Joseph?" asked Thomas.

"Uh, not recently,"

"William Shakespeare, not Robert Burns, by the way, wrote 'The Merchant of Venice'. This is what he said about music," Thomas said.

"The man who has not music in his soul, or is not touched with concord of sweet sounds,
Is fit for treasons, stratagems, and spoils. The motions of his mind are dull as night,
And his affections dark as Erebus. Let no such man be trusted." 7.6

"Scots have a history of military service, even going as far back as the Romans. The Romans never were able to conquer Scotland. The Scots fought so hard that even the Vikings were afraid to confront them. That same warrior blood is in all of the McGonagle's," John said.

"Abe Lincoln is placing his faith and hope in Scots like us to fight the Confederacy."

"Yes, indeed. Hearing those words just reminded me of the 'Faith and Hope' song that Nancy played."

"Is that the song that was also called 'The Old Man's Song to His Wife'?" Joseph asked.

"Aye, laddie. Remember, we all chuckled whenever Nancy played that song," John said.

"Everyone, except for father."

7.7

Chapter 8

"One thing that seems odd to me is that our father certainly has that warrior blood but did he marry a woman warrior? No, he didn't. Our mother's side of the family are all Quakers, you know, and they don't fight at all," John said.

"I'm glad you brought that up, John. Maybe you can explain it to me," Joseph said.

"Our mother's maiden name is Lisle. Most of those relatives on that side of the family are Quakers, including our cousin Maggie Lisle. It makes sense, now that I think about it, that Maggie Lisle is such a caring person that she would most certainly make a quilt with a peaceful pattern, like a hummingbird quilt. Maybe Thomas can give you a better explanation about the marriage between a Scottish warrior and a Welsh Quaker," John answered.

"Can you imagine any two people with totally different backgrounds and ideas of the world getting married as did our mother and father?" Thomas asked.

"I understand what you're getting at Thomas. I've thought about that from time to time but I don't think I totally understand. Is this another family secret I'm about to discover?" Joseph wondered.

"No brother, it isn't a secret but let me try to explain it to you. The McGonagle's are Scots and that Black Watch blood still courses through our veins. Like other Scots we are fighters. Scottish Highlanders never backed down from a fight, they never quit and neither do we. They just keep charging and their bravery in battle is unmatched. It's been in our blood for generations and that warrior blood has been passed on to the three of us. It's just part of us and who we are. That's why the Army of the Cumberland was anxious to have some Scottish warriors join them. And fight we have. The harder we fight the sooner this war will be over," Thomas said.

"Okay, so---," Joseph started to say.

Thomas interrupted, "I've told you about the warriors on father's side of the family. Now I'll tell you about our mother's side of the family - the keepers of the peace. Our mother's maiden name is Lisle. Isabelle Lisle, before she became Isabelle McGonagle. The Lisle's are peacemakers. They're Quakers," Thomas said.

"Aye. Mother is a keeper of the peace for sure. How many times have you heard mother quote the Sermon on the Mount?" John asked.

"Oh yeah, I know. Every time I'd get in a scrap at school, she would say 'blessed are the peacemakers, for they will be called children of God'," Joseph said.

"Quakers are guided by peaceful principles. They don't fight. They believe in what they call an Inner-Light. That Inner-Light directly works on everyone's souls. The Quaker values are simplicity, peace, integrity, community, equality, and stewardship," Thomas said.

"How do they get the name Quaker? Is it because they're so fanatic they make people quake and shake?" Joseph kidded.

"No. Their founder, George Fox, told a judge that he should 'quake and tremble' at the name of God. So, they became known as Quakers," Thomas explained.

"What is the history of the Quakers? Were there a whole lot of them in Pennsylvania where our mother's side of the family, the Lisle's lived? Joseph asked.

"You are just full of questions, aren't you? I'll tell you what I know," Thomas said.

"The Quakers were officially called the Religious Society of Friends. The Quakers first arrived from England in 1682. The leader was William Penn. The land where they settled was called Pennsylvania. The Quakers believe there is something of God in everybody."

"Everybody? Do they even think there is something of God in Jefferson Davis?" Joseph asked.

"Yep, everybody. The Quakers value all people equally. When they arrived in America, they treated the Native Americans fairly and were against slavery. They oppose anything that will harm people and rely on their conscience for morality. They are against war and fighting, no matter what. They believe in a direct experience with God, not ritual and ceremony. So, consequently, they believe that priests and rituals are an unnecessary obstruction to God," Thomas explained.

"They must read the bible though. I've seen our mother reading it." Joseph said.

"They do but they regard the bible as an inspirational book. The true Quakers don't celebrate Easter or Christmas because they believe those days shouldn't be just one-day events. They keep the resurrection of Christ in mind all year long rather than a day," Thomas said.

Thomas patted John on the shoulder and pointed at Joseph, who was deep in thought and trying to understand everything Thomas was saying. Thomas and John shared a smile.

"There will be another question coming soon," John whispered to Thomas.

And after a few minutes had passed, they noticed Joseph move. He was coming out of whatever trance he had been in. Joseph stretched and realized it was time for the changing of the quilt. Joseph framed his next question in his head, handed the quilt to Thomas, and started to ask his question.

"But mother ----," Joseph started to say. Then stopped.

Joseph thought some more. After a long pause, he decided to forge ahead and ask his question.

"But mother supports us being in the Army. She believes the war with the Confederacy is necessary and that we must fight to keep the Union together and stop slavery. How can she be a Quaker and not accept all of their beliefs?" Joseph asked.

"I was getting to that Joseph but your questions come faster than I can talk. I was just getting ready to explain that our mother shares a lot of Quaker beliefs but she is a Free Quaker," John said.

"I remember her sometimes saying that she was a Free Quaker," Joseph said.

"Mother always told me that the poet Emily Dickinson wasn't a Free Quaker but mother thought she could have been. She could tell Emily Dickinson was a free thinker just by reading some of the poems she wrote, like 'On Keeping the Sabbath'."

"On Keeping the Sabbath"

"Some keep the Sabbath going to Church, I keep it, staying at Home,

With a Bobolink for a Chorister. And an Orchard, for a Dome.

Some keep the Sabbath in Surplice, I just wear my Wings.

And instead of tolling the Bell, for Church, Our little Sexton sings.

God preaches, a noted Clergyman. And the sermon is never long,

So instead of getting to Heaven, at last –I'm going, all along."

8.1

8.2

Chapter 9

Joseph looked at Thomas and John with a perplexed look. He started to ask another question, then stopped. He tried to think about how to word his question. Thomas spoke up before Joseph could ask.

"Explain it to it to him, John," Thomas said.

"Free Quakers go back to when the Revolutionary War was going on. The Free Quakers had all the core beliefs of the Society of Friends. They also chose to exercise their right to freedom of thought and follow their conscience in all things. The Free Quakers embrace an independent spirit of thought and action. They commit to do the right thing for the right reason," John said.

"Aye. Free Quakers choose to act on a situation with freedom of thought without a consensus of a group. The responsibility for the right decision is determined by each Free Quaker who decides personally on the right thing to do. Sometimes that means fighting for freedom," Thomas said.

"I kind of understand. I can certainly envision our mother as a Free Quaker," Joseph said.

"I agree with you, Joseph. Simply put, Mother is the finest example of a Free Quaker you could think of. She knows herself well and has the confidence to always speak what she believes. She is true to her heart and embraces the Inner Light, which leads to love and caring for all," John said.

"Hands to work and hearts to God," Thomas said.

"Oh, my gosh. How often did I hear her say that!" John said

Joseph struggled to understand his brother's explanations of what it meant to be a Free Quaker. As he thought about it, he realized that his mother demonstrated her Free Quaker beliefs all the time, without him even being aware. He understood better what John and Thomas were telling him. He recalled an incident that demonstrated how their Free Quaker mother exercised her freedom of thought.

Joseph remembered that he was with his mother one day at the Wooster Mercantile. Mrs. Greenwood, who is a staunch Quaker, was also at the mercantile. She asked our mother how she could just stand by and let her sons go off to war. Mrs. Greenwood went on and on. Mother listened to her and when Mrs. Greenwood finally ran out of steam, Mother asked her this question.

"Are you a patriot? Do you put your hand over your heart when the American flag marches by? Are you a true patriot?"

"Well, old lady Greenwood hemmed and hawed. She didn't have an answer. Then Mother answered her own question."

"A true patriot salutes the flag but also does everything they can to ensure that American flag waves over a nation where every person is free".

"Was our mother the first in the Lisle side of the family to become a Free Quaker?" Joseph asked.

"Her parents and grandparents were also Free Quakers," Thomas said.

"That is so good to know. Our family made up their minds to do what they felt was right. They were patriotic. They were not afraid to always take a stand for America, even as far back as the Revolutionary War," Joseph said.

"I think I remember mother saying that Nathanael Greene was a Quaker and her great-grandfather Lisle was in his regiment," Joseph said.

"Very good, Joseph. You do know some family history. Nathanael Greene was a Free Quaker. He was the first general under George Washington to fight against the British. Two of the battles Great-Grandfather Lisle fought in under Nathanael Greene were close to the land in Pennsylvania where the Lisle families farmed, 'The Battle of Brandywine' and 'The Battle of Germantown'," Thomas said.

"You haven't answered my question though. How did a warrior and a peacemaker ever marry? Their approach to the world seems so vastly different, A warrior and a peacemaker getting married seem as different as night and day," Joseph wondered.

"I often wondered the same thing myself. Father explained it to me when I asked him that very question," John said.

John walked to the pile of cedar branches they were using to keep the campfire going. He kicked a few away until he found what he was looking for, then held up a branch that had a Y shape and held it in front of Joseph.

"Think of one limb of this branch as a warrior. A warrior doesn't fear conflict and doesn't run from a fight. They use skill, purpose, and power. A warrior uses persistence and force to come out on top. Warriors champion causes they believe in. That is a description of a McGonagle and our father as a prime example."

John handed the branch to Joseph so he could hold it, then pointed to the other limb of the branch that formed the Y.

"Now the other limb of the branch is a peacemaker. Peacemakers put their emotions aside. They try to understand people's feelings so they can make decisions to discourage conflict. Peacemakers believe dialogue will bring a solution. That is a description of a Lisle and our mother as a prime example. The warrior and the peacemaker are attracted to one another because they obtain their goal by working together and utilizing each other's qualities to become one in spirit," John explained.

"I think I'm going to start quaking after that explanation," Joseph said.

"You mule-head! I might start shaking and quaking you," John said.

"Answer me this then brother. You said the Quaker values are peace and against violence of any kind. What did the Quakers do during the Revolutionary War? Or the War of 1812? If they wouldn't fight, whose side were they on during the wars?" Joseph asked.

"The Quakers did not take sides, which was a problem for the colonists that were fighting for independence and freedom from Britain.

The Quaker religion was so opposed to fighting, they would not do it for any reason, even if it was to benefit them," John said.

"So, our peacemaker Welsh Quaker mother married our warrior Scottish Episcopal father because she was a Free Quaker and made up her mind to decide what was right for her," Thomas said.

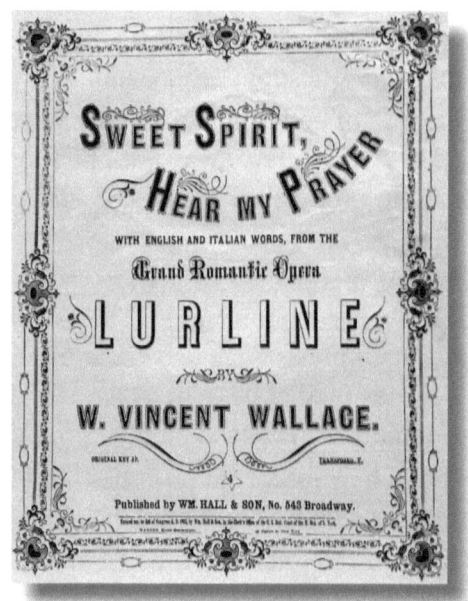

9.2

"*Sweet Spirit, Hear My Prayer*"
'*Oh! Thou, to whom this heart ever yet. Turned in anguish or regret.*
The past forgive, the future spare. Sweet Spirit, hear my prayer.'

"Mother, probably because of her Quaker background, certainly liked Nancy to play a different kind of music on the piano than what father liked her to play," Joseph said.

"Bless the Barney Stone, laddie!! You're right about that. Mother likes those spiritual Quaker-type songs like "Wings of A Dove" and father—," Thomas said.

"Father liked those foot-stomping, play it loud, Scottish ballads, like 'Coming Thru the Rye', or songs that he could bellow out, like

'Old Dan Tucker', John interrupted.

"Talk about us wrestling and fighting over what we wanted to play—," Joseph said.

"You're right. Mother and father could debate whose song was going to be played next as if they were arguing a case in front of the Supreme Court," Thomas said.

"Mother would say something like 'May you have all the luck that life can hold. At the end of your rainbow, may you find a pot of gold.'"

"Father would use his Scottish diplomacy. He could tell someone to go to hell so that they would look forward to the trip."

John crossed his arms, made a stern face, and imitated their father's low voice.

"I've been working since sun up plowing that field on the north forty and chopping down trees Isabella. I want to listen to a good old fashioned Scottish ballad. Let's hear 'Mary Of Argyle'."

Thomas tilted his head, smiled, and imitated their mother's high voice.

"Now Robert, I've been working since before sun up so I could feed you a breakfast of eggs, shortbread, Stornoway black pudding, Lorne sausage, Ayrshire middle bacon, and tattie scones. I did all that before you even started to plow today. So, I should get the first choice. I want to hear 'Wings of a Dove' or 'Sweet Spirit Hear My Prayer'."

"Now, Bella, just because your name means 'God's promise' doesn't mean you need to always listen to those religious songs. How about a good Irish jig?"

"And why, my dear husband, do you want Nancy to play things like 'Old Dan Tucker' and sing so loud they can hear you in the next county?"

"Okay, tell you what darling, we'll compromise and hear 'Roy's Wife of Aldivalloch."

"Okay."

"Okay then?"

"Okay, right after 'Wings of a Dove"

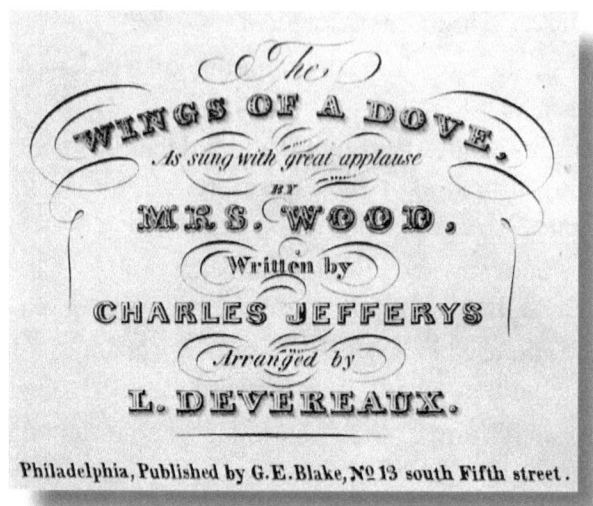

9.3

'Wings of A Dove"
"Oh! Had I wings like a dove I would fly, Away from this world of care.

My soul would mount to the realms on high, and seek refuge there.

But is there no heaven on earth, no help for the wounded breast,

No favored spot where content has birth, in which I may find a rest."

Nancy had barely played the last note of 'Wings of A Dove' when she could feel the impatience of her father as he waited for his song.

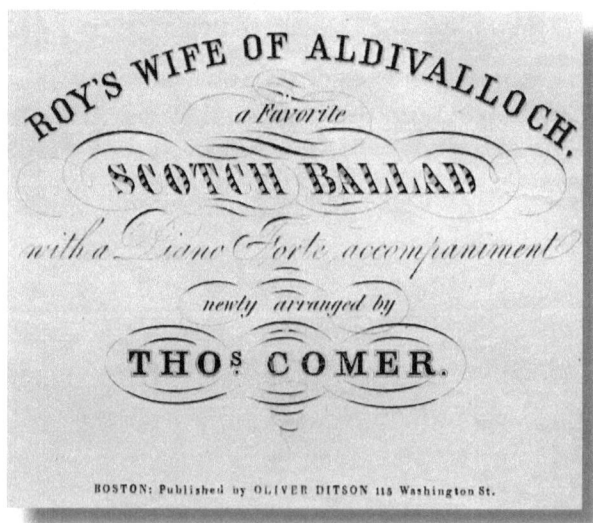

9.4

"Roy's Wife of Aldivalloch".
"Roy's wife of Aldivalloch, Roy's wife of Aldivalloch!
Wa ye how she cheated me, As 1 came ov'er the braes of Balloch.
She vow'd, she swore she wad be mine, she said that she loo'd me best of any.
But oh! The fickle faithless queen, she's ta'en the carl an' left her Johnie!"

"I think I do understand what you're saying. Two people who marry that are from totally different backgrounds are the best people to marry because they can learn from each other," Joseph said.

"That's the way I see it," John said.

"The differences in their approach to life are a compliment to each other and they form a stronger foundation. Hearing the other person's thoughts and how they live their lives will determine the other's decisions and actions," Thomas said.

"We all had a great time listening to the piano at home in the evenings. Mother and father would use different arguments so their favorite songs would be played. It reminds me, just like the title of a song I remember, that the 'Dearest Spot of Earth to Me is Home'," Joseph said.

"Just look at what outstanding brothers we became because of the way our parents raised us," John said.

"At least two of us anyway," Thomas kidded.

"Which two?" Joseph asked.

"Me. And I haven't decided who the other one is yet," Thomas laughed.

Thomas held the folded quilt next to the fire so it would warm, then handed it to John, as it was time for the changing of the quilt

Chapter 10

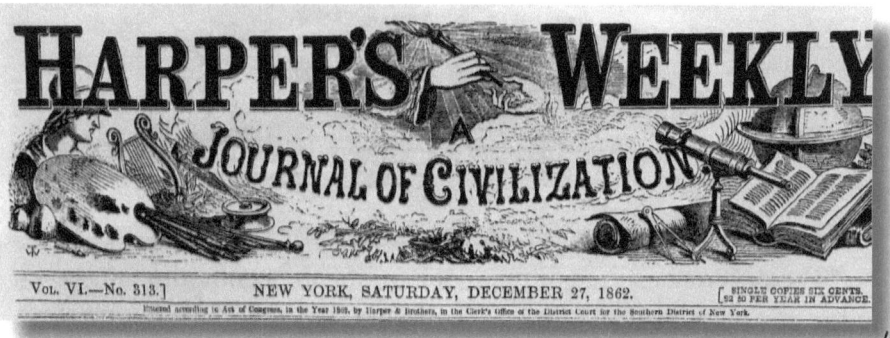

HARPER'S WEEKLY

JOURNAL OF CIVILIZATION

Vol. VI.—No. 313.]   NEW YORK, SATURDAY, DECEMBER 27, 1862.   [SINGLE COPIES SIX CENTS.
$2 50 PER YEAR IN ADVANCE.

Entered according to Act of Congress, in the Year 1862, by Harper & Brothers, in the Clerk's Office of the District Court for the Southern District of New York.

10.1

"All this talk of Quakers and family has me thinking about some of our mother's relatives that were Quakers. I remember a letter that our mother showed us a few times that was written by a relative back east. What was his name, Thomas?" John asked.

"John Reece," Thomas said.

"His family lived in Pennsylvania?"

"That's right. John Reece lived in Fayette County, Pennsylvania, and wrote a letter to his brother Jacob Reece – this would be our mother's father, our grandfather on our mother's side. John Reece wrote the letter to explain that his wife, Martha, had died from complications of childbirth and he was left with 10 children to take care of," Thomas said.

"You know, John, I just had a thought. Do you suppose that John Reece is who you are named after? Mother could have read his letter again at about the time you were born and decided that the name John would be just fine," Joseph said.

"Maybe. There is a John Lisle and a John Reese in our family. I could have been named after either one of them," John said.

"I guess life was rough back in the old days, The Connellsville letter explained how Martha gave birth to ten children, probably without help from a doctor. She died from complications giving birth to the last daughter," Joseph said.

"It's also interesting that our families on both our father's and mother's side lived in Pennsylvania and moved to Ohio," John said.

"The Lisle families emigrated from Ireland and moved to Pennsylvania. The Reece families emigrated from Wales and also moved to Pennsylvania. Our grandfather Reese moved to Ohio and wrote letters to his brothers that still lived in Pennsylvania. The McGonagle families came from Scotland, moved from Pennsylvania, then Indiana, and then back to Ohio," Thomas said.

"So, the brother that wrote the letter would have been an uncle of ours – Uncle John. He wrote the letter to his brother, our grandfather, Jacob Reece. If I've got this right - The McGonagle's are Scottish, the Lisle's are Irish, and the Reece's are Welsh. Guess we've got every country in that continent covered," Joseph said.

"Aye, laddie. All those Scotch, Irish, and Welsh relatives of ours came to Pennsylvania. Some of them stayed there and some moved to Ohio," Thomas said.

10.2

Connellsville. Fayette Co. PA
13th August 1847 A/D

Dear Brother,

After my affectionate regard for you and your family's welfare, suffice it to say that I am not conscious of ever having written to you more than once or so since you left Pennsylvania, however let that matter be as it may. I am at this time influenced by motives of brotherly feeling and respect to address you at length as follows. I am yet living and write west of Connellsville on the State road. I have been informed by brother Wallace that you was apprised of the death of my wife, through his letters to you. She died on the 9th day of March last one year ago, leaving me with ten living children. Three sons and seven daughters, namely in notion according to birth: -1- Joseph who was 24 years old the 10th day of June last, -2- Elizabeth who was 22 years old on the 12th

day of February last, -3- Emily who was 21 years old the 9th day
of March last, -4- Mary who was 18 years old on the 28th day of
February last, -5- Martha who was 16 years old the 5th day of this
present month, -6- John Andres who was 13 years old on the 1st
day of October last, -7- Anne who was 11 years old on the 12th day
of April last, -8- Isaac who was 8 years old on the 5th day of May
last, -9- Susan who was 5 years old on the 11th day of February
last and -10- Harriet the youngest who was 1 year old the 13th of
September last. Thanks be the kind providence. These one and all
so good constitute to all health, together with rational friends and
perfect natural family. 4 of my daughters are full grown young
women as you will perceive from their ages given above. Joseph is
married two years past and has one child, a daughter, he left home
the 9th of May one year ago. He went to Dayton, Ohio where he set
in clerking for Aepers, Harris & Chambers and was forwarding.
Carmeuse Michigan is continued in their employ as clerk til the 1st
day of May, last which time they made him a Captain, one of their
last Canal Boats. They having to learn at their own running at
which business he is now employed, running from Cincinnati past
Dayton to Toledo on the Lakes, he was.

His last trip to Lafayette at the head of steam navigation on
the Wabash River in the state of Indiana. He has a capable education and from all we can judge & hear he is doing well, He speaks
in his letters to me of paying a short visit home this fall to see us,
and for your further grateful time. I forthwith transmit to you his
last letter to me written by his own hand. I must now detail to you
further particulars relative to the loss of my dear companion. She
was confined to bed for seven weeks before she died. Her complaint
commenced with secret inflammation in the womb, which entirely
baffled the skill of the physician, Dr. Cumings, and finally ran into
consumption which terminated her existence in this life but thanks
be to kind Heaven she did not leave in disconsolate. She departed
this life triumphant in faith, fully a person of a blessed resurrection and a reunion of the body & spirit of the second coming of
our heavenly King & Master. A short time before she departed she
called us all up to her bedside. She told us she felt happy she knew

her time was at hand and she felt fully prepared for the change.
She then took each one by one by the hand, giving us each individ-
ually her charge and monition to be kind to each other and faithful
in the way of the Lord, bidding us all a final farewell in this life
and early by sunrise into the arms of her Savior to rest. Affectionate Brother – language fails me to express anything like what my
feelings was on that occasion. I am fully of the inspiration from
that experience that there came to be nothing more trying to a
man's soul than of being called up with ten children to the bedside
of a beloved wife to witness her last benediction and taking her
last farewell with himself and her dear children and at her expir-
ing moment. I was last night with our aged father and mother,
they are growing old and feeble, yet they are now in the enjoyment
of reasonable good health. Father has been sometime back sorely
afflicted with inflammatory rheumatism, but has now completely recovered from the same. He is now in quite good spirits, he is
drawing actually from government Pension of Ninety-Six dollars
per year which supports the two old folks comfortably. Mother complained back time of occasionally pains in her limbs which is only
common with all, as most all of her age. They both urge me much
to communicate to you of John Weevers family their affection-
al respects, saying they have little hope of ever seeing you in this
mortal life again yet they entertain high hopes of seeing you all
in that immortal life which is to come in that bright world where
we all hope to meet, you are singing and where if we meet we shall
here part more. Brother Wallace, wife & one child are living with
father & mother. They are all as well as usual. John Pistoe & wife
are both well and live well, Sister Sally has her home with father &
mother. She is well. Nancy that married Robert Defirst & family
are well. As for brothers Nathan & Andrew & their families, they
are all well for anything. I know at this time I have not seen them
or any of them for the last time two weeks. They then were all well
and doing well. Brother Nathan in particular is a very zealous
and I think an honest and pious Christian. He has been an El-
der of our Christian body for several years. He cannot be called a
fluent man as speaker. Never the less, he has the confidence of the
church and wives, as well as an officer. Brother Andrew, although

a very persevering, industrious honest man in his own mechanical
line of business, yet he is somewhat indifferent to the prosperity of
the church.

Brother, if you will believe me, I consider it a matter of not a
small magnitude, that I can state to you the truth that my four
eldest daughters have all embraced the religion of Christ and are
no members of ordinary standing in the church; here you may put
the question what church as body, I answer the Christian Church,
as in their words. The disciples of Christ, or if you will understand
it better by giving yours. I haven't envisioned that for us as a ???
phase of star is good. Camp bell tells us, and not withstanding all
the troubles, trials and difficulties, I have hither to had encounter
& contend with during my past life. I am still constrained to acknowledge that I have abundant reason to be thankful that all is as
well with me as it is, for I see daily & hourly that the very start of
God's mercies a& helping so much greater than we and I now only
lament that so many years of my full & prim. e days were spent,
regardless of the time interest of Christs Kingdom I now see clearly
that vanity of the vanity which is abound and afloat in the world.
I once, as you yourself know, loved without paying due regard to
that special treasure of the world to come and now of what avail is
it, like the evening blast it is blown through misfortune or chance of
times. I am reduced to very humble circumstances not-withstand-
ing. I am by no means discouraged. I thank God for all. It's the
will of heaven it should be so, no doubt, and whatever is the will of
heaven must and totally be. Why should we mourn for that which
was only given to us and only indirectly ours? The Earth is the
Lords & the fullness thereof. My earnest care in future will be to
serve the Lord in all his appointed ways. And to render my dear,
and mother of my children, as comfortable as my circumstance will
admit by educating them as well as I can. Striving to bring them
up in the nature and admonitions of the Lord. My children are in
some respect at least as they should be. They are agreeable, affectionate and kind to one another.

10.3

"The Connellsville, Pennsylvania letter described that John Reece's son, Joseph Reese, was a riverboat captain on the Ohio and Erie canal and also piloted a steamship from Ohio to Indiana down the Wabash River in the 1830s. We certainly have a lot of adventurers on both sides of the family," Joseph said.

"I'm glad you're taking such an interest in our family history, Joseph. It's good we're having this discussion since one of us will have to pass this information along to future generations," Thomas said.

"Now I've got even more questions. The more we talk about this, the faster the time goes and takes my mind off the cold. I also like not having to think about what is apt to face us tomorrow with all those Johnny rebs wanting us out of Tennessee," Joseph said.

"Aye, laddie. I like talking about this too," said John.

"It's important to discuss family history because when those that know the history are gone, it's gone forever and can't be passed along," Thomas said.

Thomas walked to the fire, leaned over, and picked up a few branches. Before he placed the branches on the fire, he removed the quilt from around his shoulders. He folded it in half, then rolled it up and tucked it under his arm He wanted to be careful and not arrange the quilt close to the fire. Most of the branches they placed on the fire were cedar but he recognized these branches were from a sycamore tree. Thomas remembered seeing a large sycamore tree last week as the Army of the Cumberland marched past the Murfreesboro courthouse. It was a magnificent tree, probably over 80 feet tall. It was interesting that sycamore trees grew in Tennessee, just like in Ohio. The largest trees that grew in Ohio were sycamores. Thomas placed the branches on the fire and wondered if the family history would go up in smoke like the sycamore branches that now began glowing. He hoped that the family history would be passed on to another generation by at least one of his brothers.

Chapter 11

Joseph nodded his head in agreement and stood up. Since he was standing now, he found his haversack and retrieved a piece of hardtack. He pulled it vigorously in his mouth, back and forth, in an attempt to break off a piece. No success. He took the hardtack out of his mouth and inspected it. It was so hard Joseph thought maybe it was a flat rock. No, it was some hardtack. He placed the hardtack in his mouth again, with an even larger bite, and squeezed his jaws as tight as he could.

"Watch your teeth there on that worm castle," Thomas kidded.

"Jumping Jehoshaphat! Where did hardtack get its name anyway? You could make an artificial leg out of this stuff. It never wears out," Joseph said.

11.1

Joseph attempted another bite, which was also unsuccessful.

"Okay. Since I can't bite into it, maybe I'll just skip this sheet-iron cracker across Stones River. What's the history behind hardtack anyway?" Joseph asked.

"Hardtack dates back before the Revolutionary war. The hardtack that the North uses is a cracker made by a sea captain by the name of Josiah Bent. Captain Bent discovered that his bread crackled when placed over a fire. That's how a cracker got its name," John said.

"What's it made out of? Crushed rock? It's harder than this big ole stone I'm sitting on," Joseph said.

"It's just a hard biscuit made out of flour, water, and salt. They keep forever. That's why they issue nine of them to us each day," John said.

"This one is extra hard. Wish I had some Worcestershire Sauce to soften it up so I could have at least one bite," Joseph complained.

"Well, just give it several good licks with the butt of your rifle to break it up," John suggested.

"Afraid it would break my rifle."

11.2

John looked at the box of hardtack. He wanted to make sure Joseph was trying to just eat some hardtack. He wasn't sure why, but when the weather turned cold, the hardtack seemed to become even harder. It reminded John about a funny incident when he was growing up.

A right, proper, snooty, distant relative from England stopped by their farm one day. The 'Duchess of Amesbury' asked for some afternoon tea. John never really believed she was an honest to goodness true Duchess but that was a whole different story. The McGonagle's weren't used to drinking tea, just coffee. The Duchess was aghast. After a little snit, she accepted the coffee, then asked for a biscuit to have with her coffee. Mother thought this was a little strange but wanted to be hospitable and left to go to the kitchen. A few minutes later, our mother came out with a plate of hot biscuits and gravy to serve to the Duchess. Needless to say, the 'Duchess of Amesbury' fainted and fell out of her chair. Once she was revived, the matter was all sorted out when it was explained that in England, they use the word biscuit when what they are really after is a cookie.

"Made by the G.H. Bent Cookie Company, Milton, Massachusetts," John read.

"They're the ones responsible for these?" Joseph asked as he put the biscuit on a rock and hit it with his fist several times.

"About the only way to soften them up is to fry them in pork fat," John said.

"Yes, and then they're called skillygalee," Thomas said.

"Skillygalee? Sounds Scottish," Joseph said

"Sounds like it but it's an English word," Thomas said.

"Those darn Brits. I bet this hardtack is left over from the War of 1812," Joseph said.

11.3

"You know, a soldier from the 116th Ohio was telling me just the other day that he was eating a piece of hardtack when he bit into something soft. What do you think it was?" asked John.

"A worm," Joseph answered.

"No, it was a ten-penny nail."

All three brothers laughed at John's joke. Then Joseph hit the hardtack with his fist several more times. Nothing happened to the hardtack, not even a crack. Joseph just shook his head. He might as well have been hitting a brick. He decided to give up on the hardtack or biscuit or whatever it was.

"I've got an idea. If you want a bite of that iron cracker so much, why don't you try whacking it with a cannonball?" John asked, then laughed harder than necessary.

"Well, Beat the Dutch! I thought you weren't going to bring up the cannonball incident again," Joseph said.

"I didn't bring it up, you just did," John said.

"You know, I'd like to hear your version of what happened Joseph," Thomas said.

"Well, good. I'll tell it my way."

"We were at Camp Wood, learning the ways of the Army during our training. One afternoon we had some time off. I decided that we needed a new game to pass the time. The idea of bowling just came to me. We all saw it being played back in Ohio. I got some of the rest of the regiment to help me carve some pins that would stand on their own. The 41st Ohio challenged the 11th Illinois to a game. All we needed was a bowling ball. There weren't too many round objects available to choose from. Then I got the idea we could use a cannonball and borrowed one from an artillery regiment," Joseph explained.

"Borrowed one, laddie?" Thomas asked.

"Quiet Thomas. I'm telling the story. I borrowed a twelve-pound cannonball. You have to admit, that twelve-pounds 'Napoleon' was a better choice than a twenty-four-pound cannonball. Anyway, we played the game and the 41st Ohio bowled better than the 11th Illinois. That's about all there is to tell. Although I didn't have much experience with cannonballs, I would think you'd be proud that I knew bowling was invented in Scotland. I was just keeping up the family heritage. Even though I was only in the Army for about a month, everyone congratulated and remembered me for my fine idea to have a bowling contest," Joseph explained.

"I know what you were remembered for. You want me to tell the rest of the story?" John asked, barely getting the words out while laughing.

"Oh, go ahead. I don't know why you and Thomas make such a big deal out of bowling with a cannonball. Everything turned out just fine," Joseph said.   ..

"Aye, laddie. You were one very lucky Billy Blue, that's what you were," John said.

He finished the rest of the story that Joseph had omitted.

When the bowling game finished, Joseph commented that he was taking the cannonball, that he borrowed, back to the 22nd New York Artillery.

"No, really Joseph. Where did you get that cannonball?" a sergeant from the 11th Illinois asked.

"As I said, the 22nd New York Artillery regiment," Joseph said, as he tossed the cannonball back and forth between his arms.

"Back away boys. This private is a fresh fish if I ever saw one. He's either bluffing us or he doesn't know that the 22nd New York uses only one kind of cannonball. The kind that can explode!"

Joseph suddenly stopped and held the cannonball with both hands to inspect it.

"Well, Beat the Dutch!" Joseph exclaimed and gingerly leaned over and placed the cannonball on the ground.

"When you stood up Joseph, the 11th Illinois was nowhere to be found. The 41st Ohio all scattered to the hills too. The only ones still standing close to you, although we were a little distance away, were your two brothers," John said.

"Well, I hadn't been through the mill with the Army know how yet. You're exaggerating," Joseph said.

"I never saw a regiment of Union soldiers run so fast, have you, John?" Thomas asked.

"Talk about racing into the woods from the Tennessee quickstep!"

"Who could have guessed that the very next day we were drilled in 'all you ever wanted to know about a cannonball but were scared to ask'," John said.

"It was explained that some cannonballs are non-exploding. Those are used as a battering projectile. Other cannonballs explode or are filled with shrapnel," Thomas said.

"Okay, I'll acknowledge the corn. Can we talk about something else?" Joseph said.

"Ole Cannonball Joe as he was known as, far and wide," John said.

"Cannonball Joe! Jumping Jehoshaphat!" Joseph protested.

Joseph was embarrassed whenever Thomas and John embellished the cannonball story but now he started to laugh. "Cannonball' Joe! How did they come up with that? Thomas and John joined Joseph by the campfire. They all laughed together, as brothers only know how to do. Thomas slapped Joseph on the shoulder. They both knew Joseph would recover from their teasing and would soon be asking more questions.

It was time for the changing of the quilt. John placed the quilt over Joseph's shoulders. Joseph knew this was the opportunity to get away from the current conversation topic and discuss more family history. He pondered another question. Joseph thought about another letter that his father showed him one day. He was young and didn't pay a lot of attention. Now he wanted to know more about it. He forged ahead to ask Thomas and John some more questions.

"As long as we're discussing Quakers and religion, I seem to remember something about Mormons in a letter that I saw a few times. What was that about?" asked Joseph.

"Mormons? Oh, I know what you're referring to. There was a letter that was mailed to our family from A.J. Camblein. She was one brave Scot, that one," Thomas said.

"Did you say she? A.J. Camblein is a woman? Is that the same Camblein family that we're good friends with back home?" Joseph asked.

"That is the same family and that was no ordinary letter either. A.J. Camblein sent that letter from Ft. Kearny, Nebraska, to our father, almost twenty years ago," Thomas said.

"Nebraska – or we should say Nebraska territory," John said.

"Right, it's Nebraska territory. It isn't even a state yet, you know."

"What was a woman doing in that territory? What was the name of the fort?"

"Fort Kearny. It's a U.S. Army fort way out west,"

"Who was A.J. Camblein and what does the A.J. stand for and---," Joseph asked.

"Whoa Joseph. I'm about ready to send you to Company Q. Stop with all the questions and I'll tell you an amazing story," Thomas said.

Robert McGonagle
Wooster Wayne Co.
Ohio
High Creek Missouri
From the United States
Army Station at
Ft. Kearney Missouri Territory

11.5

"The McGonagle's and Camblein's both trace their roots to Scotland. Both families emigrated from Scotland to Pennsylvania at about the same time. Some of both families eventually traveled to Ohio. Our families have been friends and neighbors for over a hundred years. A.J. Camblein was born in 1817, a few years after our mother was born. A.J. was a woman that was as tough as that hardtack we've been eating. You were right Joseph. She is related to the Camblein family that farmed next to ours. She was about 25 years older than you are Joseph, so that's why you knew most of A.J.'s nieces and nephews but didn't know her."

"This is A.J. Camblein's story. A.J. moved to Iowa Territory from Ohio because she wanted to be a farmer, own her land, and do the work herself. The land in Iowa was great for farming. You don't have to clear a lot of trees as you do in Ohio. A.J. – that's the only name I ever heard her called, just A.J. – farmed her own land. Owning land was unusual for a woman. She farmed herself, raised wheat, and corn. A.J. also had about twenty beehives. She was an expert at harvesting honey. She could quilt. And who do you think taught her to quilt?"

Thomas stopped talking and looked at Joseph for a few moments, taking time to let this information sink in. Joseph seemed to sense that there was more to the story, so he kept quiet.

"Well, the best quilter in all of Ohio taught her, none other than our mother, Isabella Lisle McGonagle. Mother and A.J. Camblein were good friends in Ohio and corresponded with each other when A.J. moved to Iowa. The letter A.J. wrote from Nebraska Territory was dated 1848. She explained that she was part of the Mormon Battalion that was headed to the Great Salt Lake Basin in Utah. At the end of the letter, she sent her love to the baby. That baby was you, Joseph. You were only a few years old when A.J. wrote the letter," Thomas said.

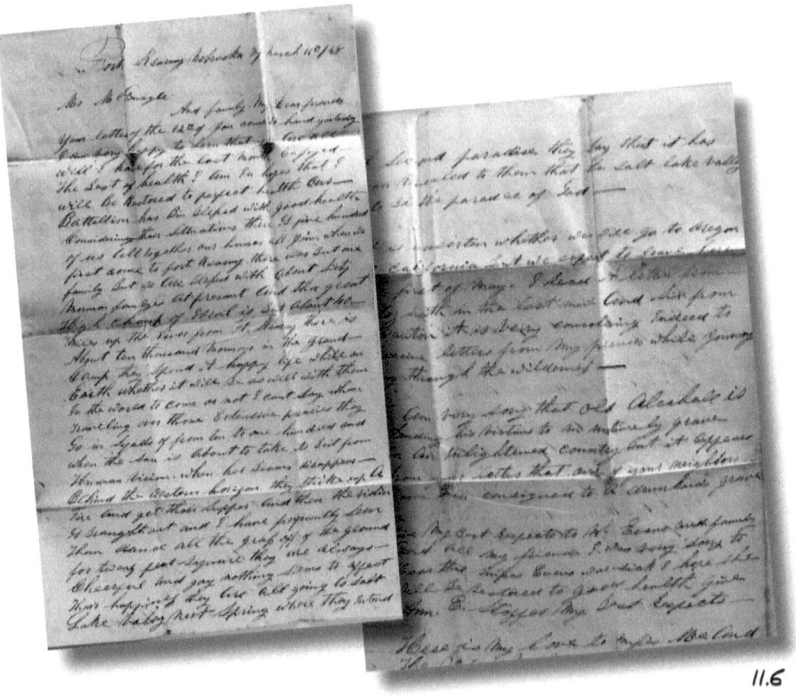

11.6

Fort Kearney Nebraska Territory   March 11, 1848
Mr. McGonagle,

And family. My dear friends your letter of the 12th of Jan
came to hand yesterday. I am very happy to learn that you are all
well. I have for the last month enjoyed the best of health. I am in
hopes that I will be restored to perfect health. Our Battalion has
been blessed with good health, considering their situations. There is
five hundred of us all together. Our houses all joined when we first
came to Fort Kearney. There was but one family. But we are blessed with about sixty Mormon families at present and their Great
High Champ of Israel is but about 40 miles up the river from Ft.
Kearney. There is about ten thousand Mormons in the grand
camp. They spend a happy life while on Earth. Whether it will be
as well with them in the world to come or not I can't say. When
traveling over those extensive prairies they go in squads of from ten
to one hundred.And when the sun is about to take it's exit from hu-

man vision, when her beams disappear behind the western horizon, they strike up the fire and get their supper. And then the violin is brought out and I have frequently seen them dance all the grass off of the ground for twenty feet square. They are always cheerful and gay. Nothing seems to affect their happiness. They are all going to Salt Lake Valley next spring where they intend a second paradise. They say that it has been revealed to them that the Salt Lake Valley is to be the paradise of God.

It is uncertain whether we will go to Oregon or California but we expect to leave here the first of May. I received a letter from Peter Smith in the last mail and six from Canton. It is very consoling indeed to receive letters from my friends while journeying through the wilderness.

I am very sorry that old alcoholic is sending his visitors to an untimely grave in an enlightened country. But it appears from your letter that one of your neighbors has been consigned to a drunken grave.

Give my best respects to Mr. Evans and family and all my friends. I was very sorry to hear that Mrs. Evans was sick. I hope she will be restored to good health. Give Ann E. Stoffer my best respects.

Here is my love to Mrs. and the baby. No more at present. Only I would not strike a girl as hard as Gill Searight did for a thousand dollars.

Ado dear friends for the present.
A. J. Camblein   Ft. Kearney [11.7]

Thomas paused again. He could see the puzzled look on Joseph's face. Joseph worked hard to just listen and not ask hundreds of questions that percolated through his mind.

"I'll answer the question you've got in your head, Joseph. The Mormon Battalion was composed of about 500 men, along with some of their wives, and just a few women. It was an official volunteer infantry battalion, part of the U.S. Army, created by President Polk. The Mormon Battalion was made up of volunteers that started from Council Bluffs, Iowa and went all the way to San Diego, California. It was the only enlistment in American history that had a religious title and was composed entirely of recruits from a single religion. They enlisted in the U.S. Army – the same Army you're in now- for a 12-month enlistment. This was during the Mexican-American war. If truth is known, many Mormons hoped Mexico would win the war since the Salt Lake Basin at the time was in northern Mexico. By the way, our commanding officer, Colonel Hazen, fought in the Mexican-American war. When the war ended, Mexico ceded the land to the USA."

"The first group of the Mormon Battalion went through the desert of the southwest territories as their route to California in 1847. That route was so perilous and so long that after that, the other groups of the Battalion went across Nebraska to the Salt Lake or Oregon or California," John explained.

"Imagine this, Joseph. There were only three women that traveled with the first Mormon Battalion group. A.J. Camblein was in one of the next battalions that crossed the great prairies in 1848. She was one of the first brave women to leave from the starting point of Fort Kearny and follow the Platte River west," John said.

"Aye. In the beginning, the Mormons were forced out of Illinois and they started west. When they reached Iowa, it was too late in the year to continue west, so they spread out to work and figure out how and where they were going. During this time, a man by the name of Kane -Thomas Kane- proposed an idea. Yes, he was Irish, not Scottish but I guess history can't hold that against him. Anyway, he convinced President Polk to let the Mormons gather along the Missouri River. It was a place called Winter Quarters, in Nebraska," Thomas said.

"I would imagine those Mormon's sang their way all across Nebraska Territory."

Chapter 12

"Tittery-Irie-Aye"
"Come all my good people and listen to my song
Although it's not so very good, It's not so very long
And sing tittery-irie-aye and sing tittery-irie-aye.'
Now young men don't get discouraged, get married if you can,
But take care don't get a woman that belongs to another man.
And sing tittery-irie-aye and sing tittery-irie-aye.
Now concerning this strange people, I have nothing more to say,
Until we all get settled in some future date.
And sing tittery-irie-aye and sing tittery-irie-aye." 12.1

"The way our father explains it is that A.J. owned her farm in Iowa, needed help when her farm grew in size, and hired some Mormons to go to work for her. Remember the Evans families from Ohio? A.J. even asked about Mrs. Evans in her letter that we're talking about. Anyway, some of the Evans families got all caught up in the excitement and left their Quaker roots for Mormonism. They became known as 'Quaker Mormons'. Our mother told Israel Evans that when he left Ohio that he should stop in Iowa to see A.J. Camblein. When Mr. Evans found her, A.J. told them they could help each other out. Her farm was becoming too large to manage all on her own and the Mormon families needed help to be able to travel onward. The Evans family and another family by the last name of Clark worked hard for her for a few months. They explained to her they were headed west in the spring to find a permanent home with other Mormons."

"A.J. realized she could join them and experience a once in a lifetime adventure. She also knew she would be a great help to a bunch of greenhorns from the east as they crossed the wilderness. She had the skills to survive. A.J. knew how to farm and how to shoot and hunt. When she also found out that some of the Mormons were taking beehives to the Great Salt Lake, she felt called to help them out. A.J. was a Presbyterian with a fiery Scottish independent streak. You know those Scots, when they make up their mind, just get out of their way. A.J. Camblein was certainly of tremendous help to those Mormons. She could handle an oxen team and ride a horse. A.J. was even known to be able to take a wild horse and break it to ride. How many women do you know that could do that?" John said.

"Jumping Jehoshaphat! That is an amazing story. Let me see if I've got this right. A. J. Camblein was in Ft. Kearny, Nebraska in 1848. I was born in 1842, so I was only six years old when she sent that letter to Robert McGonagle and family," Joseph said as he counted the years on his fingers.

"What happened to her?"

"A.J. left with the Mormon Battalion in May of 1848. They had only been on the trail a week or so when they were crossing their wagons across the Loup River in Nebraska territory. The Loup, which is a french word for wolf, was deep, swift, and dangerous. One of the men with the Clark family that had worked for her in Iowa was taking his oxen team and wagon across when the wagon got stranded on a sandbar. The wagon was stuck and the oxen struggled to move the wagon across the river. And then the darndest thing happened. A roving pack of wolves saw their opportunity. They came howling out of the hills and attacked the oxen. In the ensuing commotion, the oxen panicked. Mr. Clark was thrown off into the river and the wagon was caught in the current. A.J. quickly put the horse reins in her mouth and with a rifle in her right hand and a revolver in her left hand, charged at the wolves. She fired at the wolves until they gave up and ran away. A.J. rode her horse to the wagon, got the oxen under control, and got the wagon across the river. She saved the man's wife and three children and their wagon and supplies. Unfortunately, Mr. Clark drowned, Over the next few days, A.J. taught the Clark teenage son how to handle an oxen team. That same wagon was carrying some of A.J.'s beehives. She was able to save them also," Thomas said.

"Chills ran through every man and woman of the Mormon Battalion that evening. They heard wolves howl throughout the night and realized some of the folk songs they sang around a campfire were a little too close to home."

"The Lonesome Roving Wolves"
"The battalion was camped down by the green grove,
*   Where the pure waters flow from the mountains above,*
The hunters had returned from chasing wild bulls,
*   As we listened to the howling of the lonesome roving wolves.*
As we listened to the howling of the lonesome roving,
*   lonesome roving wolves."* 12.2

"Unbelievable! A.J. Camblein fought a pack of wolves and rescued a Mormon family," Joseph said.

"A.J. was quite the woman. She helped other families with their oxen teams or animals during the day. She would get up early and ride ahead on her horse to find a good way to take a wagon and keep it out of trouble. In the evening, she could help repair a wagon that was broken. Some evenings she would play a song on somebody's organ and sing while she was playing. Mrs. Clark gave her a 'Mormon Pioneer Songbook' to thank her for helping to get her family to the Salt Lake Valley," John said.

"A.J. Camblien was as good a piano player as there was and a purple ribbon quilter. Because she was a good farmer and had the know-how, she even took the time to help the Mormons plant some crops along the way, so some following travelers would have an easier time of it. Father would say that A.J. stood for 'Always Jumping' because she was so quick to jump into action," Thomas said.

"I also heard the story that the Mormons thought A.J. stood for "Another Jilted" because she turned down an offer of marriage so many times. She said no something like 33 times," John said.

"And that was just from Ft. Kearny to Salt Lake," Thomas laughed.

"She was determined to get to California though, so she wintered over at Ft. Boise in Idaho. A.J. trapped coyotes and wolves and sold the furs to the Hudson Bay Company in Idaho. In 1849, she became a Forty-Niner and followed the gold rush to California. She earned money by driving a mule team for the Western Express Company by the name of Cram & Rogers from Crescent City, California to Mount Shasta. She farmed in Trinity County, California until, just a few years ago. Sad to say, she died in a blizzard. Some schoolchildren were lost in a snowstorm, A.J. Camblein went to look for them, and an avalanche got her," Thomas said.

"When A.J. was found, 'The Mormon Pioneer Songbook' was tucked into the pocket of her coat. A song from that book was sung at her service. It was called 'Come, Come Ye Saints'."

"Come, Come Ye Saints"
"Come, come ye Saints, no toil nor labor fear, but joy wend your way.
Though hard to you this journey may appear, Grace shall be as your day.
Tis better far for us to strive, our useless cares from us to drive.
Do this and joy your hearts will swell. All is well! All is well!" 12.3

Joseph shivered and edged closer to the campfire. John and Thomas both stood beside him. It was a good time for the changing of the quilt. Joseph handed it to Thomas and he quickly pulled the quilt tightly over his head and shoulders.

"If I wasn't cold enough, finding out A.J.'s life ended under a mountain of snow certainly doesn't warm me up," Joseph said.

Joseph placed a few more branches on the fire. Larger branches.

"Guess you could say A.J. Camblien had a full life. As the poet, John Donne said, you just don't know 'when the bell will toll for thee'," John said.

"For Whom the Bell Tolls"
"No man is an island, Entire of itself.
Each is a piece of the continent, A part of the main.
If a clod be washed away by the sea, Europe is the less.
As well as if a promontory were. Each man's death diminishes me,
For I am involved in mankind. Therefore, send not to know
For whom the bell tolls. It tolls for thee." 12.4

"A.J. lived life to the fullest. It just goes to show, whether you're a man or a woman, whether you're a soldier of the Scottish Black Watch or an Irish quilter that life is like riding a stampeding two-ton Scottish Highland Dragon. It will buck furiously, breathe fire, and drag you through the most demented, atrocious, dreadful situations in this world. The knack is to hang on tight, and that dragon will give you the ride of your life," Thomas said.

"I'll try to remember that Thomas. I've never quite heard that approach to life before. The story of A.J. Camblein's life was one amazing story though, from the letter that came from Ft. Kearny, to her adventure with the Mormon Battalion. It was satisfying to know she made it to California," Joseph said.

Chapter 13

It was a challenge for the soldiers that gathered near Murfrees-boro to try to keep warm. The December wind came at them in different directions. The temperature dropped steadily downward. The Tennessee ground was frozen where the sun was out of reach. Areas that did get some sun on the clay soil turned to deep mud. Gentle rain showers changed into hard and fast storms without notice. Just now, one of those gentle showers gave way to a burst. The ensuing downpour threatened to put out the McGonagle campfire that struggled against the night. As Thomas rearranged the quilt around his shoulders, he inspected it closely. He wanted to ensure that the waterproof side of the quilt was on the outside. Mother McGonagle not only made a beautiful quilt for them to share, but she also anticipated that the quilt would have to hold up through rain and snow. She used close-woven duck cloth and then boiled it in linseed oil. The unusual construction made the backing of the quilt waterproof. Each brother raised an occasional prayer, usually when he had possession of its warmth, thanking their mother for the quilt. John wrote more letters home to their mother than did Thomas or Joseph. Each letter would thank her for helping to aid them, in her special way, in fighting the rebels.

"You've told me some interesting history about our great-grandfather Thomas McGonagle One. Do you have any family history about Thomas McGonagle – Two – our grandfather?" Joseph asked.

"Aye, laddie. Thomas McGonagle Two was born in 1778 in Scotland. He came to America to settle in the land that was awarded to his father, after his service in the Black Watch, in Pennsylvania. Thomas McGonagle Two was a farmer and a carpenter. However, his plans for a quiet life of growing wheat in Pennsylvania were interrupted by the British. Seems like we had to fight the War of Independence all over again. Our grandfather was in a Scottish regiment, part of the Ohio Militia, during the War of 1812," Thomas said.

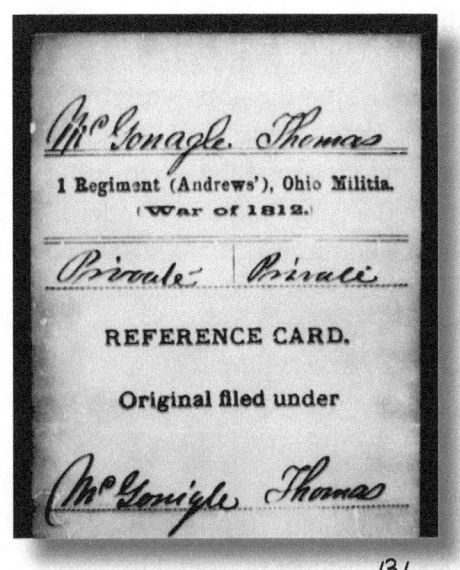

13.1

"Before you tell Joseph how our family history was involved in the War of 1812, you should tell him about the Burr Conspiracy in 1806, and how that intertwined into our family history," John suggested.

"Oh yeah, that did come first and ---," Thomas started to say.

"You mean Aaron Burr, as in, the Aaron Burr and Alexander Hamilton, who fought the duel?" Joseph interrupted.

"That's right. That duel took place in 1804. Aaron Burr was then the Vice President and he shot and killed Hamilton. A few years later, Aaron Burr tried to organize a group that supported the secession of the land west of Ohio. Burr wanted to be the president of this new nation," Thomas said.

"What? Well, I'll eat my bummer's cap! That no-good jailbird!"

"Why wasn't he successful in his attempt to secede? Who stopped him?" Joseph asked.

"Your grandfather, Thomas McGonagle Two stopped him," Thomas said.

"Holy Cow! Bully for grandfather McGonagle! I haven't heard this family story before," Joseph exclaimed.

"That's why we're telling you. This is the story. The President during 1801 was Thomas Jefferson and the Vice President was Aaron Burr. Aaron Burr convinced President Jefferson's Commanding General of the U. S. Army, General James Wilkinson, to help him in his scheme to secede from the Union. A wealthy businessman by the name of Harmon Blennerhassett, who owned a mansion on an island in the Ohio River, was also involved and offered his island as the place to store all the supplies they needed for their secession mission," Thomas said.

"I think I see how this is going to involve grandfather McGonagle. He is living in Ohio now, right?" Joseph asked.

"Aye, laddie. He is in Ohio at this time, which becomes the 17th state added to America in 1803. The Burr Conspiracy occurred in Ohio just a few years later. Burr plotted to split the northwestern territory away from America into another country. General Wilkinson, at the last minute, had a change of heart and informed President Jefferson of Burr's plan. Jefferson then ordered a cease and desist order for Aaron Burr. The Ohio militia, of which Thomas McGonagle Two belonged, was ordered to storm the Blennerhassett island. Grandfather McGonagle knew the Ohio River better than anyone and guided the Ohio Militia to the island. They succeeded and captured all of Aaron Burr's boats and supplies. Thomas McGonagle Two and the Ohio Militia ended the attempt to separate the Western United States from the Union," Thomas explained.

"So, Thomas McGonagle Two fought to help keep the Union together and avoid a secession attempt by Aaron Burr. That's just what we're fighting for, over 50 years after the Burr Conspiracy. We intend to stop the South from secession," Joseph said.

"What happened to Aaron Burr?"

"A few months after the island in the Ohio River was captured, Aaron Burr was caught and arrested for treason. A trial found him not guilty," John said.

"Not guilty? In a pig's eye! Burr actively tried to organize a group to form a separate nation by seceding from the Union. That is treason," Joseph said.

"A lot of people would agree with you, Joseph. Before Burr's trial was over, the Supreme Court decided that Aaron Burr had not committed an overt act, as defined by the Constitution. Chief Justice Marshall ruled that intent alone was not sufficient for conviction. Burr had not committed an act of war. His opinions regarding the government were protected by the First Amendment, freedom of speech," John said.

"Sounds like there was some political intrigue involved with that decision," Joseph said.

"Aye. The Supreme Court had to define what types of speech are and aren't protected by the Constitution. There are always clashes of personalities and conflicts over the interpretation of the law. I think the decision to find Burr not guilty of treason was constitutionally correct. Ethically correct is another matter," Thomas said.

"I'm not so sure it was the correct decision. It seems to me that freedom of speech could not be protected when inciting action against the nation in an attempt to harm it," Joseph said.

"A citizen does have the right to express information, ideas, and opinions without any government restrictions though," John said.

"Jumping Jehoshaphat! The three of us can't even agree on this, let alone a bunch of lawyers," Joseph said.

"Thank goodness we don't have any lawyers in our family or we'd argue even more than we do now," Thomas said.

"Imagine that. Three brothers can't agree on everything. Let's leave this constitutional dilemma discussion to the barristers. I'm ready to exercise our freedom of speech and talk about how grandfather Mc-Gonagle was involved in the War of 1812," John said.

"The War of 1812 was fought over maritime rights on the Great Lakes, particularly Lake Erie. Private McGonagle---"Thomas said.

"Rank of Private! That's just what we are now," Joseph interrupted.

"That's right. Our grandfather, Thomas McGonagle Two, joined the 1st regiment of Ohio Volunteers under the command of Colonel Duncan McArthur. McArthur and Thomas McGonagle Two grew up in the same area of Pennsylvania. They were friends early on, due to their common Scottish ancestry," Thomas said.

"Birds of a feather, flock together," Joseph said.

"Aye, laddie. They were just like two Scottish birds. By the by, Joseph, not to throw too much information at you but just so you know, there is a red finch called a Scottish Crossbill that is unique to Scotland. It lives in the pine forests in the Scottish Highlands," Thomas said.

"My two dear brothers, I must say that you are full of family history which I like knowing about. But the Scottish Crossbill? Just knock me into a cocked hat."

Joseph realized he was learning huge chunks of family history. And facts of the world, along with all the family stories he was learning. He was appreciative of that but then Thomas or John would just throw random information into the family history stories. Jumping Jehoshaphat! How could they know all of this stuff? Aaron Burr. Freedom of Speech. Indian tribes. The Black Watch. Scottish Highlands. The Mormon Battalion. Joseph hoped he could remember everything.

"Well, Joseph, there is family history. And there is the history of our nation. The two histories are intertwined. So, pay attention. The history lesson continues," John said.

"Colonel McArthur and grandfather McGonagle worked together on a surveying expedition in the Ohio Territory in 1796. The two of them surveyed and laid out the town of Chillicothe, Ohio which, if you didn't know, was the first state capital of Ohio," Thomas said.

"Not Columbus?"

'Actually, Chillicothe was the first capital. Then it moved to Zanesville, then back to Chillicothe, then Columbus after that," Thomas said.

"That's balderdash," Joseph said.

"Nope, it's all true. Your Ohio government at work. Anyway, here's your history lesson, Joseph. The Treaty of Paris in 1783 ended the American Revolutionary War and Great Britain gave up rights to the Ohio Country. However, British troops continued to occupy forts in the territory. Also, the native American Indians in the Ohio Territory refused to recognize America's claims to areas northwest of the Ohio River. In 1785, Britain allied with the Native American Indians," John said.

THE TIPPECANOE QUICK STEP
Published by SAM¹ CARUSI Baltimore

/3.2

"As a private in the 1ˢᵗ Regiment of Ohio militia, Thomas McGonagle Two fought in several battles against the British and Indian alliance. The most significant battle he fought in was the Battle of Tippecanoe. That was fought in 1811 on the Indiana and Ohio border," Thomas said.

"Tip and Ty"
"Oh, who has heard the great commotion, motion, motion
All the country through? It is the ball a-rolling
*   For Tippecanoe and Tylor too.*
And with him, we'll beat Little Van, Van,
Van is a used-up man. And with him, we'll beat little Van."
/3.3

"Tippecanoe County, in Indiana, right?" Joseph asked

"Right. Governor Harrison ---,"

"You mean William Henry Harrison, who was elected president in 1840, just before I was born?" Joseph interrupted.

"Right. Stop interrupting Joseph. Thomas McGonagle Two was part of the American troops under command of Governor Harrison that fought against a great Shawnee leader called Tecumseh. Tecumseh envisioned an independent Native American nation east of the Mississippi River, under British protection," Thomas said.

"Tecumseh lost the Battle of Tippecanoe. Remember how you lose a battle, Joseph?" John asked.

"You run out of ammunition."

"Aye, laddie. So, don't let that happen to you," John said.

"Governor Harrison was impressed by how determined Thomas McGonagle Two and the 1st Andrews Regiment of Ohio fought. The Governor chose the 1st Andrews regiment and ordered them to make a final charge at Tecumseh's warriors," Thomas said.

"A final charge? That would have been an unbelievable sight. Can you picture it? The Andrews Regiment of Ohio and the Shawnee warriors charging at her other. What happened?" Joseph asked.

"The Scottish Highland regiment forced them to retreat. This last successful charge helped win the Battle of Tippecanoe. The defeat was so pronounced that Tecumseh's alliance never recovered." Thomas said.

"William Henry Harrison earned the name 'Tippecanoe' for his heroism. I must say, that Scottish regiment that grandfather McGonagle was part of made 'Ole Tippecanoe' look really good," John said.

"So that's why he used the campaign song 'Tippecanoe and Tyler Too' during his 1840 election," Joseph said.

"It was titled 'Tip and Ty'. Maggie played this on the piano for us sometimes. She always used to say that the refrain in the song was euphonious, as it had a triple alliteration, an internal rhyme, and formed an iambic tetrameter," Thomas said.

"Oh sure. That's just what I was going to say," Joseph said.

"I just bet you were Joseph."

"I remember Nancy playing 'Tip and Ty' anyway. I also remember that Harrison wasn't president for very long. And I remember President John Tyler was in office when I was born," Joseph said.

"That's a lot of remembering for you Joseph. But you're as right as a month of Sundays. Harrison talked for so long at his inauguration that he got a cold, then got pneumonia, and soon he was pushing up daisies. He was only in office for a month," John said.

"So, brothers, let me see if I've got this right. Obtain the services of a Scottish Regiment to fight your battles. Name a song after the battle you win and use it to campaign for President. Don't go getting any pneumonia. And try to keep out of the cold," Joseph said.

"Aye, laddie."

Thomas looked down at his muddy, ragged, worn boots.

"You'd think Mother Nature would respect a shoemaker better than this."

He shook his head in dismay. Thomas eased the quilt off his shoulders, snapped the rain off, and handed it to John. John gave him a nod of thanks.

John McGonagle
in the U.S. Civil War Soldiers, 1861-1865

Name:	John McGonagle
Side:	Union
Regiment State/Origin:	Ohio
Regiment:	27th Regiment, Ohio Infantry
Company:	I
Rank In:	Private
Rank Out:	Corporal

13.4

Chapter 14

"We've talked a lot about our Scottish bloodlines, warrior instincts, our ancestors fighting in the French and Indian War, and the War of 1812. Now we're fighting another war in this country between the Union and the Confederacy. At least our father didn't have to fight in a war," Joseph said.

"You sure about that Joseph?" John asked.

"Oh no. I'm wrong about that too? Sounds like I'm about the learn some more family history."

"Ever hear of the Toledo War, Joseph?"

"No, but I think I'm about to."

"The Toledo War was fought between Ohio and Michigan. Our father, Robert McGonagle, was right in the middle of it," John said.

"Ohio and Michigan went to war against each other?" Joseph asked.

"Aye, they did. At the end of the French and Indian War the 'Northwest Ordinance of 1787' established the northern boundary of Ohio as the southern bend of Lake Michigan," John said.

"Ohio became a state in 1803. So, when was this war?" Joseph asked.

"That's when it started, in 1803 when Congress voted Ohio into the Union. At that time, they also accepted a boundary provision that was attached to the Ohio Constitution. The provision stated that the Ohio northern boundary included where the mouth of the Maumee River flows into Lake Erie. Congress accepted Ohio's Constitution but did not act on the northern boundary provision. This led to a conflict between Ohio and Michigan," John explained.

"Well. Beat the Dutch! How was it originally decided where the northern Ohio boundary would be?" asked Joseph.

"Funny you should ask. The boundary between the two states was decided when the land was surveyed," John said.

John looked at Joseph as if he should know what he was going to say next.

"You don't mean—," Joseph started to say.

"Aye laddie. You catch on fast," John said.

"You said Thomas McGonagle Two was a surveyor. So, you're telling me that our grandfather McGonagle started the war between Ohio and Michigan?" Joseph said.

"Yup. He was on the surveying team of three or four men that established the boundary. Of course, Michigan did their survey and they disagreed where the boundary should be," John said

"Well, imagine that."

"When Michigan wanted statehood, this dispute had to be settled. The argument about the boundary went on for 30 years. Finally, in 1833, the U.S. Senate sided with Ohio but the House of Representatives refused to agree," John said.

"Again - Imagine that."

"Huh. I thought the House and Senate always worked together to find solutions to problems," Joseph said.

"Oh, grow up," Thomas kidded.

"What happened next was Ohio used the boundary where grandfather McGonagle and the other surveyors established it and formed an Ohio county in the disputed territory," John said.

"And Michigan didn't like that," Joseph said.

"They didn't like it one little bit. Michigan sent their state militia to the boundary. Ohio responded by sending their militia and other landowners in the northern counties of Ohio to the boundary," John said.

"Even though grandfather McGonagle had already died by this time, our father got involved to make sure the boundary that his father had set was correct and not changed. He was ready to go to war with Michigan to preserve our family honor. Also. if Michigan successfully won the argument over this disputed boundary, what would be next? Would Michigan continue to argue over boundaries, including the county where our farm is?" Thomas said.

"So, in a sense, this was all about 'Home, Sweet Home'," Joseph said.

There it was again. *"There's no place like home. There's no place like home!"*

The Union and Confederate bands had played the song back and forth so many times that now 'Home, Sweet Home' was stuck in Joseph's head. The song was in every soldier's head. Not just the melody, and words to the song, but the longing for 'Home, Sweet Home'. Home was in their thoughts with every breath they took.

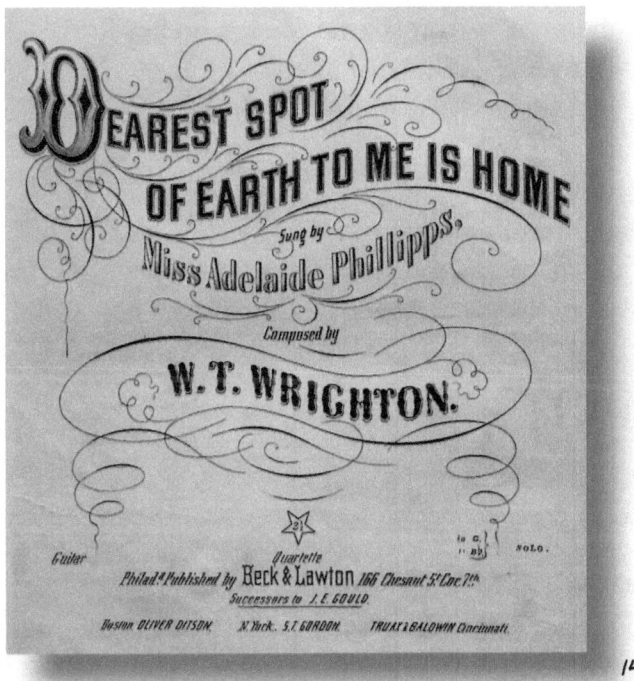

14.1

"The dearest spot of earth to me is home, sweet home,
The fairyland I've longed to see is home, sweet home!
There how charmed the sense of hearing,
There where hearts are so endearing,
All the world is not so cheering, as home, sweet home.
The dearest spot of earth to me is home, sweet home."

"The dearest spot of earth of me is home. Home, sweet home," John said.

"Amen, brother. While we listen to the regimental bands play 'Home, Sweet Home', I'm sure one of us has another question," Thomas said.

"Beat the Dutch! You can't stop in the middle of a story. We're at the point where Ohio and Michigan are set to fight each other over the boundary between the states. What happened next?" Joseph asked.

"You know we've talked about the Scottish warrior blood that we have. Our father was so passionate about defending the surveyed boundary that he organized about twenty of the surrounding farmers and neighbors that had roots from Scotland. They formed a little county militia and named it the 'Scotch McBuckeyes'," John said proudly.

"Everyone always said Robert McGonagle had a sense of humor, didn't they," Thomas said.

"He always carried some humor and determination throughout his life. When the militia was formed, he packed his Greenwood musket, several tomahawks, a month's worth of supplies, and rode with the other 'Scotch McBuckeyes' to the boundary," John said.

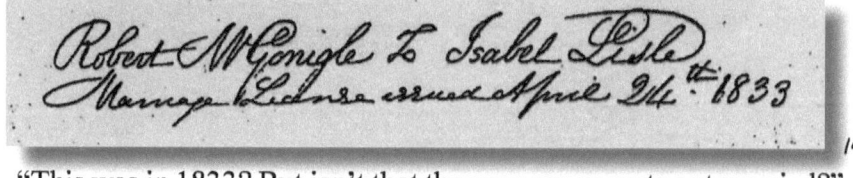

14.2

"This was in 1833? But isn't that the year our parents got married?" Joseph asked.

"Aye, laddie. Robert and Isabella McGonagle got married in April of 1833. A few months later, Robert left his lovely Quaker bride to run the farm while he went off to war," Thomas said.

"What was her opinion about father running off to fight in the Toledo War after only being married a few months?" Joseph asked.

"I believe she sang the words to 'Sweet Spirit, Hear My Prayer' over and over."

"It is well known that Isabella Lisle McGonagle, due to her Quaker upbringing, was a peacemaker to everyone she ever met. Now that her husband was off to fight, she pushed down all her frustration and focused on the things she could control. Mother realized that one could never know when life would take you down an unexpected path. She did what she could to support her husband and keep the home fires burning. She accepted that the storms of life, that occur to us all from time to time,

 forced them into an untenable situation." John explained.

"Storms of life, eh?"

"Aye. And she prayed for his safe return every day."

"Talk about 'Home, Sweet Home'! Isabella made sure Robert would have a home to return to when the Toledo war was over," Thomas said.

"So, what happened to end the Ohio-Michigan War? Did the Ohio wives and the Michigan wives have a quilting bee to settle the controversy?" Joseph kidded.

"Far from it. The 'Scotch Mc-Buckeyes' and the rest of the Ohio militia gathered on one side of the Maumee River and the Michigan militia gathered on the other side. Michigan has always had a reputation for being vicious and bloodthirsty people. The Ohioans called them wolverines, a name for them that still exists to this day. Both sides had their rifles pointed at each other and some started exchanging rifle fire," John said.

"Robert McGonagle waited to see what would happen and didn't fire his rifle," Thomas said.

"He could have told everyone after the Toledo War was over that he had shot a genuine Michigan wolverine," Joseph said.

"What he liked to tell everyone was that he fought in a war but never fired his gun," Thomas said.

"The president of the United States at the time was Andrew Jackson who requested that both sides try to negotiate a peaceful resolution. Mother's Quaker background must have had some effect on her warrior Scottish husband because our father agreed to be one of the Ohio representatives in the negotiations. He thought, at first anyway, he would be helpful in the discussions with the wolverines – uh, Michigan," Thomas said.

"How did that work out?"

"As you might expect. That Scottish blood not only is known for fierce fast-moving fighting. It's also known that Scots are very stubborn and do not back down from a fight. It is not in a Scots nature to negotiate. Father's position was that the boundary had been surveyed correctly. After all, it was Thomas McGonagle Two who was one of the surveyors, so of course, our father knew it had been surveyed correctly. He would not concede an inch of land to Michigan," John said.

"So much for negotiation. How did it end?" Joseph said.

"President Jackson eventually just replaced the Michigan Governor and gave Ohio the 400 square miles of disputed land, The Toledo War ended," John said.

"Michigan eventually gave up their fight over the boundary and became a state in 1837, the same year I was born. That's how I remember the year," Thomas said.

"What did you think about that family story Joseph?"

"Fine as cream gravy."

"Understand everything?"

"Let's see. We had a Revolutionary War and gained our independence and some land. Then we reclaimed that land in the War of 1812, which then granted land to America all the way to the Mississippi River. Those horrible Michigan wolverines took their licks and finally received their statehood in 1837," Joseph said.

"Bully for you, Joseph. You did pay attention."

"Father was proud of the Ohio volunteers he put together - the Scotch McBuckeye's. He said those lads were certainly 'Gems of Scotland', just like Scottish ballads.

"There would be five states other than Michigan that would come out of what was considered the northwest territory. Ohio in 1803. Indiana in 1815. Illinois in 1818. Wisconsin in 1848," John said.

"Gems of Scotland! Didn't you also say that about grandfather McGonagle and the Black Watch?" Joseph asked.

"Aye, laddie. That I did."

Chapter 15

John placed one knee on the ground by the campfire. He arranged some branches, realized they were too green to burn, and replaced them. John watched as the branches started to burn, then stood up and stretched. The rain had now mostly subsided except for a few drops that still found their way to the campfire. He took his cap off and brushed the rain away. He scratched the back of his neck a little. Then a little more. Then vigorously.

"John – do you have some of Bragg's bodyguards bothering you?" Joseph asked.

"You're telling me that your eyes are sharp enough to spot some lice on my neck from the distance you're sitting Joseph?" John asked.

"That would indeed require eyes good enough to be a sharpshooter," Joseph said.

"Aye. We all know the only person with eyes good enough to be a sharpshooter in our family is another Thomas in the family. None other than our cousin, Thomas Lisle," John said.

"Yep. We are all pretty good shots but Thomas Lisle qualified to be assigned to Birge's Western Sharpshooters. Remember that time we went hunting with Tom for Thanksgiving turkeys? I can understand why he's a sharpshooter. He was shooting a turkey that was so far away I could barely even see any feathers," John said.

"We all are accurate with a rifle. Thomas or John – one of you always wins the county shooting contests. I'm not too far behind you. I usually come in second or third. That cousin Thomas Lisle though – he's a whole different kettle of fish," Joseph said.

"When we would go over to his farm and have a shooting contest he was amazing," Thomas said.

"Yep. We never could outshoot him. Now Thomas Lisle is in the

66th Illinois. I don't know which state they're in right now," John said.

"The last I knew he wrote a letter and said he had been at the Battle of Williamsburg and the Seven Days Battles of Richmond."

"Those battles took place in which state?" Joseph asked.

"I'll give you a hint. It is the only state to split into two states since the civil war began," Thomas said.

"Oh, I know. Those battles took place in Virginia. That state divided into West Virginia and Virginia," Joseph said.

"Aye. I almost feel sorry for those Johnny Rebs in battle with Thomas Lisle. I'd bet my best Arkansas toothpick that his sharpshooting skills would be better than anybody's," John said.

"You know, to be a sharpshooter you have to pass a pretty stiff rifle test. You have to be able to place ten shots in a circle of ten inches – from two hundred yards away," John said.

"Two hundred yards? How many soldiers can do that?" Joseph asked.

"I heard there is only about ten or twenty or so from each state that can pass the rifle test. Then they combine them all into several sharpshooting units," Thomas said.

"If you are a sharpshooter, you even get issued a Sharps rifle. If I had a Sharps rifle I could pass that rifle test, even at three hundred yards," Joseph said.

"You think so? I think you'd better go check into Company Q. You seem to be hallucinating Joseph."

"Company Q?"

"So many questions. You know, the fictitious unit for all the sick soldiers."

"Oh, that Company Q."

"Did you know that they issue a sharpshooter a green uniform?" Thomas said.

"They do? Why is that? Or are you trying to see if I'm a pie eater again?" Joseph asked.

"Nope, no joshing. Their uniform is green rather than the standard Union blue. This gives a sharpshooter some camouflage," John said.

"Special Sharp's rifles and special uniforms. I bet the sharpshooters are treated so well that they get all the john barleycorn they want," Joseph lamented.

"I don't know about that Joseph. I don't think a wallpapered sharp-shooter would do too well at a rifle test."

John walked back to sit on one of the large stones again and situated the quilt over his back. As the quilt brushed against him, Joseph rubbed part of the quilt be-tween his fingers. Joseph enjoyed the family history that

Thomas S Lisle in the U.S., Civil War Soldier Records and Profiles, 1861-1865	
Name:	Thomas S Lisle
Age at Enlistment:	22
Enlistment Date:	15 Mar 1862
Rank at enlistment:	Private
State Served:	Ohio
Survived the War?:	Yes
Service Record:	Enlisted in Company 3rd Indp, Ohio 3rd Sharp Shooter Company on 17 Apr 1862. Promoted to Full Sergeant. Mustered out on 26 Apr 1865.
Birth Date:	abt 1840
Sources:	Official Roster of the Soldiers of the State of Ohio

15.2

his brothers were telling him. He just wished the stories weren't being told on a freezing, wintry, windy, rainy night in Tennessee. He wished he and Thomas and John were all in Ohio, sitting by their fireplace and listening to Nancy or Maggie play 'Home Sweet Home' while mother worked on a quilt. Joseph was reminded of something about his mother and a quilt. He just couldn't place exactly what it was. The thought was just out of reach. What was it? He pictured his mother in the rocker with a quilt in progress on her lap. Joseph tried hard to focus so it would jog his memory. The memory was just out of reach but another question came to mind.

"It's hard to imagine A.J. Camblein being the same person to plow a field or hunt an elk during the day and then work on a quilt in the evening. Those things don't seem to go together. How do you know she was a quilter? Just because she was a girl?" Joseph asked.

"No, I remember once when I was at the Camblein's farm helping them repair the roof on their barn and I got soaking wet in a thunderstorm. I went in their house to warm up and ole lady Camblein, A.J.'s mother, gave me a quilt. She told me it was the 'Fox and Geese' pattern and that A.J. had made it. A.J. gave it to her brother as a birthday present," Thomas said.

"Thinking about that 'Fox and Geese' quilt reminds me of our mother. Think back to any cold evening when we would gather around the fireplace in our house. Mother would always cover her legs with the same quilt all the time. Remember that quilt?" John asked.

Joseph had a sudden moment of realization. He remembered what the memory was that he was trying to recall.

"I do remember that quilt very well. Very well indeed," Joseph said.

"Why is that Joseph?"

Joseph smiled at the remembrance. He had not thought about this particular incident for a long time. He had a particular memory of his mother's favorite quilt. Joseph envisioned the quilt in his mind. John and Thomas would be surprised when he revealed that he knew the pattern of their mother's quilt. As the memory flooded back to him, he realized something else about the quilt.

"Well, I'll be a blue tick hound," he murmured to himself.

"Okay, brothers. Now I've got a family story to tell you," Joseph said.

"This should be interesting, Thomas. We're going to get a history lesson from Joseph," John said.

"When did this happen?" Thomas asked.

"This happened when I was eleven years old, so it must have been the winter of '53. It was one of those cold, drizzly days in Ohio where the cold can go right down to your bones. I was inside the house because it was such a nasty day. Mother was in her rocker with a bowl on her lap and was peeling vegetables, getting ready to make soup for dinner. She had that same quilt that she always used, wrapped around her legs as she worked. She was all situated and working away on some potatoes when she asked me to bring her a cup of coffee so she wouldn't have to get up. So, I did and----"

Joseph paused and looked up at the dark night sky. He realized the rain had stopped, for now anyway. Try as he might, he couldn't see the

Big Dipper because of the cloud cover. He thought about the rest of the story. Should he tell his brothers the story he was remembering? It would just give them more ammunition so they could tease him about something else.

"You okay Joseph?"

"Yeah, it's just something I haven't shared with you or anyone since it happened so many years ago."

"Well, what happened? What did you do Joseph?' Thomas asked.

Joseph looked to the ground, then up to the trees, then back to the ground. He looked at Thomas. He looked at John. Joseph watched some cedar branches sway back and forth. He wished the wind would stop blowing. Joseph realized that his brothers knew he was stalling. Should he continue with his story? It was too late to stop now. He had already let the cat out of the bag. Joseph took a deep breath.

"I spilled some of the coffee on her quilt as I handed her the cup," Joseph admitted.

Thomas and John looked at each other, both almost not believing what they had just heard Joseph say. Their mouths dropped open wider and they could not have been more surprised than if a herd of buffalo had charged through their campsite.

"Good Glory Hallelujah! That quilt was one of her most favorite things in the world. How could you spill coffee on it?" Thomas said.

"I was young and not as careful as I should have been."

"I've never heard this story before," Thomas said.

"I haven't heard this before either. You must have gotten a good whupping for doing that," John said.

"That's what I expected too but I didn't get a whupping, just a lifelong lesson," Joseph said.

"Well, Joseph, it's hard to believe you didn't receive the whupping of a lifetime but tell us what happened."

"Well, this is the rest of the story. As soon as I spilled that coffee on the quilt, I started crying because I knew how much that quilt meant to her. I was so sorry and upset with myself that I had disappointed her.

Mother said, "Oh Joseph! You need to be more careful!"

Then she took the cup of coffee and set it on the floor, along with the bowl of vegetables. She put her arms around me and hugged me until I stopped crying.

"Let me tell you why you need to be more careful Joseph. The things you do in life can have a lasting impression, just like the coffee stains that are on the apples of this quilt," Mother said.

"What apples on the quilt? I don't understand."

She spread the quilt out on the floor and we both got down on our hands and knees. Mother had a paper tape measure. She helped me measure it. The quilt was square, six feet long, and six feet wide.

"Let me explain about this quilt. This is called an Apple Tree Quilt," Mother said.

She took my hand and traced around two red patches on the quilt.

"Each one of these pieces of material represents the apples on the tree. Each one is called a block and a quilt is made up of a number of blocks."

She took my hand again and traced around the green blocks on the quilt.

"These four blocks are the leaves on the tree and there are a few more brown blocks that are the trunk of the tree."

Joseph paused as he looked up at the dark sky again. He could envision exactly what the quilt looked like. Thomas and John were still speechless, waiting for Joseph to continue his story.

"It made sense to me then. I could see that it was a pattern of an Apple Tree. I had never realized it before and now it really jumped out at me. I could see that the fabric matched with the apples, the branches,

the trunk of the tree," Joseph said.

"Mother, I am so sorry. I can see now that one of the apple blocks has been stained by the coffee. Will the stain come out?"

"I can get some of it out but no, that coffee stain will be there forever. So, just like the permanent change the coffee made to the quilt, other decisions that you make in this

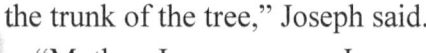

15.3

life can also cause permanent changes that can't be undone. You have to be careful with the words that you say and the things that you do – those can also be permanent."

She looked at me with those bright blue peacekeeper eyes.

"Understand?"

"I know now that mother was very wise for handling my mistake the way she did. She used the Quaker teachings she knew and used my accident to illustrate how I should live my life. Then she explained even more about the Apple Tree Quilt. She told me a good friend had given her the quilt and that it was a symbol of their friendship. Her friend decided to quilt the Apple Tree pattern because of all the connections they shared with apples. The McIntosh apple was their favorite variety. The apples on the Apple Tree Quilt were most certainly a McIntosh. What a great Scottish name for an apple – a McIntosh. It has to be the best of all the apple varieties. Mother explained

15.4

that she and her friend also liked apple pies. When her friend was at an early age, mother taught her how to quilt and make McIntosh apple pies. Soon, her friend became a great quilter and baker, with an apple pie her specialty. The friend gave mother an Apple Tree quilt to thank her for teaching her how to quilt and bake," Joseph said.

Thomas and John exchanged a knowing glance. The story Joseph told was so typical of their mother. The peacemaker. The Quaker. The teacher. They all had similar experiences growing up when their mother inevitably would use an opportunity to teach them a lesson. A lesson that would make them better people and something they would remember for the rest of their lives.

"You know, Thomas and John, this is what you explained to me earlier. Quilts have a secret meaning sometimes. The apple tree quilt was very meaningful and held some secrets that just mother and her friend shared. Mother explained that her friend picked wonderful colors for the quilt. I could see that the apple blocks looked just like a McIntosh. She explained to me why this particular quilt design was so special. She explained how it was made with great accuracy and construction. The binding was finished with particular care. Mother took my hand again and traced around the binding, all the way around the edges of the quilt. She appreciated that the color of the binding was so beautifully chosen."

Then I said, "Mother this quilt is so meaningful to you. Now I know why you like to use it so much. It not only keeps you warm, but it also has warm memories whenever you use it. It is made so perfectly and now I've made it imperfect by spilling coffee on it."

Joseph took a deep breath. He thought about 'Home, Sweet Home'. Then he smiled, knowing Thomas and John would be surprised at what he was now going to tell them.

"That's when mother explained to me that the quilt was not perfect. There was a mistake on the quilt that had been made on purpose. This was done as just a reminder that the only perfect person in heaven and on earth is God. The quilt wasn't perfect even before I spilled coffee on it. Then mother shared the secret where the mistake was located on the quilt. On one of the bottom blocks she pointed out a small mismatched area, with some tiny initials inside that spot. I only noticed them when she pointed them out. The initials on the quilt were 'J.A.'."

Joseph stopped his story. He wanted to see if Thomas or John could figure out who it could be that had the initials 'J.A.' He smiled at them as they struggled to come up with a name. Thomas and John looked at each other to determine if the other one had a clue. Now they were both scratching the back of their necks. Neither one was able to name the person that those initials might be.

"Give up trying to figure out who 'J.A.' was? The mistake was her friend's initials really were 'A.J.' – not 'J.A.'. She had purposefully sown the initials on backward. That way, the quilt would not be perfect and the backward initials would be a little secret between the two of them'," Joseph said.

He smiled at Thomas and John broadly again and slowly pronounced, "A.J."

The understanding of whose initials were on the quilt was realized by Thomas and John at the same time. Joseph saw the expression on their faces and recognized that they had figured it out.

"I never realized until a little while ago that mother's friend that made the quilt was---," Joseph began.

"A.J. Camblein," they all said at the same time.

The McGonagle brothers smiled at each other, then Joseph started to laugh. His laughter was contagious and soon Thomas and John were laughing too. When their laughter would die down after a while, one brother would start laughing again and soon they were all laughing together again. One brother would start to say something but found he was unable to talk because he would start laughing again. Then another brother would attempt to talk and then laugh again. Finally, Thomas got the words out.

"Well, you certainly did give us a family history lesson, Joseph. I never knew all those things about that quilt and I never knew mother taught you so much about quilts. I saw mother with that Apple Tree quilt on her lap almost every day and didn't realize all the hidden things about it," Thomas said.

"Well Joseph, you outdid yourself with that Apple Tree Quilt story. As a reward for telling a story that Thomas and I hadn't heard before, you can use the bear paw quilt," John said as he presented the quilt to Joseph. John bowed graciously to Joseph.

"A.J. could do everything. She was good at anything she tried. The surrounding farmers in Iowa went to her for advice because her wheat crop was the best of any in that part of the country. We forgot to tell you, Joseph, she was also a boulangere," John said.

"Bou—what?"

"Boulangere. It's a French word that means a baker. A.J. acquired her apple pie making abilities from our mother. Her pastry and bread making skills came from an aunt of A.J.'s that worked at the 'Des Gateaux et Du Pain', the finest boulangerie in Paris. Mother said that A.J. always won the grand champion ribbon at the county fair whether she made an apple pie or chocolate cake. Or beignets," John said.

"Boulangeries and beignets. Think I've had enough French for to-night," Joseph said.

"This French talk reminds me of another song Nancy or Maggie played on the piano. The name of the song in French is 'La Priere Dune Vierge'. In English, it is called 'The Maidens Prayer'. That was a great piece."

"Father would object though if she played it too much. He liked the Scottish ballads."

"La Priere Dune Vierge"

"Oh, may my life be free from every care.
No stain of earth ever blight each promise fair
Joy, peace and hope like flowers in Eden bloom.
And love triumphant rise above the tomb."
15.5

Chapter 16

"It has always astonished me to realize that the letter A.J. Camblein sent to our family was dated 1848 because Ft. Kearny had only been in existence for a few months before A.J. arrived there," Thomas said.

"That reminds me – do you know what I've heard? I can quote General William Tecumseh Sherman regarding Ft. Kearny," John said.

You better have an accurate quote if you're going to quote a general," Thomas said.

"It's accurate alright. General Sherman described the whiskey at Ft. Kearny as so incredibly horrible that he called it 'tanglefoot'," John said.

"Tanglefoot? How did you know that John?" Joseph asked.

"Well, General Sherman is from Ohio, just like us, and I heard this story when we were all there at the Battle of Shiloh. By the way, when we were talking about the Shawnee Indian chief Tecumseh, I forgot to mention something you might find interesting. I happen to know that General Sherman's father admired Tecumseh so much that he used that for his son's middle name," John said.

"I wondered how General Sherman got the middle name of Tecumseh. Wish I had some of that 'tanglefoot' right now," John said.

"That might help warm me up too," Joseph agreed.

John and Joseph both shivered at the same time. Thomas smiled. He would soon share his secret that would help warm them all up.

"How did A.J Camblein's letter make it from Nebraska to Ohio?" Joseph asked.

"Letters were not too common during that period of time, especially in that wild part of the country. Letters were delivered sporadically by stagecoach. That letter was dated 1848 and the pony express didn't deliver mail across Nebraska and Ft. Kearny until 1860."

"Fort Kearny - that's the real west, part of the great plains. There are even different Indian tribes in Nebraska Territory. Cheyenne, Omaha, Pawnee, Missouri, Iowa," John said.

"Those are certainly different-sounding names," Joseph said.

"I'm just familiar with the Indian tribes in Ohio – the Iroquois, Shawnee, Miami, and Ottawa."

"A.J.'s letter described being part of the Mormon Battalion. She described the Mormons dancing and singing and wrote about their religion in the letter. She planned on taking the Mormon Trail to the Salt Lake Valley," John said.

"What else do you know about the Mormons?" Joseph asked.

"I'll tell you a few things about the Mormons. They started west from Nauvoo, Illinois in 1846. Because of disease, supply problems, and bad weather, they were only as far west as Nebraska territory in late June of that year. They decided not to travel further across the unknown territory ahead and wintered over at Winter Quarters, Nebraska. In the spring, they followed the Platte River and stopped at Ft. Kearny on their way to Utah. This route across Nebraska Territory and onward became known as the Mormon Trail. At the time A.J. Camblien wrote the letter to Robert McGonagle, some of the very first Mormons were using oxen teams. Later, a lot of the Mormons also pulled handcarts the entire 1200-mile journey," Thomas explained.

"Handcarts? Why not use a horse?" Joseph asked.

"A lot of them didn't have the money for a horse or oxen, so they would build a cart, put whatever belongings in, and start walking," Thomas said.

"That must have been rough," Joseph said.

"Almost as rough as you sitting on this huge rock in the middle of winter, freezing and shivering as you wait for whatever the big bugs decide for tomorrow," John said.

"Well, just like those Mormons, I guess you do what you believe in," Joseph said.

Thomas and John nodded their heads in agreement. Sometimes their little brother surprised them.

"Aye. You do what you believe in. That's why we all joined the Army."

16.1

"I understand they're working on a railroad so people won't have to travel by horse or stagecoach," Joseph said.

"They're trying to organize it. The Union Pacific Railroad Company is supposed to head west from Omaha and the Central Pacific Railroad Company is headed east from California," John said.

"You know Lewis and Clark started across Nebraska Territory on the Missouri River in 1804 and---," Thomas started to say.

Joseph interrupted, "I suppose now you're going to tell me we have a letter sent to our grandfather McGonagle from Sacagawea and Meriwether Lewis."

Joseph slapped his knee and laughed.

"Well, Beat the Dutch! What are you, the camp canard? Sacagawea writing a letter to our grandfather! I hope you're absorbing some of this family history Joseph. I don't know why but I just feel like now, right now, is the time to pass on all the family information that I know about," Thomas said.

"I do like hearing all these family stories Thomas. I just have to kid you some. I never knew or didn't know all the details anyway that you're telling me," Joseph said.

16.2

"The Lewis and Clark expedition took place in 1806. It is astounding to realize that our father was only about 4 years old when Lewis and Clark took their trip and started their journey across northern Nebraska," John said.

"I guess it was hearing "Home Sweet Home" that got me thinking about our family and how the events in their lives intersected with U.S. history," Thomas said.

"I've learned a lot about history. I've enjoyed talking about the piano music that sister Nancy and cousin Maggie played for us. It makes me aware of how important music was to our family. It kind of bound us together every day," Joseph said.

"Remember whenever Maggie Lisle came to visit?" John said.

"You know, Maggie was kind of sweet on you John," Joseph said.

"That's balderdash."

"No, that's true. She kept wanting you to sing that certain song. You're the only one she wanted to sing it with."

"Double balderdash."

"I think the private 'doth protest too much'."

"What was that song, John?"

"I forgot."

"Oh, I remember. It was 'When You and I Were Young, Maggie'."

"Can I help it if I was the most charming of all her cousins?"

"Charming, eh?"

John placed his hand in front of his mouth so his brothers wouldn't see him smiling. He wasn't being very successful though. Thomas and Joseph knew him well and knew John and Maggie shared something special. John truly was Maggie's favorite cousin and neither Thomas nor Joseph could figure out why. It was just a bond, a special friendship between two family members. It was obvious to the most casual observer. Maggie would play special songs on the piano for John and write special poems and stories for him. She would always bake him a pie or a cake when she visited. Usually blackberry pie, his favorite.

Those two could hike out into the woods, talking for hours while they looked for those blackberries. Sometimes, hours later they would return, after dark. Sometimes without the blackberries. Then they would sit out on the porch and talk more, caring little whether they ate supper or not. Not a day would go by when Maggie was visiting their farm that she didn't coax John into singing 'When You and I Were Young Maggie'. The verses in the song were about being older, having gray hair, and the difficulties in life being over. All things that they could not imagine. They laughed together about the words in the song. The sharing of the song started one day after John had been plowing a field. As he unhitched the horses, he bemoaned how much his back hurt from the work.

"Oh, my Lord, my back hurts after working all day. Makes me feel feeble with age," John said.

"What have you been doing today?" Maggie asked.

"Just plowing up half the county," John said as he rubbed his back.

"You're not old and feeble, John. You'll feel better after you wash up, have some of my blackberry pie, and listen to some piano music," Maggie said.

Suddenly, John started to sing in a loud voice, so much so that it startled the horses.

He gestured with his left arm as his right arm rubbed the small of his back.

"The green grove is gone from the hill, Maggie. Since you and I were young, Maggie. Since you and I were young."

John surprised even himself. He didn't think about singing the verse from that song. He just belted it out. Then he could feel his cheeks turning red. Maggie loved it though. She realized right away that something special had just occurred. She knew that the impromptu singing of a verse from the song would become a meaningful song between just the two of them. She sang the verse back at John.

"The green grove is gone from the hill, Maggie, since you and I were young, Maggie, since you and I were young."

Maggie's smile and delight made John's tiredness dissolve. John had to admit to himself that he enjoyed that they had a special song, He liked that the name Maggie was repeated a lot throughout the music.

"When You and I Were Young, Maggie"

"I wandered today to the hill, Maggie, to watch the scene below,
    The creek and the creaking old mill, Maggie, as we used to
      long ago
The green grove is gone from the hill, Maggie, where first the
    daisies sprung,
    The creaking old mill is still, Maggie, since you and I were
      young.
And now we are aged and gray, Maggie, and the trials of life
    nearly done,
    Let us sing of the days that are gone, Maggie, when you and I
      were young."

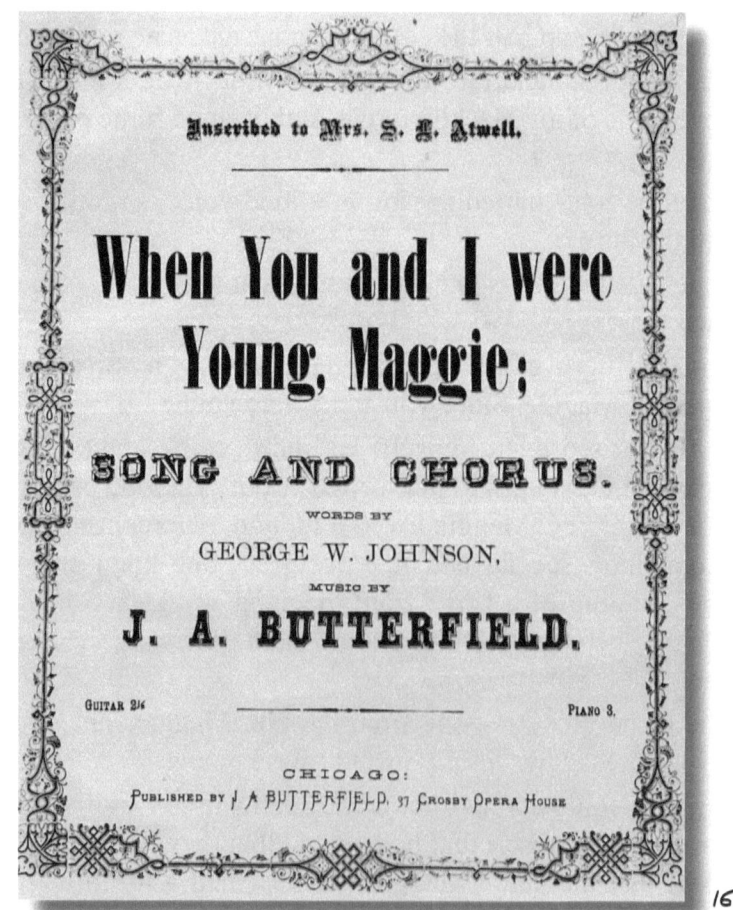

16.3

"I heard Maggie play that song so much, I think I know all the words myself.

"Let us sing of the days that are gone, Maggie, when you and I were young," Joseph said.

"Good Glory Hallelujah! I heard it so much, I know all the words too," Thomas said.

"Did you know that the quilts that Maggie made were different than the ones that Mother made?" John said.

"Oh no. Not more quilting stories," Joseph complained.

"Just part of your family history that you should know about Joseph," John said.

"Jumping Jehoshaphat! We have discussed the quilts mother and A.J. Camblein made. Now you're going to tell me about the quilts Maggie made? Is this some more family history you're going to cram into my head?" Joseph asked.

"More history, yes. Do you remember which country Mother and the Lisle side of the family came from?"

"Wales," Joseph replied, proud that he remembered.

"Aye, laddie. When Maggie quilts, she always makes her quilt in the traditional Welsh tradition. Mother quilts in a style that is associated more with Pennsylvania or the Amish," John said.

Joseph raised his hands to stop John from talking. He held his head in his hands. He walked over to the campfire and stared out into the night. The wind shifted. He could hear Stones River. It was difficult to imagine how many Confederate troops were just on the other side of the river. And yet, here he was. He was discussing family history and heaven knows what else with Thomas and John. It was the strangest conversation he had ever experienced with his brothers. He took a deep breath, let it out slow like he did when he sighted a target with his rifle. Then Joseph turned, looked at his brothers, and started to speak.

"You talk about our grandfather Thomas McGonagle in the War of 1812 and I like that. Then you meander off and tell me about the Scottish Crossbill and the careful construction of an Amish quilt. It makes me feel like my head is full of goobers. That reminds me---,"

"It reminds you that your head is full of goobers?" John interrupted.

"It reminds me of something I learned about Amish men. They always have beards but they never have mustaches. Military men often have elaborate mustaches. Because the Amish are pacifists and are against war, they don't have mustaches at all," Joseph said.

"Your mind certainly works in mysterious ways Joseph," Thomas observed.

"Sorry. Things just pop into my head sometimes and it has to get out. Now go ahead and explain the difference a Welsh quilt has from an Amish quilt. If you must," Joseph lamented.

"Here's your family history lesson Joseph. Maggie explained quilts to me once and-----,"

"Of course, she did. It must have been one of those nights that the two of you were famous for. You know, when the two of you talked long after the rest of us had gone to bed," Joseph interrupted.

"You're right about one thing Joseph. Things just pop into your head and off you go," John said.

"Sorry again. No more commentary from me. Tell me about the quilts," Joseph said.

"The Amish quilts are similar to Welsh quilts because they both settled in Pennsylvania. Welsh quilts are whole cloth quilts, that is they are made from one piece of fabric. Amish quilts use fabric that is cut into many pieces, then stitched together in a precise pattern. The Welsh quilts have stitching patterns that have a theme, like a maritime theme. Then they use an intricate design, which is more important than how closely spaced the stitches are. There is no repetition in the quilt-

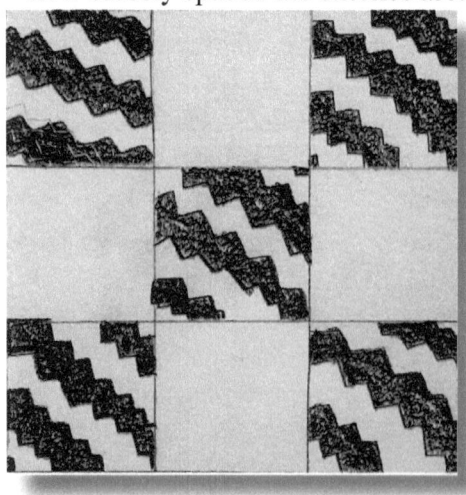

ing pattern of the Welsh style and they are heavily quilted. The Amish quilts use a block design that is pieced together. When the Welsh quilts are finished, they also have an edge that is like a knife-edge. Amish quilts have an edge that has a binding, that is, they use a long narrow piece of fabric to cover the raw edges," John explained.

16.4

"Jumping Jehoshaphat! I guess this will come in handy if I'm ever a quilting judge at the Ohio State Fair," Joseph said.

"Well, you paid attention Joseph, so I won't talk anymore about quilting tonight," John promised.

"I've learned something else from all this talk about quilting. If I ever do decide to make a quilt, I'm going to talk to myself. That way I can get expert advice," Joseph said.

Thomas and John smiled at Joseph. Talk to himself for expert advice! Soon all three brothers were laughing together again. Joseph's advice comment reminded Thomas of something else.

"Expert advice. That reminds me of what the prettiest lady in Wayne County would say about you Joseph," Thomas said.

"What would she say?"

"A man and a quilt will both keep me warm at night. But a quilt never says anything stupid."

Chapter 17

Nancy McGonagle enjoyed playing and singing her father's favorite Scottish ballads. Occasionally, he would request something different. When it was a really hot day, father might ask Nancy to play 'The Long, Long Weary Day'.

She looked forward to the evenings when the family would gather to listen to her play the piano. The music Nancy played depended on what had happened that day. If mother had seen some robins building a nest, while she pulled weeds from the garden, she requested that Nancy play 'Robin Red Breast' on the piano that evening. Nancy practiced the piano every day, whenever she could. Of course, hanging clothes on the line or peeling carrots for vegetable soup came first. Even if she only had a half-hour, when she didn't need to be helping her mother, she would practice on the piano. She always played for the family in the evenings. The music could be sad if they had buried a relative that day. Or it could be a 'sing as loud as you can' song to celebrate the Fourth of July.

It was both a blessing and a curse for Nancy to be the oldest and first McGonagle to be born to Robert and Isabella McGonagle. The blessing was that she had three younger brothers. The curse was that she had three younger brothers. Her brothers could help on the farm and do all the back-breaking chores that were required, so she was able to practice the piano during the day. They were typical brothers though and would tease her as much as they could get away with. Nancy was confident and could hold her own usually. Sometimes, when it was three against one though, they could make her pray fervently that she could be an only child. She also had some of that tenacious Scottish blood and could find ways to take care of Thomas, John, and Joseph. Nancy used the piano and her music to express what she was feeling on any particular day. She often would play a song to cheer somebody up. Or to dole out some musical punishment stemming from a naughty brotherly incident.

The three brothers and her parents had their favorite songs. Nancy could predict what music would be requested in the evening according to how everyone's day went. When she was asked to play 'I Hear the Wee Bird Singing', she knew her mother had probably heard birds chirping in a nest that day. Probably cardinals or blue jays. Or maybe all her pies had turned out just the way she wanted. Of course, Nancy knew her mother could listen to nothing but hymns and be perfectly content. Father usually wanted to hear a Scottish ballad like 'Within A Mile of Edinburgh Town'. She could get even with those three brothers of hers by playing 'Three Fishers Went Sailing', a story where she could substitute the word fishers for brothers and lustily sing how they were lost at sea.

"Three Fishers Went Sailing"
"Three fishers lay out on the shining sands,
In the morning gleam as the tide went down,
And the women are weeping and wringing their hands
For those who will never come back to the town.
For men must work and women must weep,
And the sooner it's over, the sooner to sleep.
And goodbye to the bar and its moaning."

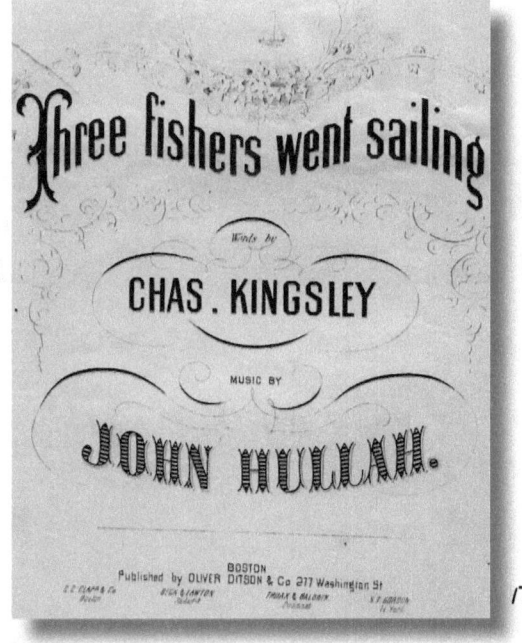

17.1

"We were so fortunate to have both our sister Nancy and cousin Maggie able to play the piano so well," John said.

"Those are good memories of home," Thomas said.

"I looked forward to the evenings when we relaxed and listened to the music they played," Joseph said.

"It's great thinking about all the times we listened to them play, even if it was just an hour in the evening," Thomas said.

"On holidays they practically played and played all day long," Joseph said.

"The one song that gave me the shivers is when, after someone had died, Nancy would play 'Under the Daisies'," John said.

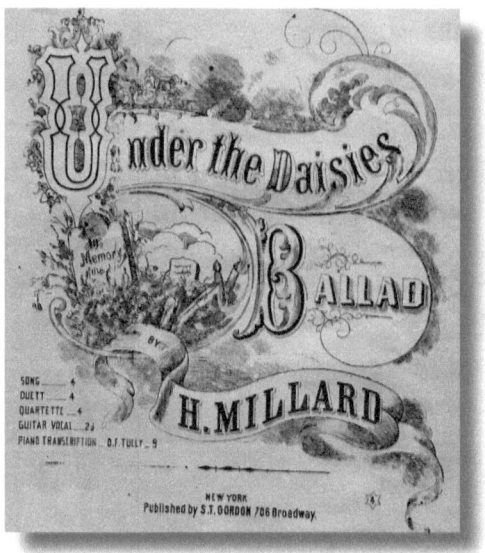

17.2

"Under the Daisies"

"I've just been learning the lesson of life. The sad, sad lesson of loving.
And all of its powers for pleasure or pain. Been sad and slowly proving.
And all that's left of the bright, bright dreams, With its thousand brilliant phases,
Is a handful of dust in a coffin hid. A coffin under the beautiful, beautiful daisies."

"You know, those Confederate states have their favorite songs that they play on the piano," Thomas said.

"Dixie."

"Bonnie Blue Flag."

"I never heard Nancy play those songs on our Steinway," John laughed.

"Can you imagine? We would have thrown her in the creek if songs like that were played on our piano," Joseph said.

"I do remember the last time we heard Nancy play the piano for us," Thomas said.

"Who can forget that night! It was the only time Nancy and Maggie played duets for us. Maggie visited a few weeks early just so the two of them could practice. They put on a special music show just for us," John said.

"Aye, laddie. That was special. Just before we went off to war the next day. I remember they played 'Yankee Doodle' and 'The Star-Spangled Banner'."

"'Hail Columbia' and 'May God Save the Union'."

"I remember they played 'Battle Cry of Freedom' and 'Red White and Blue'."

17.3

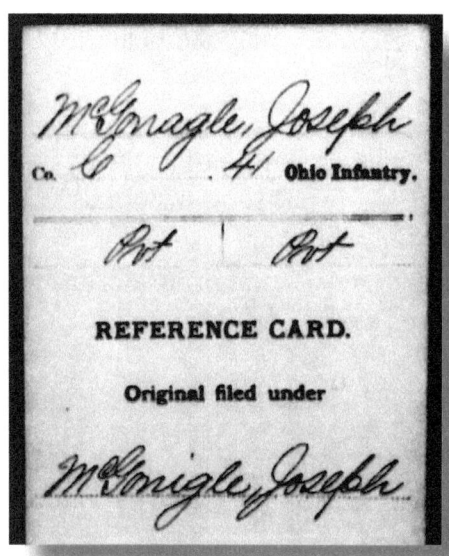

Chapter 18

Major Aquila Wiley limped among the troops of the 110th Illinois, 6th Kentucky, 9th Indiana, and 41st Ohio. These were the soldiers of the Second Brigade commanded by Colonel Hazen, part of the Second Division, under Brigadier General John Palmer. They formed the Left Wing under Major General Thomas Crittenden of the 14th Army Corps with Major General William Rosecrans, commanding officer of The Army of the Cumberland.

18.1

Colonel Hazen ordered Major Wiley to make an assessment of the men and then report back to him. The Major inspected the soldiers as they rested, talked, and prepared for the next day. He ensured that each soldier scraped the pounds of mud off their boots and clothes. The additional weight of mud on their boots would slow them down when they formed the picket lines. He wanted to make sure they were ready. The sixteen-mile march that day through the Tennessee clay layered mud upon mud on every soldier's boots.

Major Wiley limped more noticeably now that he was almost finished with his inspection of the troops. As hard as he tried not to limp, his leg rebelled and gave him some problems at the end of a long day. He rested against a tree for support and rubbed his left leg. He quietly uttered a few choice words into the northern wind. The tree branches above him rocked to the rhythm of the wind. In actuality, he

18.2

was relieved that his leg hurt. A sawbones had threatened to amputate it above the knee when he was wounded last April. He felt the deep depression in his leg where the bullet had lodged and thought back to that day, the Battle of Shiloh, April 7, 1862. The Confederates had surprised them with a morning attack. Major Wiley managed to gather and position his troops. He didn't want to be totally routed by the Rebs. Colonel Hazen ordered Major Wiley to advance his regiments.

"41st Ohio! Change front to rear on the left company!"

Major Wiley observed that the 41st Ohio now was positioned at right angles with the 9th Indiana.

"Picket line, advance."

His troops did so in unison and marched through open woods with some underbrush for six or eight hundred yards. The Confederates rained heavy fire upon them as the Ohio and Indiana troops moved to the front of the battle,

"6th Kentucky! Change front to rear on the right company!"

The ground now became more densely wooded as they advanced to within one hundred and fifty yards of the rebels. Major Wiley remembered that it was at this point in the battle that he would later write in his report that the rebel fire was 'exceedingly destructive'.

"Fire! Everything you got boys! Fire!"

Soon the rebel ranks started to fall apart. The Major saw that the middle of the Confederate line was completely open wide. He didn't hesitate.

"Second division! All advance!"

Major Wiley was at the front of the advance and stood next to the color bearer of the 9th Indiana. The color bearer held the national flag, having 33 stars. The center star was not there yet. It would be placed when West Virginia was admitted into the Union. After advancing fifty yards, a Minnie  ball impacted the shoulder of the color bearer. He fell, his flag falling *18.3* into the Major's hands. The Major raised the flag high into the air and considered his next command.

The unrelenting artillery fire, the overwhelming noise of muskets, and rifles were so powerful that the Major's steadfastness started to waiver. This was his first major engagement and was unlike anything he ever imagined in this war. The ugliness tugged at him in all its power. He hesitated to proceed with his next order but still held the 9th Indiana colors high. At that moment, he was aware of Colonel Hazen. Remarkably, the Colonel spurred his horse and calmly, firmly rode, and directed each area of his command. The Major absorbed the heroism of the Colonel more than any imposing Union weapon could have bolstered him. Major Wiley shouted his order.

"41st Ohio! Halt and fire! 9th Indiana! Halt and fire."

Soon after his last order was executed, a bullet hit the Major's left leg with incredible force. He started to fall backward. Everything seemed to be in slow motion. He regained his balance and placed his right knee on the ground. The flag remained upright and waved gloriously in the smoke of the battle. It was one of the most beautiful things he had ever seen in his entire life.

Major Wiley tugged at the pain in his leg with one hand. His vision blurred. A fading, a haze, enveloped his senses. The Major grappled with the flag to keep it erect and not touch the ground. He was fighting through pain and the haze but felt he was losing control. His strength receded and he struggled as a dark fog overcame him. Just as the flag started to leave his grasp, a private from the 41st Ohio retrieved the flag. Major Aquila watched as the soldier placed the colors in one hand, his rifle in the other, and charged onward. The Major succeeded in keeping the flag aloft until someone could take over for him.

18.4

A gust of frigid Tennessee wind brought Major Aquila Wiley back into the present. He shook his head and chased away the past. He had just relived his experience at the Battle of Shiloh. That had been eight months ago, in April. Now it was a frigid, rain-soaked night at the end of December. He willed his body to focus on the present. Duty called. The Major needed to finish his rounds and walked a few steps. His leg rebelled and forced him to stop. He needed to rest for a while before he carried on.

The flag that he viewed through the smoke at the Battle of Shiloh rushed back into his thoughts again. He envisioned again the incredible glory of the red and white stripes as the flag folded into the smoke. The image of those colors was etched into his memory forever. He remembered the first few lines of a poem he had read, written by Julia Ward Howe.

18.5

"The Flag"

"There's a flag hangs over my threshold, whose folds are more
    dear to me,
Than the blood that thrills in my bosom, it's earnest of liberty.
And dear are the stars it harbors, in its sunny field of blue,
As the hope of a further heaven, that lights all our dim lives
    through." 18.6

Major Wiley had so far resisted using a cane but might be forced into it. He sat on a large stone and rubbed his left leg, thankful that he still had it to rub. The Major observed the three Union soldiers around a campfire. He recognized two of them, they were in the 41st Ohio. He knew most of the men's names, particularly the 41st Ohio. He recognized these soldiers. They were the McGonagle brothers, from the same state of Ohio, as he was. Not only that, they were from the same town, Wooster. As his leg regained some strength, the Major listened as the brothers talked. He could tell they were deep in conversation. Major Wiley took advantage of an old sycamore tree and leaned against it. He enjoyed watching and listening to them for a few minutes.

The Major inhaled a deep breath of the cold Tennessee air, knowing he soon had to finish the orders of Colonel Hazen. The Colonel directed Major Wiley to check on his troops and he went from campfire to campfire. What he accomplished when he 'checked' on the soldiers was that he assessed the strength and character of each of them. Fierce battles would soon be fought and as he made his rounds, he evaluated each soldier's battle readiness.

The McGonagle brothers reminded him of his home and brothers in Ohio where he too left to join the Union Army. He rolled a cigarette, inhaled, and held it in. When he exhaled, the smoke quickly evaporated into the trees. Major Wiley thought of the 'Home Sweet Home' music he had heard earlier that evening. The Major smiled briefly as he thought about his two brothers that he had grown up with in Pennsylvania. He recalled that his family, just like the McGonagle family, had moved to Ohio from Pennsylvania. How he wished he could sit and talk with his brothers now, just as the McGonagle's were doing.

Major Wiley inhaled the cigarette smoke again. A strange thought came to him. Could the tobacco in this cigarette have been grown in a Confederate state? Could it have been harvested by a slave and sent North before the war started? The Major looked at the rolled cigarette in his hand as if it would give him the answer. He wondered if he would ever see his brothers or home again. He didn't even know where his brothers were. The last he knew one brother was with the Army of the Potomac, commanded by General Winfield Hancock. The other brother was with the Army of Virginia, commanded by General John Pope.

His duties consumed all of his attention. Aquila Wiley rarely afforded himself the luxury of thinking of home and family. Now that he had stopped to rest for a few moments, memories of his brothers and incidents in their lives in Ohio flooded back to him. Family recollections rushed into his consciousness, like waves in the ocean thrown up by a storm. He listened to the McGonagle brothers as they reminisced about the influence music had on their lives. The Major was keenly aware of the impact music had on his life also. He focused on a memory and a song that prompted him to join the Union Army. It was the song 'We are Coming Father Abraham'. Aquila Wiley and his brothers had gathered in town for a harvest festival. At the celebration was a choir from a local church. They performed a new song, written by a Quaker, James Sloan Gibbons, who was stirred to writing the song after reading that Abraham Lincoln had requested 300,000 volunteers to fight the Confederacy.

"We Are Coming Father Abraham"

"We are coming, Father Abraham, three hundred thousand more,
From Mississippi's winding stream, and from New England's shore;
We leave our ploughs and workshops, our wives and children dear,
With hearts too full for utterance, with but a silent tear;
We dare not look behind us, but steadfastly before:
We are coming, Father Abraham, three hundred thousand more!" 18.7

The song stirred powerful emotions for Aquila Wiley and his brothers. After hearing the song, they realized they needed to enlist and join in the war between the states. The very next day they all volunteered to join the Army. 'We Are Coming Father Abraham' propelled the Wiley brothers to literally 'leave our plows and workshops, our wives and children near'. This was especially true for Aquila Wiley. He went off to war a few months after he had been engaged.

Major Wiley smoked his cigarette and smiled in between breaths of smoke, as he listened to the bantering between the three McGonagle brothers. The Major appreciated the unique comradery that existed between Thomas, John, and Joseph. He had a special bond with his brothers also and wished his brothers were all serving in the same regiment. From a military perspective, he also appreciated that the McGonagle's were very fine soldiers. They had a Scottish bloodline, so they fought ferociously and gallantly with every ounce of their being. The Major exhaled the cigarette smoke and a thought occurred to him. The thought was so pronounced, he quietly said the words out loud. Even though it was only the river, Stones River, that carried his words into the bitter cold of a winter night on a rush of wind.

"If I had an entire regiment of nothing but Scots, we'd win every battle we were in."

Major Wiley knew that the brothers were intently aware that a major battle was to commence more than likely tomorrow. Still, here they were, drinking coffee in the bitter cold, as relaxed as if they were sitting on a sofa sharing a bottle of brandy.

He easily could have watched and listened to the three brothers for much longer but he had to soon report back to Colonel Hazen. He stepped over to the McGonagle's campfire and rubbed his hands together over the coals to warm them.

Chapter 19

"Evening' boys."

"Major Wiley, sir,"

"It's just like the three of you were sitting around your parlor at home listening to a piano, singing songs, playing checkers, and enjoying an extra slice of rhubarb pie," Major Wiley said. .

Unsure whether the Major was approving or disapproving of their family reminiscing, the three brothers did what any private in the Army would do in just such a situation. They kept their mouths shut.

Major Wiley turned his back to the campfire and said, "I envy you all being in the same company so you're able to talk to each other like this."

"Yes sir, we are quite fortunate," Thomas said.

"Thomas – I know you and Joseph are in Company C, 41st regiment but why isn't your other brother in the 41st?" Major Wiley asked.

"Well, I hate to tell you this sir but ole John here isn't much of a marksman. The 41st won't have him," Thomas said solemnly.

"Ha! I could outshoot and outride you any day of the week and twice on Sunday," John said.

"Looks like I stirred things up," Major Wiley smiled.

The Major enjoyed the sparing between the brothers. He knew that each one of them could probably outshoot and outride almost everyone else in all the regiments that were gathered by Stones River. If he had to bet on which brother would win in a shooting contest, he wasn't sure which one he would bet on.

"Reminds me of my brothers growing up in Pennsylvania. Laughing and joking one minute, wrestling and fighting the next," Major Wiley said.

"The real story is that our brother John lived in a different county in Ohio than Joseph and I did," Thomas explained.

"We were living in Wayne County, Ohio and John was living in Cuyahoga County when we enlisted," Thomas said. "So, Joseph and I were assigned to Company C in the 41st regiment."

"If John enlisted, he would have been in Company K, 62nd Ohio. You could say John was just unfortunate and lived in the wrong county," Joseph said.

"First Thomas insults my marksmanship and now Joseph insults Cuyahoga county," John said.

"What do you think of that sir?" John added.

"Yeah, you're brothers all right. Since you were in a different county, how were you able to be in the 41st Ohio with your brothers John?" the Major asked

"I'll tell you the true story, Major. The real story is that John wanted to enlist but he lived in a different county in Ohio. He wouldn't have been in the same regiment as his brothers. He wasn't quite sure what to do. The other factor in John's decision, more so than his other brothers, was our mother. She was raised as a Quaker. A Free Quaker, I should say. The one son that her peacekeeping spirit grabbed hold of more than anyone was John. Not that he's not a fighter, sir," Joseph said.

"He for sure is, especially if something really gets him riled up. It's just that we are all a little different in our approach to things. John, for example, has somewhat of a more gentleness about him. A little bit of 'Quakerness' in his fiber, so to speak. Anyway, there was a friend that I had in Wayne County. Jacob was his name. He had enlisted also in the 41st Ohio, but before we were sent off to camp, his wife died suddenly from typhoid fever. Jacob had six young children, with no one to raise them with his wife gone. John knew about this and offered to be a substitute," Thomas explained.

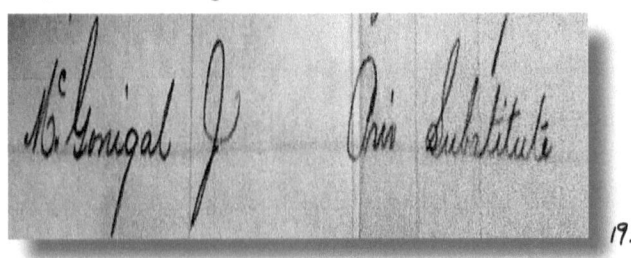

19.1

"Bully for you, John. A substitute. Outstanding. That explains it. Very admirable. You performed a great act of compassion and as a bonus, you got to be with your brothers for a while. As I'm sure you're aware, as a substitute, you will more than likely get transferred to a different regiment sometime soon. Substitutes tend to get transferred a lot, to wherever they're needed the most," Major Wiley said.

"Yes sir, I know. It's just good to be with Joseph and Thomas for a few months. I should say, most days it's usually good. Some days---,"

"There is something else I admire about your volunteering as a substitute John," Major Wiley said.

"What is that sir?"

"You volunteered as a substitute out of kindness and empathy, not as a mercenary," Major Wiley said.

"That's right. As I explained, Major Wiley, John has a gentle side to him," Thomas said.

"Think you called it 'Quakerness'," Major Wiley said.

"I just helped someone that had some hard knocks in his life. I do have to tell you though, I received three hundred dollars to take Jacob's place," John said.

"Guess what John did with those three hundred dollars, Major? He gave one hundred fifty to our mother and gave the other one hundred fifty to our cousin, Maggie Lisle, so she could study at the conservatory of music in Oberlin College in Ohio," Joseph said.

"Yep. Our brother John is not a muggins, not in the least," Thomas said.

"I'd say he has a lot of grit. The story you've told me about John is about as scarce as hen's teeth," Major Wiley said.

The Major deeply breathed in the last of his cigarette, tossed the remainder into the campfire, and took several steps away from the boys. It was time to resume his rounds. Something Thomas had said about their cousin Maggie reminded him of his sister Laura. She majored in music at Ohio University.

A song named 'Jeannette and Jeannot' suddenly flowed back into Major Wiley's memory. His sister used to play it on their piano. Now, in a terrible twist of fate, his life had taken on the essence of that song. Aquila Wiley had left the girl he planned to marry and joined the Army of the Cumberland. The realization hit him almost as hard as that Minnie ball had hit his leg. Major Wiley turned to look at the boys again.

"I heard you discussing some ballads, like "Annie Laurie" that your sister played on the piano. Your ancestors were Scottish. My ancestors were French. Thinking of music that I used to hear reminded me about some of the French piano pieces my family played on our piano. I always liked a French song about a maiden named Jeannette and her lover named Jeannot who goes off to war. It is rather ironic that I liked that song because it describes my life now. I haven't thought about that for a long time. Thanks for letting me forget about this horrible war for a while."

Major Wiley seemed lost in his thoughts for a few moments.

Then he stretched his arms wide and said, "You know, a piano in a home is only slightly more important than a kitchen stove. I don't know who invented the piano but it was a grand invention."

"Yes, sir," Thomas said.

"Our mother always said a piano was the grace of life and the best 105 dollars she ever spent," Joseph said.

"I just hope all of us can hear some grace of life with our mother when all these battles are over," John said.

"Jeannette and Jeannot"
"You are going far away, far away from poor Jeannette,
  There is no one left to love me now, and you too may forget.
But my heart will be with you wherever you may go,
  Can you look me in the face and say the same?
Jeannot! When you wear the jacket red and the beautiful cockade,
  Oh! I fear you will forget all the poems as you made,
With the gun upon your shoulder and bayonet by your side.
  You'll be taking some proud Lady and be making her your bride." 19.2

One of the verses of the song haunted Major Wiley. 'You'll be taking some proud Lady and be making her your bride'. He thought of the girl he had left in Ohio - Linda Sue Montgomery. Those dimples of hers when she smiled felt like sunshine. How many battles would he need to live through to make her his bride? He had almost lost his leg once. How many more chances would he have? Her eyes were so blue and so focused on him when they rocked on her porch swing. She was so afraid he wouldn't return from the war. It hadn't helped lessen her fears when he was wounded at the Battle of Shiloh in the spring of this year. Aquila Wiley resolved again to fight as hard and do as much as he could to defeat the Confederacy, so he could propose to Linda Sue Montgomery and make her his bride.

Major Wiley thought of his family and 'Home, Sweet Home'. He had been so busy getting soldiers to where they were supposed to be and planning for tomorrow that he had thought of nothing else. Now that he had paused to give his stubborn leg a respite, his thoughts went to Pennsylvania, where he grew up. His mother still lived there. The Steinway piano in their home was beautiful. He would have to visit her soon.

Major Wiley rubbed his leg and had another memory of The Battle of Shiloh. The day before the battle, he had given Lieutenant Opdycke his pumpkin rinds. Ironically, during the battle, Major Wiley saved the Lieutenant's life when he pushed him out of the way of a direct artillery hit. The shrapnel missed Lieutenant Opdycke but some fragments lodged in Major Wiley's shoulder. The Major evaluated the wound, then decided it wasn't too bad. He would seek medical treatment later. He continued to issue orders and direct the troops under his command. Moments later, he was severely wounded in his leg while securing the colors and transported to a medical tent.

As he waited for his turn at treatment, Lieutenant Opdycke brought Major Wiley a bottle of whiskey to deaden the pain in his leg and shoulder. The Lieutenant arrived just as the sawbones prepared to work on the Major. The doctor was trying to decide whether to remove the shrapnel from the Major's shoulder first or remove the bullet from his leg. Probably dig the metal out of the Major's arm, then use the saw on his leg. The Lieutenant handed the whiskey to Major Wiley. The surgeon wanted to inspect the contents before his patient started drinking the medicine. The sawbones held the bottle up to the light for a second, then took a big swig of the whiskey for himself. He needed it as much as the Major.

The sawbones made his decision. He would remove the fragments from his patient's shoulder first. The doctor ascertained that this was good whiskey, not the rotgut type. He decided to not amputate the Major's leg. He took another long swig and poured the rest of the ole red eye over the Major's wounds. The surgeon reasoned that a whiskey this good just might prevent infection and make it unnecessary to amputate his leg. He gave his surgical blade a swipe on his pants and went to work. Major Wiley protested and accused the doctor of wasting good whiskey.

Now, looking back on the incident, Major Wiley was thankful the sawbones made a good decision. Amazingly, the whiskey had indeed stopped any infection. The only explanation was that the 'O Be Joyful' must have been a really good whiskey. His leg healed up in a few weeks and he only had to limp a little now.

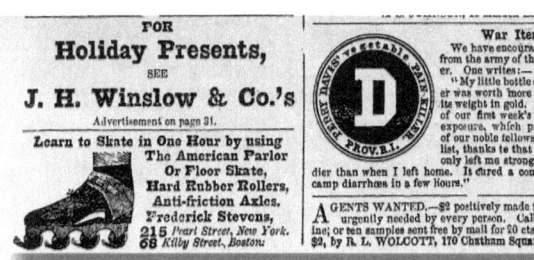

Major Wiley rubbed his leg as he considered the medicinal healing power of whiskey. He was ready for tomorrow, for then it would be New Year's Eve. It would be a new year, 1863. The war can't last much longer, can it? Another verse from 'Jeannette and Jeannot' entered in his thoughts. Each day that he wore the 'gun and bayonet by his side' would be a day closer to when he would be back at 'Home Sweet Home'. His mother played a Steinway piano at their home too. He had not thought of that for a while. He tried to remember some of the songs she used to play. There was a song he tried to think of. It wasn't coming to him. What was it? Something about a song, a mother---. Well, it would eventually come to him.

He was expecting a letter from Linda Sue, thanking him for the roller skates he had mailed to her for Christmas. He hoped the skates worked better than the 'Perry Davis Vegetable Pain Killer' he ordered to help heal his leg. The Major realized he didn't have any more time to think about piano serenades and Linda Sue Montgomery. He had orders to accomplish, supplies to check on, things to ready for a battle tomorrow. Major Wiley walked into the darkness to find some other soldiers to check on. Then he suddenly stopped. The song he had been trying to remember popped into his head. He knew what he had been trying to recall and wished he hadn't remembered. It was the song 'Just After the Battle Mother'.

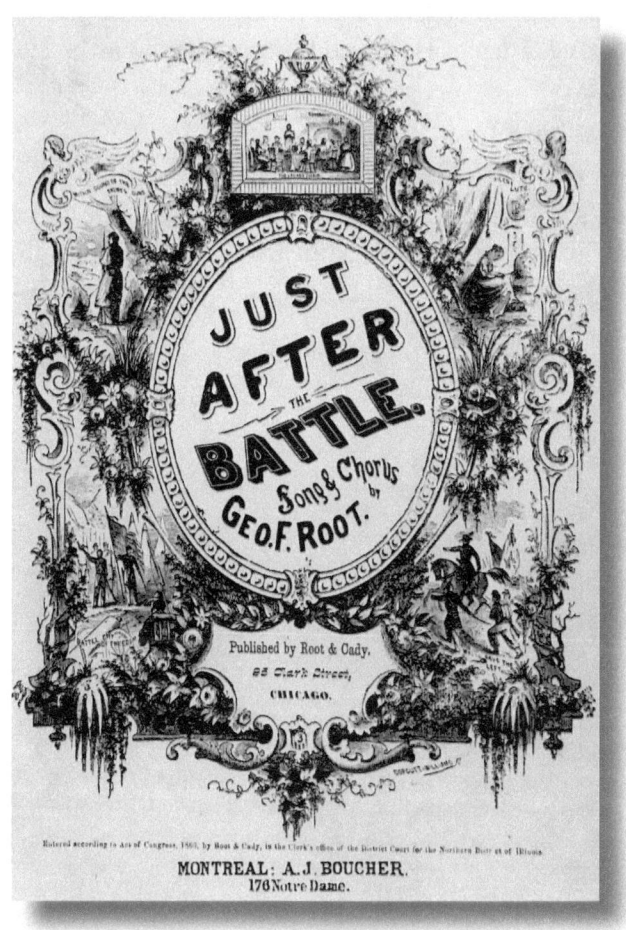

19.4

"Just After the Battle"

"Still upon the field of battle, I am lying Mother dear,
  With my wounded comrades waiting, for the morning to appear.
Many sleep to waken never, in this world of strife and death,
  And many more are faintly calling, with their feeble dying
    breath.
Mother dear, your boy is wounded and the night is drear with
    pain,
  But still, I feel I see you and the dear old home again."

The verses flooded Major Aquila's memory. He forced the battle song away, the words too difficult to think about for any length of time. There were other troops to check on and he needed to report back to Colonel Hazen. He started limping again as he called back to the brothers.

"Carry on, boys."

The brothers watched Major Wiley as he stepped over a fallen tree. The Major shivered and drew his coat tighter. The December cold grabbed at his left leg, the warmth from the campfire already faded into the darkness.

Chapter 20

"It was interesting that the Major took some time and had a chat with us," Joseph said.

"He always seems to spend a few minutes talking to us. He likes to be part of our conversations for a while when he makes his rounds," John said.

"Not all the officers do that. Some just bark orders and walk around like they are God's greatest gift to the world," Joseph said.

"Aye, Joseph. Major Wiley is an officer who can talk to a lowly private like me and be interested in what I'm thinking, whether it's Ohio, farming, or a maneuver on the battlefield. I have a lot of respect for him," John said.

"You know, there are only three men in this world worthy of respect. A teacher, a soldier, and a poet. To know, to kill, to create," Thomas said.

Joseph and John stared at him in amazement. They both knew Thomas had a bit of a philosopher in him. This philosophical statement though came out of nowhere. After a long pause, neither Joseph nor John knew what to say. Finally, John cleared his throat.

"Wow Thomas. That's pretty deep. I've never heard that before."

"It's exactly right though," Joseph said.

"A teacher knows, a soldier kills and a poet creates."

"Where did you read that?" John asked.

"I just now made it up," Thomas said.

"You did not," Joseph said.

"Sure, I did," Thomas said.

"Thomas?" Joseph asked in an inquisitive voice.

"Okay. I didn't just make that up. I read it somewhere. I don't remember where."

It was time for Joseph to give up the quilt. The Army issued them blankets, which they always kept with them in their packs but the quilt was certainly much warmer and gave them just a little extra shot of comfort. They first started sharing the quilt and it was just before the Shiloh battle that Joseph decided to do what they do in England. At Windsor Castle, shift changes were called 'changing of the guard'. Joseph decided they should adopt the custom. When one brother gave the quilt to another brother to use, they called it 'changing of the quilt'.

"Here you go, Thomas. Time for changing of the quilt," Joseph said.

Thomas no sooner had wrapped the quilt around his shoulders than Joseph asked another question.

"Just who did invent the piano?" Joseph asked.

"Aren't you ever going to run out of questions?" Thomas said.

"When you answer my question with a question, that probably means you don't know the answer," Joseph said.

"Bartolomeo Cristofori," Thomas said, pulling on the quilt.

"Bart who? Doesn't sound Scottish," Joseph said.

"It isn't Scottish. Scots didn't invent everything you know:"

"According to our father, the Scots invented everything."

"Yes, he was very proud of Scotland but the inventor of the piano was Italian. Around 1700 Bartolomeo Cristofori invented the piano."

"Who invented those expensive Steinway pianos?" Joseph asked.

Thomas and John looked at Joseph like he had asked the most foolish question ever.

"What? What are you looking at?" Joseph wondered.

John shook his head, looked at the ground for a bit, then raised his head again, and smiled at Joseph.

"Think his name was --- Steinway."

"Oh yeah, Dumb question, right?" Joseph said as he felt the back of his neck blushing red.

"Right," Thomas and John said at the same time.

"Any more dumb questions, Joseph?"

Joseph scratched his head and thought. He shuffled his feet, pulled on his ear, and rearranged his cap.

"I do have another question, now that you ask. Do you suppose President Lincoln listens to piano music? I wonder if the White House even has a piano? Maybe there's a Steinway or a Hallett and Crumston or a Bradbury---"

"I've heard Nancy say that the White House has a piano made by the Schomacker Company of Philadelphia. She read about it in 'The Song Messenger', that monthly paper that is mailed to her. She even told me that two of President Lincoln's favorite songs are 'Battle Cry of Freedom' and 'Annie Laurie'," John said.

"Battle Cry of Freedom"
(Union version)   20.1

"Oh, we'll rally round the flag, boys, we'll rally once again,
        Shouting the battle cry of freedom!
And we'll rally from the hillside, we'll gather from the plain,
        Shouting the battle cry of freedom!
The Union forever, hurrah! boys, hurrah!
        Down with the traitor, up with the star;
While we rally round the flag boys, we rally once again,
        Shouting the battle cry of freedom!" 20.2

20.3

"Battle Cry of Freedom"
(Confederate version)

"Our flag is proudly floating on the land and on the main,
Shout, shout the battle cry of freedom!
Beneath it oft we've conquered, and we'll conquer oft again!
Shout, shout the battle cry of freedom!
Our Dixie forever! She's never at a loss!
Down with the eagle and up with the cross,
While we rally 'round the Bonnie flag, we'll rally once again,
Shout, shout the battle cry of freedom!" 20.4

"The 'Battle Cry of Freedom' is another piece of music that the North and South share. Just like 'Home Sweet Home". They each call it their own. As you might expect, 'Battle Cry of Freedom' has a Union version and a Confederate version. The melody is the same but there are different words," John said.

"I like to think that President Lincoln is inspired by the music he hears. The burden of the nation is on him and I believe he draws inspiration from the music he listens to. He is a Presbyterian and enjoys church hymns, from which he also derives an inner strength," Thomas said.

"What hymns would be some of his favorites?" Joseph asked.

"I would guess 'Rock of Ages' and 'There is a Fountain'. Maybe 'Whatever of Earthly Bliss'," Thomas volunteered.

"President Lincoln has some of the same favorites that I do. I like singing "Battle Cry of Freedom'. The Union version that is. I especially like singing the verse 'shouting the battle cry of freedom'. As loud as I can," Joseph said.

"President Lincoln's other favorite, 'Annie Laurie', is a top rail sparkling melody. 'T'was there, that Annie Laurie gave her promise true'," John repeated one of the verses.

"Annie Laurie? I wonder why President Lincoln likes a Scottish ballad like that?" Joseph wondered.

"I know the answer to that. Sister Nancy keeps up on anything related to music. She told me when Abe Lincoln was a child that his mother sang to her children every evening. She liked both English and Scottish ballads," John said.

"Then I would say that our commander-in-chief has some excellent tastes," Joseph said. "It's hard to imagine that President Lincoln has any time to listen to singing and piano playing. What do you think Thomas?"

Thomas rubbed his hands together. Was it his imagination or was it getting colder? He remembered reading that music wasn't just entertainment. It had a purpose. Thomas agreed with a Virginia poet, John Thompson.

'And fair the form of music shines. That bright, celestial creature. Who still, amid wars embattled lines, gave this one touch of nature.'

Thomas considered repeating the quote. He decided not to. He was concerned that just might push Joseph to run screaming into the woods for certain. He would keep his answer a little less philosophical. He'd let Joseph yell 'Jumping Jehoshaphat!' for some other comment.

"Well, let's think about this for a minute. Almost every home has a parlor. Parlors are a central room in any house and pianos are the central part of any parlor. I do know that President Lincoln listens to piano music at the White House and goes to the opera sometimes. I read an article where a reporter asked him this very question and Lincoln was quoted as saying, 'The truth is I must have a change of some sort or die'."

"Aye, laddie. Just like us. We fight hard but then it's nice to just sit around a fire, put some long sweetening on some hardtack, have some Scottish coffee, and talk with your brothers," John said.

"I've read that President Lincoln listens to piano music every Sunday at the White House. I read in 'The Belmont Chronicle' that President Lincoln was very moved by a song called 'Your Mission'. I liked it too when I read the verses in the sheet music and even memorized one of the verses. Would you like to hear it?" Thomas said.

John and Joseph looked at each other in somewhat disbelief. They had never heard Thomas talk as much as he had tonight, let alone quote music verses. They both nodded their heads.

Thomas stood up, cleared his throat, and placed his hand inside his coat, like a true orator.

"If you cannot, in the conflict. Prove yourself a soldier true,
If, where fire and smoke is thickest, there is no work for you to do;
When the battlefield is silent, you can go with careful tread,
You can bear away the wounded, you can cover up the dead."

20.5

The three brothers were quiet for a while after the sobering music verse that Thomas had recited. They felt comfortable not talking if there wasn't anything worthwhile to discuss. Joseph poured each one of them some more coffee. It was hot but was barely keeping them warm on this December night. They had endured wind, rain, sleet, and mud, just in the last few hours. They swallowed the coffee and studied the campfire. John repeated the verses of 'Your Mission' in his head. He was amazed that Thomas could recite poems and verses to songs that he wasn't even aware of. When his cup of coffee was finished, he knew what he wanted to say.

"Well brother, that verse was something you've had tucked under your bummers cap for quite a while. Those were powerful and beautifully written words. 'Your Mission' is a beautiful piece of music. It just illustrates that music binds people and families together, just like at our home. Music helps people remember events in their life. Just like we're remembering tonight," John said.

"That's right John. Music does bind people together, whether it's a family just like ours from Ohio or Abraham and Mary Lincoln in ---, in ---,"

"Cat got your tongue, Joseph?"

"Yeah. What state is the White House in? It can't be Virginia because that state is in the Confederacy," Joseph said.

"The White House is in Washington D.C. because the Constitution provided for a federal district under the jurisdiction of the U.S. Congress. So, it is not a part of any state. The District of Columbia is the nation's capital," Thomas said.

John and Thomas studied Joseph's face. They could both tell he was thinking hard. They knew Joseph was soon to pop another question. All it would take would be a little coaxing.

"Okay Joseph, let's have it," John said.

'Have what?" Joseph asked.

"You've had as many questions as forty dead men," John said.

"What does a full cartridge box have to do with me?" Joseph asked.

"John means that a full cartridge box has forty rounds, just like you've asked forty questions tonight," Thomas said.

"Guess I have asked a lot of questions. They just pop into my head and before I know it, I've got a question and I need an answer. Here's a question. We've discussed the Revolutionary War, the French and Indian War, and the War of 1812, Why is it that the only thing we've avoided discussing is this war?" Joseph asked.

"Easier to talk about things that happened in the past. Isn't it?" John said.

"What's your question about the Civil War now that we're about 500 feet from an Army in gray uniforms. They are just on the other side of Stones River and would like nothing better than find their Remingtons and chase us until we're back in Ohio," Thomas said.

Chapter 21

Joseph stood up, then sat back down. He stood up again, then sat back down.

Thomas and John could feel that this was going to require some deep discussion. Joseph had been going over a question in his mind for a while. Since Thomas and John were older, maybe they could help him sort things out.

"Are we fighting the South to stop secession or to stop slavery?" Joseph finally asked.

John thought about Joseph's question before he answered. The answer was somewhat complicated. It was a good discussion to have. He would try to answer Joseph's question.

"Abraham Lincoln's main goal in this war is to preserve the Union. That's what we are doing – fighting to prevent the country from splitting, I can tell you what President Lincoln said in August of this year when he wrote a letter to the New York Tribune.

"If I could save the Union without freeing any slave, I would do it, and if I could save it by freeing all the slaves, I would do it, and if I could save it by freeing some and leaving others alone, I would also do that."

"So, we're fighting foremost to stop secession and save the Union," Joseph said.

"That's right. The keyword is foremost. President Lincoln foremost wanted to preserve the Union. In an attempt to appease the Southern states and stop secession, his position initially was to prevent slavery in any new state entering the country," John said.

"So, Lincoln was first just opposed to the spread of slavery in new states?" Joseph asked.

"Initially, yes. That's what he said in speeches during his campaign to become president. But the very day after President Lincoln was elected, South Carolina took down the American flag at their capitol and raised their flag in its place. By replacing the American flag, they said they no longer wanted to be part of the United States. South Carolina and the rest of the Confederate states wanted to form a separate nation. They called it 'state's rights' but that just meant they wanted to secede and continue slavery, both in the south or in any new state," Thomas said.

"President Lincoln soon realized that the U.S. cannot endure permanently as one-half free and one-half slave. He said 'it will become all one thing or the other'. That's what the outcome of this war will decide," John said.

"The following month after he had written the letter to the New York Tribune, Lincoln signed the Emancipation Proclamation. It will be effective the day after tomorrow, on January 1, 1863," Thomas said.

"A start to a new year and a start to freedom for many that didn't have it before," John said.

Joseph stood up again and poked at the branches in the campfire. He considered everything Thomas and John were explaining to him. He thought President Lincoln was a great person. Joseph agreed that it was impossible for a nation to exist when some states allowed slavery and some did not. His thoughts turned to the founders of the Constitution and the slavery that existed then.

211

"Why didn't the Constitutional Convention settle this issue of slavery back in the 1780s? Why didn't they put it in the Constitution that slavery was prohibited? Then we wouldn't be fighting," Joseph said.

"It's complicated. You could say that the civil war being fought now is due to the sins of our founding fathers. They formed a new nation that was a beacon for liberty to the rest of the world and yet, they compromised on the issue of slavery," Thomas said.

Joseph nodded his head but didn't speak. He wanted an explanation for something that he couldn't figure out. He had always consulted with Thomas or John about things that he couldn't resolve on his own. Joseph looked at his brothers. The expression on his face told them that he wanted an explanation, regardless that it was complicated. How could the founders of America form a nation based on liberty and equality when they were directly or indirectly dependent on slavery?

"Well, the first thing to know Joseph, when Thomas Jefferson wrote the Declaration of Independence, his initial draft condemned Great Britain's support and continuance of slavery as one of the reasons the colonies wanted independence. He was forced to delete that passage when the Southern states objected. The Convention in 1787 would never have been ratified because the Southern states would never have agreed to sign without some provisions for slavery, So the Northern states had to agree to some compromises or there never would have been a Constitution," Thomas said.

"What compromises?"

"This is where it gets muddled. The Convention agreed that the Southern states could count slaves as 3/5 of a person, which helped the Southern apportionment in Congress. The other compromise denied Congress the power to prohibit bringing new slaves to the south until 1808. Also, the free states could not enact laws to protect the slaves," Thomas said.

"The South was so far along with slavery that even when our Constitution was written, they could stipulate how it was written. Unless there was some provision for slavery, any common union between North and South would never have existed," John said.

"Which allowed slavery to continue in the south," Joseph said.

"Aye. The practice of slavery goes way back to when the colonies were first settled. Even George Washington and Thomas Jefferson had slaves. It was a struggle of deciding whether to use slaves to enhance your financial position or to decide that slavery was morally wrong," John said.

"The Northern states, after a few states initially allowed slavery, knew slavery was wrong. Pennsylvania was the first state to abolish slavery," Thomas said.

"The Confederation Convention in 1787 also passed the Northwest Ordinance," John said.

"How did that treat the slavery issue?" Joseph asked.

"The Northwest Ordinance laid out how new territories and states would be formed. That law prohibited slavery in the new states that would be formed from this large tract of land," John said.

"Why did the South agree to that?" Joseph asked.

"The South thought the territory would be populated by Southerners. Although they would not have slaves of their own, they believed they also wouldn't join the swell of the abolition movement in the North," Thomas said.

"The Supreme Court is supposed to make intelligent decisions where they rule on things that are best for the country. Why doesn't the Supreme Court just make a ruling that slavery is wrong?" Joseph asked.

21.2 "Because the Supreme Court doesn't always make the right decisions. The Court has always been somewhat political. During the founding of our country, a number of judges had Southern sympathies," John said.

"That's right. They even concluded in the Dred Scott case that a slave was not entitled to freedom. In terms of the law, a slave was just an ordinary article of merchandise. They also ruled Congress had no power to limit the expansion of slavery," Thomas explained.

"Well, Beat the Dutch! You're essentially telling me that the Supreme Court is broken. They don't always do the right thing," Joseph said.

"For the Southern states, their economy depends on slaves providing labor for their agriculture, so they will not give it up and are willing to fight and form their own Confederate nation for it," Thomas said.

"I heard someone say that if cotton was selling for 12 cents a pound, you could expect a slave to be auctioned for $1200," Joseph said.

"Yep. They not only wanted to continue doing that in the Confederate states but the South wanted to expand slavery into the new territories and states that become part of the United States. The South pushing for that made the civil war inevitable," John said.

"At least our great-grandfather McGonagle never had to fight over the slavery issue. There wasn't any slavery in Scotland and they never had a war over it and tore the country in two, like is happening in the United States," Joseph said.

Thomas and John were silent. Thomas kicked at the ground. John rubbed his eyes.

Their silence told Joseph that slavery had been present even in Scotland at some period in time.

"What? That isn't correct?" Joseph asked.

"Slavery in Scotland was outlawed a hundred years ago but sadly, it was part of their past," John said.

"At least they abolished it without a civil war," Joseph said.

"That's right. Scotland has just one flag, unlike America now. The North has stars and stripes as our flag. The South has stars and bars as their flag."

"What does the white cross on the blue flag of Scotland represent?" Joseph asked.

"The white x shaped cross represents the cross of the patron saint of Scotland, Saint Andrew," John said.

"Why is the cross on the flag an x shape anyway?" Joseph asked.

"Glad you asked that question, Joseph. Andrew was a disciple of Jesus and many of the disciples were also crucified. Saint Andrew said that he could not emulate Jesus and wasn't worthy enough to die on the same shape of a cross as Jesus. Andrew asked to die on a diagonal cross. The flag of Scotland is called the saltire. The diagonal cross design is also called a Saint Andrew's cross," Thomas said.

Thomas walked over to the campfire, selected two branches, and placed them in an x shape over the fire. The McGonagle brothers watched as the flames began to burn one branch, then the next. The fire crackled, the Tennessee wind fanned the flames. The moment was so sobering that not even Joseph asked a question. They were all quiet for several minutes.

"Speaking of Scotland, Harriet Beecher Stowe visited Scotland several times to discuss abolition for America," John said.

"Who is Harriet--- what was her name?" Joseph asked.

"When this war is over Joseph, you will have to read a book written by Harriet Beecher Stowe. It's called 'Uncle Tom's Cabin', written in 1852. She visited England and Scotland a year after her book was published to discuss slavery in America," John said.

"Did she ever come to Ohio to discuss slavery? I've heard of the book but what is the book about?" Joseph asked.

"Harriet Beecher Stowe did have an Ohio connection. She lived in Cincinnati, Ohio for a while but moved to Maine to write her book. It's an anti-slavery book and the first American novel with a negro hero named Tom. It is so well written that it stirred up deep sympathy for the slaves. It brought to light the terrible inhumanity of slavery in the United States," Thomas said.

"According to our mother, 'Uncle Tom's Cabin' propelled America to the civil war," John said.

"Mother might have been partially right about that. President Lincoln even met Harriett Beecher Stowe at the White House and told her 'so you're the little woman that started this war'."

"How do you and Thomas know all this stuff?" Joseph asked.

"Because we're the smartest ones in the family. It's a known fact that if you are a McGonagle, the smartest kids are the firstborn. The ones that come later, like you, are just a lot dumber. The younger they get, the dumber they are," Thomas kidded.

"That's funny. I heard it was the other way around," Joseph said.

It was time for the changing of the quilt again.

"I don't suppose you'd be wanting this quilt for a bit, would you?" Thomas asked.

"Don't mind if I do. You may not be as smart as me but at least you have a kind heart," John kidded.

John placed the quilt over the front of his body and edged closer to the campfire. Maybe if he let the quilt warm up by the fire he could place it over his back and warm up even more. John knew he didn't need to bring up anything to talk about. He knew Joseph would soon be asking another question. He looked at Joseph as if to say 'just get on with it, ask another question', Joseph. John didn't have long to wait.

"I was too young to vote in the presidential election but if I could have voted, I would have voted for Abraham Lincoln. I'm smart enough to figure that out," Joseph said.

"You know, once Lincoln was elected president, it pretty much ensured the war was going to happen," John said.

"I read that Abraham Lincoln didn't win a single state in the South, so how was he elected President?" Joseph asked. "That's right. Lincoln only got about 40 percent of the popular vote but won in the electoral college. Lincoln believed that the Constitution granted states control over slavery in their own borders but also the Constitution gave the federal government power through Congress to prohibit slavery in the national territories," John said.

"So, when the Confederate States fired on Ft. Sumter, the war began. The flag at Ft. Sumter had 33 stars, the number of states at that time," Thomas said.

2l.3

"Why didn't the South negotiate more instead of going to war? Didn't they say the issue was 'state's rights?" Joseph asked

"The Confederate States may say this war is about state's rights but it is about allowing the right of states to continue slavery. And not just in their states but to expand slavery into new states," John said.

Chapter 22

You've just got question after question, don't you Joseph?"

Joseph was formulating a response and started to speak but Thomas got the words out first.

"Okay Joseph, to help you understand this better, let me play Devil's advocate. Let's say I am a plantation owner that grows cotton in Virginia, which by the way, is the state that has the most slaves. The only way I can pick all my cotton and harvest all my crops is to use slave labor. Our representatives in Congress have tried to settle the question of slavery but typically and, as you might expect, Congress does nothing to resolve this issue. I can say that the Constitution gives men inalienable rights. So, the southern states believe they have an inalienable right for secession," Thomas said.

"Secession was not mentioned in the Constitution, right Thomas?" asked John.

"Right, so secession was not a violation of the Constitution. Continuing to be the Devil's Advocate, I can say, as a Virginia citizen and property owner, that slavery is my constitutional right," Thomas said.

"Beat the Dutch! Jumping Jehoshaphat! Slavery is a right according to the Constitution? What lawyer dreamed up that argument?" Joseph blurted.

"It was a Supreme Court decision made in 1857. It was called the Dred Scott decision. The Court ruled that the South had a constitutional right to go into the new territories with their property, including their slave property. The Confederacy also argues that they can declare secession because of the Northern state's failure to enforce the Fugitive Slave Acts. Do you want to talk about the rights that the Constitution gives to its citizens? Okay. The North says the South does not have the right to have slavery. The South can use the same argument to say that it is the North that does not have the right to not oppose slavery," Thomas said.

"What a bunch of lawyerly gibbity-gab. I don't agree with the reasons the Southern states are using to justify slavery. I don't agree with the Supreme Court rulings either. It is morally wrong to argue that a slave is your property and you can do whatever you want with them. I must say you're a pretty good Devil's Advocate Thomas," Joseph said.

"Just trying to give you their side. You and John and I don't agree with the Confederacy. So much so that we've put on this uniform and we're sitting on this side of Stones River instead of the other side," Thomas said.

"I can't imagine anything worse than wearing a 'CS' on my belt buckle," John said.

"You know, the Republicans have never had a president before. Abraham Lincoln is the first Republican president. All the others have had southern connections. Politics is one strange beast. When the colonies first formed, they adopted the Articles of Confederation, which explicitly stated that the Union would be perpetual. Therefore, there was no legal basis for a state to secede. Later, when the Constitution was signed, compromises had to be made," John said.

"There also can be an argument that the Preamble to the Constitution prohibits the right of any state to secede," Thomas said.

"The Preamble. Let's see. We the people in order to form a more perfect union---. What's the rest?" Joseph asked.

"We, the people of the United States, in order to form a more perfect Union, establish justice, insure domestic tranquility, provide for the common defense, promote the general welfare and secure the blessings of liberty, do ordain and establish this Constitution of the United States," Thomas said.

"I'm impressed you have that memorized Thomas. Maybe you are the smartest brother after all," Joseph said.

"All thanks to my fourth-grade teacher," Thomas said.

"Is that the teacher you picked mother's roses for, gave them to your teacher, and got in trouble with mother? Maybe you don't have as much horse sense as I thought," Joseph said.

"That wasn't me, that was John," Thomas said.

"Me? Oh, go boil your shirt," John said.

Thomas could feel a warmth coming over him. He knew Joseph and John told the correct version of the flower story. He admitted to himself he enjoyed thinking about Miss Hessler. It was like she grabbed moonbeams and they filled the classroom when she entered.

Thomas liked Miss Hessler, liked her a lot. He remembered those large red roses he had snipped at the height of their beauty. Giving her those roses was worth the trouble I got into for picking them. That was long ago though. As much as he enjoyed thinking of his first love – what had he been, all of 11 years old - he decided to direct the conversation back to the conflict between the thinking of the North and the South.

"Jefferson Davis is the President of the Confederacy. He graduated from West Point and was the Secretary of War for President Franklin Pierce. The Vice-President of the Confederacy is Alexander Stephens. If you are from the South and want to justify slavery, the Devil's Advocate argument could quote Vice President Stephens. This is what he said about slavery."

"The great truth is that the negro is not equal to the white man, that slavery, subordination to the superior race, is his natural and normal condition'. The South believes that a negro is not affected by the stifling heat, working in the cotton, and tobacco fields 16 hours a day. They believe a negro doesn't feel pain when they are whipped, that---,"

"What? How can they think that? That is balderdash! Alright, Thomas, it is complicated. I've had enough of this Devil's Advocate. Let's talk about some more family history or complain about this cold, dark, rainy night," Joseph interrupted.

A gust of wind swept over the Tennessee valley. The McGonagle brothers leaned into the chill as it passed over them. An eerie silence settled over the Union camp. Gentle rain and mist began. It felt like it could be this way for the rest of the night.

"Into each life, some rain must fall," Joseph said.

"Jumping Jehoshaphat! Joseph just quoted a line from a Henry Wadsworth Longfellow poem," John said.

"I did? I mean, I did!" Joseph said.

"The Rainy Day"
"The day is cold and dark and dreary,
  It rains and the wind is never weary.
The vine still clings to the mouldering wall.
  But at every gust, the dead leaves fall.
Thy fate is the common fate of all.
  Into each life, some rain must fall.
Some days must be dark and dreary." 22.1

"Okay, Joseph. The night may be dark and dreary but let me tell you a story about another President that is a little more cheerful," Thomas said.

"Which President?" Joseph asked.

"President John Tyler," Thomas said.

"Is this the story about Charles Dickens visiting President Tyler and calling the White House a 'charming English clubhouse?" John said.

"No. Not the Charles Dickens story," Thomas said.

"Is it a similar story? Like Vice-President Aaron Burr, once being in one of the highest positions in our government and then forgetting about his constitutional oath?" Joseph said.

"No, not that story. I'll give you one more guess," Thomas said.

"I know that former U.S. President John Tyler now has a seat in the Confederate House of Representatives. Is it that story?" John asked.

"Beat the Dutch! Hearing that a previous president is now a Confederate legislator makes me feel like I've been through the mill," Joseph said.

"No, not that disloyalty story. I have a true story to tell you when President Tyler was in the White House. This is a story that you'll like. Then, I have a surprise for you to celebrate New Year's Eve," Thomas said.

"Great. I'm ready for a good story," Joseph said.

"And a surprise," John said.

"This story is about President John Tyler and a famous composer and singer named Anton Philip Heinrich, who was so talented he was referred to as 'America's Beethoven'. In 1841, Heinrich had completed 'Jubilee', a very complex work written for an orchestra and chorus. It was a vast commemoration from the landing of the Pilgrims to all the struggles along the way for liberty forever. 'Jubilee' took two or three hours to perform. Anyway, Mr. Heinrich visited the White House and was invited by President Tyler to play the piano and sing his piece. Heinrich launched in, playing his incomprehensible work. It involved the breaking of ice over the Niagara, the thunder of naval ships, and Army artillery. 'Jubilee' was the wildest and weirdest music ever composed.

After about an hour, President Tyler walked over to Heinrich, put his hand on his shoulder, and said, "That may all be very fine, sir, but can't you play us a good old Virginia reel?"

Heinrich was astounded and shocked as if he had just been struck by lightning. He yelled, "No, sir, I never play dance music."

Philip Heinrich gathered up his sheet music and immediately ran out the door of the Executive Mansion. Heinrich told his friend that was with him, "The people that made John Tyler president should be hung! He knows no more about music than an oyster!'"

Chapter 23

"That's a great story, Thomas. Who told you that?" Joseph asked.

Before Thomas could answer, John said, "I bet it was Maggie."

"That's right and because you two liked my story so much, I have a little surprise. Tomorrow's New Year Eve but since it's such a cold, nasty night, let's start a little early and have some Scottish coffee," Thomas said.

"Scottish coffee? Is that the same as Irish coffee?" Joseph asked.

"Good grief. I don't believe you, little brother. You don't know the difference?" John lamented.

"No. And don't try making up some wild story. It will just confuse me with all this family history you've been cramming in my head," Joseph said.

"You've got to know your family history to get by in this world, Joseph."

"If we only had the secret ingredient for true Scottish coffee. Unfortunately, I think we'll have to settle for a little rye whisky and sugar in our coffee to even make it Irish coffee," John said.

Thomas retrieved his haversack and placed it on the large rock he was sitting on. He rummaged through it, pulled out some letters, a few small books, and some hardtack. Next, he grabbed a wad of cloth with something wrapped inside. He pondered what it could be for a moment, then held it up to his nose to smell. Immediately, he recognized what it was and tossed it into the fire, which elicited a large poof. He looked at a few photographs, found some more hardtack, and kept going until he got to the very bottom. He found what he was looking for, pulled out a small bottle, and stuffed everything else back in the haversack.

"Well, my dear brothers. Not to worry. We don't have to settle for Irish coffee. I've got the secret ingredient to add. We're going to celebrate early and have some real Scottish coffee, my hardy laddies," Thomas said.

"Secret ingredient?" Joseph asked.

"And you just happen to have it?"

"That is correct, little brother. Let's call it your initiation. Hopefully, when you've sipped some Scottish coffee your little brain won't explode from all the things you've learned about tonight," Thomas said.

"I just hope it's something better than John Barleycorn," Joseph kidded.

"It will be much better. What is in this bottle will make us some honest to goodness Scottish coffee. I just happen to have the secret ingredient. It's Drambuie," Thomas said.

"Good Glory Hallelujah!! I can't believe you have been packing that bottle of Drambuie around since we left Ohio," John said in amazement.

"What's Drambuie? What's it made out of?" Joseph asked.

"You are going to like it," John said.

"Aye, laddie. Drambuie is made from Scotch whisky, honey, lemons, nutmeg, saffron, and probably some other stuff that's a secret," Thomas explained.

Thomas handed the bottle to John so he could inspect it. John thought maybe Thomas was playing a practical joke. He inspected the green bottle and saw the Drambuie label. John was astounded that Thomas had carried this in his haversack for several months. He also was surprised the bottle hadn't broken. To think that Thomas had been saving the Drambuie for a special occasion was beyond comprehension. Celebrating New Year's Eve a day early was just fine. John handed the Drambuie bottle to Joseph to inspect. The bottle was a dark green color, small, and had a curved shape. Joseph had always been told big things come in small packages. He hoped that was true for Drambuie. Although he wasn't too knowledgeable about spirits, he knew enough that the smaller the bottle outside, the stronger the contents inside.

"Scottish coffee! I'm looking forward to this. Give me my history lesson so we can get on with the tasting," Joseph said.

"Okay. Here's your history lesson. Drambuie is actually a Scottish Gaelic word. It's what is known as a liqueur. The recipe for this liqueur was given to a Scottish family by the name of MacKinnon from Prince Charles, the heir to the British throne. The prince was given sanctuary on the island of Skye after the Battle of Culloden in 1746. He was so grateful to the MacKinnon family for saving his sorry hide - the Scots had defeated the British, of course - that he gave them the Drambuie recipe. When Scots began coming to the United States, Drambuie found its way over," Thomas explained.

"And eventually to Ohio," Joseph said.

Joseph carefully handed the bottle back to Thomas. How it had survived in Thomas' haversack without breaking, he had no idea. He was extra careful. He didn't want to hit the bottle by accident against the large stones they were sitting on and have it break at this point. Joseph had first 'seen the elephant' during the Battle of Shiloh. Now he was about to have another 'see the elephant' experience and taste Drambuie for the first time.

"I would have thought you might have celebrated Christmas with your Drambuie but we are going to toast 1863 a day early now. Right?" Joseph asked.

"Well, Father Christmas put the Drambuie under my pillow on Christmas Eve, so I thought we'd use it to celebrate New Year's Eve," Thomas kidded.

"Father Christmas didn't leave me anything," Joseph said.

"No surprise there. Not to worry though Joseph, I'll share my Drambuie with you," Thomas said.

"Wish we could have been home this Christmas. Mother fixes all the Scottish favorites. She makes the best cock-a-leekie in all of Ohio," John said.

"My favorite is her clootie dumpling that we have for Christmas. And on New Year's Day we would have Scottish black bun," Joseph said.

"Don't worry, laddies. We'll probably be home next time Father Christmas comes around. For now, we are going to have a taste of Scotland for this New Year's celebration. We're going to have Drambuie to make authentic Scottish coffee. This will be our version of Hogmanay," Thomas said.

23.1

"To celebrate the coming of 1863 a little early, with a special treat, I'll make a fresh pot of coffee," Joseph said.

Joseph stoked the campfire some more and placed a few more logs. Not so large a fire that it was going to attract attention from the Confederates that were close by, but enough for some fresh coffee. The three brothers were quiet again, as they waited for the coffee to get hot. The fire crackled. They listened to the sounds of the Tennessee woods. An owl hooted. Another owl answered. The pair of owls seemed to be having their own discussion. The smell of the fresh coffee blended with the other smells of the woods – oak and cedar trees, moist earth, goldenrod, evergreens, Tennessee coneflower, Mountain mint. The Scottish coffee would soon warm them up. As usual, it was Joseph that broke the silence.

"While we're waiting for the coffee to get hot, you can answer another question I have," Joseph said.

"I have a question. Are you ever going to run out of questions?" Thomas asked.

"Well, we were talking about Abraham Lincoln listening to the piano. What piano piece do you think Jefferson Davis has as his favorite? What piano music do you think they play in the Confederacy capital?" Joseph asked.

The brothers considered this question for a while and did some more head-scratching. Thomas and John exchanged a smile. That Joseph, they were thinking. He comes up with the most unusual questions that many people don't even think about. And he always wants a well thought out answer.

"We know they like 'Home Sweet Home' because the blue and the gray both sang it a little while ago," Thomas said.

"I imagine in Richmond, Virginia, the Confederacy capital, where Jefferson Davis lives, they play 'Dixie' and 'Bonnie Blue Flag'.'"

"Jefferson Davis! If the Confederacy wins this war and is successful in seceding from the Union, they will have 'Dixie' be their national anthem," Joseph said.

"And that is why we're here with all these Union troops in Tennessee to prevent that from happening," Thomas said.

"I support Abraham Lincoln with all my heart and soul. It's vital that the Union stays together," John said.

"As we sit by this campfire, I can look around and see men from Wayne County and other Ohio counties - Geauga, Huron, and Carroll County. They have all pledged to the Army and Lincoln that we will remain one nation. My heart swells with pride to be a part of it. Army discipline can be galling but I'm here to end this war. And keep the Union together," John said.

"There were some skirmishes when we were marching south from Murfreesboro a few days ago. We got a taste of war at our first major battle at Shiloh. There were some boys from those Ohio counties you mentioned that are in the bone orchard at Shiloh. There are images from Shiloh that I will never forget. A soldier marching with his drum went down. Another soldier picked it up, started drumming, took 5 or 6 steps and he went down. It was a chaos of blue and gray uniforms," Joseph said.

Thomas and John could sense that Joseph wasn't finished talking about this yet, so they waited for him to continue. After a few moments, he did.

"I think back on that battle and remember our flag with the stars and stripes waving in the smoke and haze of battle. The smoke was so thick, it was hard to breathe. The 41st Ohio charged bravely into a hailstorm of gunfire. The regiment formed triumphant defenses to stop the rebel flank. We raced into victorious counter attacks. For the 41st Ohio, it was no longer what we envisioned war to be. It was real. Those days of grandeur, when we paraded in the streets, are over now that we've seen the ugliness of war. The grandness of wearing an Army uniform with shiny brass buttons, wearing a dog collar to impress the ladies, the feeling of being invincible is over. The confidence that nothing will ever happen to you is gone. Ever since Shiloh----," Joseph said.

"You're thinking that it could have been you that fell at Shiloh. Right, Joseph?" asked Thomas.

"Guess you can read me like a book," Joseph admitted.

"Aye, laddie. You're just like a brand-new book that has been barely opened," Thomas said.

"And I suppose you're like a well-worn, scuffed up, tattered book," Joseph answered.

Thomas said, "Well, I am a few years older than you, Joseph. Let me tell you one of the last pieces of advice I got from our mother. The day before we left for camp, I was bringing up some water from the well and mother was telling me to look out for you Joseph and------."

"She told me the same thing – to look out for you Joseph," John interrupted.

"Well, that's interesting. Not one, but two brothers told to watch over you. Anyway, she gave me some advice and now I'm going to pass it on to you Joseph," Thomas said.

Thomas paused and smiled at the memory. He thought back to that day. The day of his enlistment in the Army. It wasn't easy telling his mother that he was headed off to war, that he would be leaving the next day at first light. He was ready for an argument, certain that she would plead with him not to go, to let someone else fight this war. He was certain that she would use every Quaker verse and peacekeeper skill that she possessed to prevent him from leaving. She surprised him though when she draped a bear's paw quilt she was working on over her rocking chair.

Mother squeezed her arms around him. He got the longest hug he had ever had. Then she wiped tears from her eyes and handed him a basket. She told him to pick some blueberries for her to make him his favorite pie to have that evening. As he went out the door, she spoke the words to him that he would now pass on to Joseph.

"Never be afraid to trust an unknown future to a known God."

Joseph smiled also. He pictured the rocking chair by the fireplace.

He could almost smell and taste his mother's blueberry pie. He could hear his mother, with all of her Quaker leanings, certainly giving out this kind of advice.

"Mother quoted Deuteronomy 20 to me," John said.

John smiled at the memory of his mother's advice to him. Mother was in her rocking chair and had finished the bear's paw quilt. John pulled that very quilt tighter around his shoulders as he recalled the sensation he had then. He remembered that mother wrapped the quilt in her arms and walked over to where he was sitting. She gently placed the quilt over his shoulders and smoothed out the folds.

Mother kissed me on my cheek. She somehow knew that I had volunteered as a substitute for a soldier in the Army. I would be leaving the next day. I had not told her I was leaving but she knew. She wanted me to take the quilt and share it with my brothers. Mother picked up her Bible and read the Deuteronomy verse.

"When you go out to war against your enemies and see horses and chariots and an army larger than your own, you shall not be afraid of them, for the Lord your God is with you."

Joseph nodded his head. He could picture the room in their house with mother in her oak rocking chair. He could picture the rocks that had been used to construct the fireplace and the thick oak mantle. Joseph pictured the quilt that mother had given them that was now draped around John. He remembered the old walnut Scottish emigrant trunk where his mother stored some of her quilts. The sailing ship 'Aberdeenshire' carried that trunk, which held all the possessions that belonged to the McGonagle family. It sailed across the Atlantic from Scotland to Amerika. Amerika – that's how his family believed the spelling to be for the land where they were headed. A quilt or two might even have been placed in the trunk. With or without a binding? What was it Thomas and John had explained to him about bindings on a quilt?

Joseph once again admired the care she had taken to make the quilt. He realized that mother had quilted patterns other than the bear's paw. She made a quilt just for Joseph that he used year-round. He couldn't remember when she quilted it. He had just always used it. Joseph asked his mother one day why every bed in the house had a different pattern quilt.

"A bed without a quilt is like a sky without the stars," she said.

The quilt on his bed kept him warm and safe for years. It was a 'Corn and Beans' pattern. Appropriate for a country boy, no doubt.

Joseph could hear his mother's voice in his head quoting from the Bible. It was exactly the kind of thing she would say, exactly the quote she could knowingly find. She knew what chapter a Bible verse was in without having to hunt for it. John said that mother had read him a verse from Deuteronomy. That must be in the Old Testament.

"What advice did she give you before you left for camp Joseph?" John asked.

"She told me that having two brothers to watch over me was as scarce as hen's teeth," Joseph said.

"Well, it's about time you acknowledged the corn," Thomas said.

The coffee was ready. Joseph poured three cups. Thomas added a splash of Drambuie to each cup. All three brothers clinked their coffee cups together. The coffee was warm. The Drambuie warmed the brothers as well as being tucked under a quilt on a snowy Ohio morning. Joseph's first sip was like the percussion section of the United States Brass Band played in his head.

Chapter 24

"Haug Hogmanay, John and Joseph," Thomas said.

"And I give you this traditional Scottish toast."

"May the best you've ever seen, be the worst you'll ever see. May a moose never leave your home, with a teardrop in his eye. May you keep hale and hearty, till you're old enough to see. May you be just as happy, as we wish you all to be."

"This is my toast to you, my brothers dear," John said, as he raised his cup.

"May you never steal, lie, or cheat. But if you must steal, then steal away my sorrows. And if you must lie, lie then to shield me all the days of my life. And if you must cheat, then please cheat death, because I couldn't live a day without you."

"Happy New Year to you both. My toast to you goes like this," Joseph said.

"May your glass be ever full. May the roof over your head be always strong. And may you be in heaven half an hour before the devil knows you're dead," Joseph said.

"I hope you know that was an Irish toast, Joseph. The Drambuie is great. It warms me up all the way down to my toes."

"I think I'm dreaming that I'm sipping Scottish coffee around a campfire."

"It does help take the chill out of that Tennessee wind, eh?" Thomas said.

"I can't think of a better way to celebrate a New Year."

'The Scottish coffee feels great going down. I'm so warm I hardly even need the quilt around me. It is time for the changing of the quilt though, so here you go Thomas," John said as he handed him the quilt.

"Aye. Guess I'll be double warm then," Thomas said as he pulled the quilt over his back.

The brothers enjoyed the warmth of the coffee, the Drambuie and just being together.

They were quiet again for a while and listened to the sounds around them. It seemed when they stopped talking that the owls would begin their conversation back and forth.

Thomas and John knew the silence wouldn't last for the rest of the night.

"When this war is over, will slavery be over once and for all?" Joseph asked.

"If the North wins the war, slavery will be over," Thomas replied.

"What do you mean --- If --?" Joseph asked.

"Well, the North hasn't done too well since the war was declared. The Confederacy was the victor at the Battle of Bull Run, the North did win at Antietam. The Confederacy also won the Battle of Fredericksburg just a few weeks ago. The North really needs another victory," John said.

"I can't envision the South winning the war. That would mean slavery would continue. Why does the South need slavery and the North doesn't?" Joseph asked.

"The South is mostly farms that use the slaves as labor for planting and harvesting their crops," John said.

"The North has farms. We grew up on an Ohio farm and we didn't need slaves," Joseph said.

"Yes, but the North also has a lot more factories and industries. The Southern states are almost entirely agricultural," John answered.

"The losses on both sides have already been horrendous. When it's said that the North won this battle or the South won that battle, the losses are so great on either side, I'm not sure if there is a winner or a loser. But just so you both know, I am not doubting my commitment to preserving the Union," Joseph stated.

"I know that Joseph. You just have a lot of questions and there is nothing wrong with talking about anything you want to talk about. The tensions that eventually lead to this war has been brewing for decades. As much as I am willing to fight for what I believe, it is a hard fact that America isn't perfect. The Constitution states that this country was founded to form a more perfect union. This war is testing that American idea," John said.

"I think all three of us are also realizing that there is a big difference between what you think war is like and actually being in a battle. As a battle starts, in mere moments we see men dropping around us. There is incredible noise and the fighting is ferocious. Shrapnel and bullets are hitting the ground all around us. The rivers run red. And yet you hear music in camp. And here we are, two armies on opposite sides of Stones River."

"Music in Camp"

*"Two armies covered hill and plain, where Rappahannock's waters ran deeply crimsoned with the stain of battle's recent slaughters. And fair the form of music shines, that bright, celestial creature. Who still, 'mid war's embattled lines, gave this one touch of Nature."*24.1

"We are committed to continue to shape our democracy and by the time this war is over, one army or the other will be victorious. The outcome of the war won't be decided by a North and a South regimental band trying to outplay one another. We either form a more perfect union or there is no more Union," Joseph said.

"Aye, laddie. This is our time to be tested. I can say what I believe when I'm warm, safe, and dry at home. Now it is cold, dangerous, and wet and I still believe in what I'm doing. Our McGonagle ancestors that fought in wars before our time were all also at this point. The enemy you are fighting wants to force their values and way of living upon you. You have to make a stand. The McGonagle's and the Lisle's before us shared the virtues of courage and patriotism during their time on this earth. Now we are being greatly tested. We will, with every lasting bit of our strength, fight for our great cause. We – and by we, I mean all of us, will use whatever we have to fight, whether it's a gun, a rifle, a sword, or a bayonet. We will use whatever means to defend the place assigned to us. And never give up. We are fighting Confederates but also fighting an evil that would be too devastating to even imagine if the evil wins. We have that Scottish champion blood in our veins. We fight to the last man. We will save the Union if every soldier in the Union Army has the same courage in the perseverance of his duty," Thomas said.

"Couldn't have put it better myself," Joseph said.

"You were talking about im-  ages from the Battle of Shiloh that you can't get out of your head, Joseph. I have some of those same images that play over and over. I think about General Nelson taking us on that exhausting march through a sea of mud. I thought we were on some grand mission. Then we find out we're marching on a fool's errand, with no military benefit whatsoever. This is just because General Nelson is from Kentucky and a great admirer of Andrew Jackson. He wants to visit Andrew Jackson's old home – the 24.2 Hermitage," John said

"And he did it on his own hook too," Thomas said.

"Beat the Dutch! General Nelson didn't even clear that wild goose chase with General Buell?" Joseph asked.

"That's right. They should have taken those chicken guts away from General Nelson. We were just fortunate that the Rebs were firing Quartermaster hunters at us," John said.

"You're right about that. We got as far as the Tennessee River. Then, no sooner than we find the river, we're aware of a battle going on. We're forced to stop because it's getting dark. We're exhausted but nobody sleeps because a gunboat, a Union gunboat to boot, is firing over our heads every 20 or 30 minutes," John said.

"I thought one of those artillery shells would land on us for sure," Joseph said.

"Then, after no sleep or rest, we are engaged in our first major battle. It doesn't matter that we've had no battle experience. We're ordered to charge the Confederate line. In an hour, the fierce battle is over and there are 10,000 Union boys in the bone orchard. I certainly hope this doesn't repeat itself before we fight our next battle here at Murfreesboro," John said.

"When Shiloh was over, I realized that I can put up with all the hardships of the Army and the war. I can endure thirst, hunger, Greenwood muskets that misfire, incompetent officers, marching through mud up to my knees, and being wet and cold most of the time. But I've discovered the worst of it is life after a battle. That's when you have time to think of the soldiers that you knew that are lost to all time," Thomas said.

After that depressing thought, Thomas poured more Drambuie in their cups and added the coffee. The three brothers were silent for a while, each one enjoying the Scottish coffee. John attended to the campfire, then patiently waited for Joseph to begin his questions again. Joseph surprised them when he started talking but it wasn't a question.

"I need to correct you about one thing though John. Shiloh was our very first battle, but we've already fought our second battle. You know, the battle that took place before we marched into Murfreesboro," Joseph said.

John looked at Joseph, confused at first. Then he realized what he meant, swallowed some coffee, and smiled broadly.

"I know what you're thinking about," he said.

"Me too," Thomas said.

"The 41st Ohio and the Battle of the Texas Black Horse Cavalry."

Chapter 25

The brothers all smiled knowingly at each other. War bonded soldiers together. War bonded brothers that were soldiers together even tighter. The smiles they shared were smiles about the unique episodes they experienced, even in the midst of danger.

"Okay Joseph, since you brought it up, you can tell the story," John said.

Joseph poured some more coffee into his cup. Then he poured some more for Thomas and John. Thomas looked at the Drambuie bottle to see how much was left. Joseph thought about how he was going to tell this crazy story as he went over the details in his mind. He had saved some room in each of their coffee cups for some more Drambuie and held his cup out to Thomas. Thomas obliged and they now all had one last full cup of Scottish coffee to drink while they reminisced.

"A toast to the 41st Ohio and our victory at the Battle of the Texas Black Horse Cavalry," Joseph said.

The brothers clinked their coffee cups together to toast their victory of the great battle.

Joseph placed his hands around the coffee cup to warm them as he started to retell the episode.

"One evening, a group of soldiers from the 41st Ohio were talking about cavalry units. Someone started talking about the Black Horse Calvary of Texas. It was explained that this was a very special

Calvary troop. Every horse is a midnight black color. The Black Horse Calvary of Texas is an awesome, fearsome, dreadful, forbidding, formidable sight. They are known for their blood-curdling appearance and fierce charges, with sabers swinging wildly. Just the sight of them is enough to inflect you with the most serious case ever of the Virginia quick step. Every evening someone would tell another story about the Texas Black Horse Cavalry. Their military renown grew and grew. Every soldier in the camp would hear dreadful story after story about the Cavalry. Their legend grew larger by leaps and bounds.

And then, wouldn't you know it. A Confederate cavalry unit charged a Union steamship on the Cumberland River that was nearby to our camp. The steamship was quickly destroyed. The rumors started flying that it wasn't any run of the mill Confederate cavalry unit. It had been the famed Texas Black Horse Cavalry. Everyone was on edge, imagining that the Black Horse Calvary of Texas would be attacking the 41st Ohio infantry at any moment. The tension became so unbearable that when a private sneezed, he looked up to see everyone else in camp pointing their rifles at his head. One night, by accident, a sentry fired his carbine back toward our camp. The Union cavalry troop that was placed away from the camp to guard it immediately jumped onto their saddles and rode back to camp at a full gallop. This tremendous clatter of hoofs sounded like a thousand cavalry horses charging towards the regiment and everyone yelled, "It's the Texas Black Horse Cavalry!" We prepared for the worse. Then somehow it was discovered that the thundering horses were our very own Union troops. It was just a misfired shot. Everyone was amazed that our troops had not shot each other to pieces," Joseph said.

Thomas and John and Joseph now laughed at the incident and the mistake of seeing enemies everywhere. At the time of the incident though, the McGonagle brothers had a serious discussion. They agreed this episode gave them a chance to learn a valuable lesson. It was a lesson to not let rumors and wild talk fill your head with things that could turn out not to be true at all.

"I heard recently about some Army soldiers by the name of McCook. Daniel and John McCook and thirteen of their sons from Carrollton, Ohio are all enlisted in the Army. They're from a family of Scots that settled in Carroll County," John said.

"There seems to be a lot of Scots in Wayne County and the nearby counties that have joined the Union cause," Joseph said.

"Aye. Carrollton is in Carroll County to the east of us. Thinking about other Ohio towns where there are Scots reminds me of Loudonville, Ohio. Loudonville is just west of Wayne County, in Ashland County. That's where our father's friends, the Kirkpatrick's, live. I remember father telling me that he became close friends with the Kirkpatrick family during the Toledo War," Thomas said.

"I think I remember this. The Kirkpatrick clan was from Dumfriesshire, Scotland. I've heard our family talk about them from time to time. Good people for sure," Joseph said.

"Aye, laddie. Good Scots – all around. And to think that the McCook brothers have thirteen sons between just the two of them. That is amazing. It's even more amazing to know that they're all fighting for the Union. That's impressive," Thomas said.

"Extraordinary."

"I can't imagine having six or seven more brothers in addition to you two," Joseph said.

"I can't imagine any one of them asking more questions than you do, Joseph."

"Carroll County and Ashland County have a majority of people in them that support the Union," Thomas said.

"That reminds me of a few interesting things about Carroll County. It was named in honor of Charles Carroll from Carrollton, Maryland. He was the last surviving member of the Declaration of Independence. He died in 1833," John said.

"How do you know all this stuff?" Joseph asked, yet again.

"You can bet your wages that with a history like that, that the people in Carroll County are totally for the Union," Thomas said.

"Unlike our county. Wayne County has a lot of southern sympathizers for some odd reason," John said.

"Odd. Very odd. That means mother and the quilts she uses to help the underground railroad is even more important in a county with a lot of Copperheads," Joseph said.

When the McGonagle brothers talked about the quilts their mother made helping the slaves escape to freedom, each brother often touched the quilt, thinking of home. They each knew their mother was at this very minute more than likely in her rocking chair. By the fire, covered under her favorite quilt – with the initials 'J.A.' on a corner – that A.J. Camblein made for her. She would be working on another quilt, maybe just a simple nine square block quilt, or reading the Bible. The broth-

25.2

ers all had similar thoughts, without the other one being aware that they each were thinking about the same things. Thoughts of mother, quilts, piano concerts. Thoughts of 'Home Sweet Home.'

More coffee was ready. Three cups were filled with hot coffee and some sugar. The Drambuie bottle was empty but each brother could feel it chase away the December cold. The Drambuie had been a great addition to celebrate the soon to be New Year. Tomorrow would soon come and it would be New Year's Eve. Then a new year. The coffee still felt good going down, even if it was no longer authentic Scottish coffee. Thomas took some hardtack and dipped it into the Scottish coffee to soften it up. He raised his cup to John and Joseph.

"Happy New Year brothers."

They clinked their cups together to celebrate 1863, even if they were a day early.

"Here's to the Union. May it last forever," John said.

"Here's to Ohio and our family back there," Joseph said.

The coffee was hot but they hardly even blew on it to cool before they swallowed. They didn't want to waste any warmth that the winter was trying to take away from them.

Thomas had been holding some hardtack in the hot coffee since they poured the last cup. He attempted to bite a bit off but the hardtack resisted. He placed the hardtack back in the coffee and decided it need-ed to soak some more. Maybe a lot more. Joseph watched as Thomas attempted to deal with the hardtack. Joseph decided to wait longer before he started talking. He would give Thomas or John a chance to start an interesting subject. After a few moments, he couldn't stand it any longer.

"What else can you tell me about our family history, about where our farm is?" Joseph asked.

"I'll bet you all the spondulix you have that you didn't know that the land where the farm where we grew up used to be part of Virginia," Thomas said.

"Your bums out the window," Joseph said incredulously.

"Not this time," Thomas said.

"Run that by me again Thomas. Ohio used to be part of Virginia?" Joseph said.

"Aye. This is what happened. It was about 80 years ago, in 1784, that Virginia was granted a huge area of land called the Virginia Military District. The land was used to provide military land grants to veterans of the Revolutionary War. It later was divided to become the state of Kentucky in 1792 and Ohio in 1803."

"I guess that is why there are southern sympathies in Ohio - due to that connection to Virginia," John said.

"Speaking of Ohio, I can tell you a story too," Joseph said.

It was difficult for Joseph to decide whether to drink the coffee to stay warm or just hold his hands around the cup. He decided to take a quick sip and place his hands around the warm cup as soon as he could. Then he started his story.

"There was a big storm along the Ohio River about 10 years ago. It flooded a number of farms. The water rose so high it flowed into their houses and barns. A Scottish farmer by the name of McLachlan built his barn too close to the river and the water was so high, that his cows started floating down the river. Then pretty soon, a table from the house floated away. Then some chairs. Then a desk. The water rose into the parlor and floated a mahogany piano down the Ohio River. Farmer McLachlan's wife jumped aboard the piano and played and sang as she floated away."

"I see the Drambuie has started to have an effect on you, Joseph," Thomas laughed.

"No, it's not the Drambuie. It's a true story. The soldier that told me is a Zouave. He plays the bugle over at the 54th Ohio. In fact, he is from Cuyahoga County, Ohio – the same county John is from," Joseph protested.

"What song did Farmer McLachlan's wife sing on the piano as she floated down the Ohio River?" John asked.

Joseph took a big swallow of coffee as he thought about several songs that might be appropriate to the question.

"Think it was something like, 'I Love Nae a Laddie But Aye'," Joseph said.

"Not just a Scottish ballad but one of your favorite ones to boot, eh? If that's a true story, I bet that laddie probably never saw his lassie again," Thomas said.

"Just telling you what I heard," Joseph said.

253

"I Lo'e Nae A Laddie But Aye"

"I lo'e nae a Laddie but aye, He loves nae a Lassie but me,
He's willin' to mak' me his ain, And his ain' I am willin' to be.
He gave me a Rockley O' blue, A pair o' new mittens o' green,
The price was a bussie or two, And the debt I did pay him yet reen.
O'! I lo'e nae a Laddie but ane, He loves nae a Lassie but me,
He's willin' to mak' me his ain, And his ain' I am willin' to be."

Chapter 26

"Well, here it is almost New Year's Eve. Christmas was different this year, wasn't it? This was your first Christmas away from home, right, Joseph?" John asked.

"Yep. At least we got a little bit of a break, seeing as how we got to spend Christmas day in Nashville," Joseph said.

"That was good. We had lots to eat. There were clear skies, a warm breeze ---,"

"Don't remind me. That was the last fairly nice day we had. Then General Rosecans gave the order to march towards Murfreesboro on December 26. The clouds were black and the mist started as soon as we started to march. The mist turned to heavy rain that plagued us all day long," Joseph interrupted.

"It didn't take long before we started taking Confederate fire the following day either," John said.

"Remember we marched in the fog the following morning. 'Ole Rosie' ordered Colonel Hazen to attack and take control of that bridge at Stewart's Creek. We were just feeling our way through that fog until it lifted. Then General Hazen brought up the cavalry from the Fourth Michigan regiment," Joseph said.

"That was a good move by the Colonel. There must have been close to a hundred horses that charged through the rain as we ran as fast as we could to secure the bridge," John said.

"The Rebels panicked and we drove them back across the bridge," Thomas said.

"They ran back to Murfreesboro and informed Confederate General Bragg

26.1

that he couldn't settle in for the winter there, like he expected," John said.

"I remember thinking I was glad to spend the night guarding that bridge instead of tramping through the mud. I must have spent an hour trying to scrape the mud off my boots. These muddy roads in Tennessee are the worst I've ever seen," Joseph said.

"We got our marching orders the next day, on Sunday, December 28. It was fairly quiet until the rebels started to test our position and we shot back and forth at each other. We exchanged fire in that cornfield until it got dark. I remember the following morning, Monday the 29th, it dawned bright but there was thick hoarfrost on everything," John said.

"Colonel Hazen marched us quickstep until our brigades joined up with General Crittenden. That's when the wind increased. Now we're still enduring this cold north wind," Thomas said.

"The rain has soaked the ground so much, it can hardly get into the soil," John said.

The McGonagle brothers worked to keep their campfire going. Between the wind and the rain showers, it took some doing. Their coffee pot was empty now. The Drambuie was finished. Joseph rubbed his eyes and yawned. The Drambuie had kept him warm and was now making him a little sleepy. The brothers would try to keep the campfire going through the night, mostly for warmth but also it would be easier to get some breakfast going in the morning.

"These dry cedar boughs and some of the dead oak branches burn well. This fence post that we've chopped up burns well too," Joseph said.

"Some Tennessee farmer isn't going to be too happy to see his fence posts used for firewood," John said.

"Maybe not but whether you dress in blue or gray, you've got to do what you can to stay warm now that winter has arrived," Thomas said.

"We better get some sleep if we're going to fight tomorrow."

"I think it's too cold to sleep,"

"Maybe it is too cold to sleep but sometime tomorrow or the next day, it is not going to be too cold to fight. I can feel it. We've got a major battle that's going to take place on one side or the other of Stones River," Thomas said.

Thomas stopped talking when he watched Major Wiley walk near their campfire again. He could tell from the expression on the Major's face that this wasn't going to be another pleasant chat. Thomas knew the Major was bringing some important information. Major Wiley waved his arms to gather all the soldiers that were nearby and called to them to circle up.

"Boys, gather around the McGonagle's fire. I have an order issued by General Rosecrans that you need to listen to," Major Wiley said.

The Union soldiers tramped through the mud, their boots squished in the clay as they gathered around. Most pulled their blankets tightly around them to keep the wind out. Some chomped tightly to a pipe as the wind tossed the smoke into the surrounding forest of trees. The McGonagle boys all stood together. Thomas rearranged the quilt over his back and head and firmly grasped it with his left hand. He placed his rifle over his right shoulder. The other soldiers joined the McGonagle brothers around the campfire or stood on the large stones that were nearby. Major Wiley read the letter.

"Soldiers, the eyes of the whole nation are upon you. The very fate of the nation may be said to hang on the issue of this day's battle. Be true, then, to yourselves, true to your own manly character and soldierly reputation, true to the love of your dear ones at home, whose prayers ascend to God this day for your success. I need not ask you to be brave. Keep ranks. Do not throw away your fire. Fire slowly, deliberately, above all, fire low, and be always sure of your aim. Close steadily in upon the enemy, and, when you get within charging distance, rush on him with the bayonet. Do this and the victory will certainly be yours."

Major Wiley folded the letter and momentarily looked at the stones that were all around the

26.2

soldiers. He looked briefly in the eyes of a few of the soldiers, then walked away.

It was quiet now. The campfire crackled, it was the only sound. Slowly, the soldiers squished back through the mud and drifted back to their campfires or shelters.

"Did he say the eyes of the whole nation are upon us?" Joseph asked.

Thomas and John remained quiet. Those same words played over and over in their heads also. Thomas was the first one to answer Joseph's question.

"Aye, laddie. I would agree with that. Think about it. The Union Generals haven't had too many victories to notch in their belts. General Burnside was beaten at Fredericksburg. General Pope was beaten at the Second Battle of Bull Run. The Union needs this victory. This is what we signed up for – to keep the Union together. Slavery isn't right. We all know that. Unless the regiments are gathered here to give this a full effort, the Union won't stay together. If that happens, the morass of slavery will continue."

"General Rosecrans was right in his letter when he said to be true. True to yourself. True to your character. True to your family. True to our nation," John said.

Thomas and Joseph nodded their heads in agreement.

"As brothers, we live together, we fight together, and if necessary we die together," Thomas said.

After Major Wiley's words, the night plunged further into darkness. The campfire flickered and succumbed to the darkness. The rain pinged on the rocks. The north wind whistled dismally through the trees. Thomas, John, and Joseph prepared for battle. They filled their canteens, placed hardtack into their knapsacks, and checked that mud was not jammed into the barrel of their rifles.

"Fill your canteens, boys," John said.

"That sounds familiar. Where did I hear that before?" Joseph asked.

"At the Battle of Shiloh. Remember what the Colonel told us?"

"Fill your canteens, boys! Some of you will be in hell before night and you'll be needing some water!"

They located their bayonets and packed spare ammunition into their haversacks. When they had finished their preparations, the McGonagle brothers situated themselves on the ground with their backs against some of the huge stones. As they each closed their eyes and drifted off to sleep, Joseph could not resist one more question.

"Ever wonder why they call this place Stones River?"

Thomas opened one eye and raised an eyebrow.

"Goodnight, sweet prince."

Joseph thought for a moment and tried to think where he had heard that expression before. Then he remembered. He knew there was another sentence that came after 'sweet prince' but he was too tired to think anymore.

"That's Hamlet, right? From Shakespeare?" Joseph mumbled.

John was settled in on the other side of Joseph. Without opening his eyes, he said the line Joseph was trying to think of.

"And flights of angels sing thee to thy rest."

Joseph fought trying to sleep just yet. There were so many things to talk about. Joseph recognized that was the line from Hamlet that he tried to think of, which made him think of another question.

"That's what----," Joseph started to say, half-asleep

"Just close your eyelids, Joseph."

Joseph blinked several times but it became harder and harder to open his eyes after a blink. This reminded Joseph of another song Nancy played on the piano. Something to do with closing your eyes. Now he remembered and recalled the name of the song. It was 'Darling, Kiss My Eyelids Down'. Joseph started to recite the verses to the song but fell asleep before he could say the first few words. The exhaustion took over. Joseph, along with his two brothers, fell asleep. Without consciously thinking about it, somehow the bear's claw quilt was passed from Thomas to John to Joseph throughout the night. Joseph usually secured the quilt in his haversack when it was time to start another day. As was their custom, the older brothers slept on either side of Joseph to keep him safe, as older brothers are want to do.

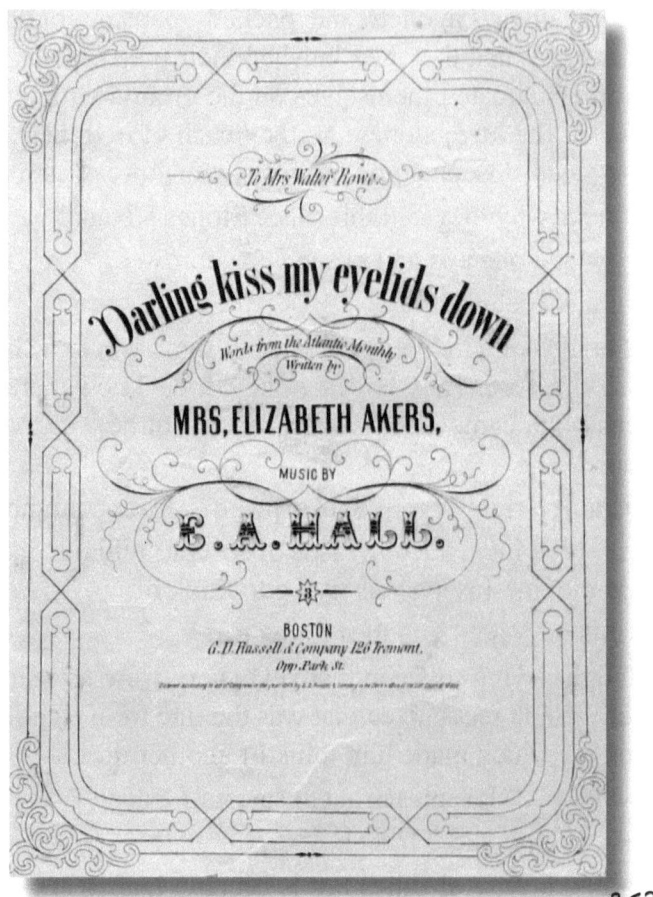

26.3

"Darling Kiss My Eyelids Down"

"The light is fading down the sky. The shadows grow and multiply.
 I hear the thrushes evening song,
But I have borne with foil and wrong. So long. So long.
 Dim dreams my drowsy senses drown.
So, darling kiss my eyelids down. So, darling kiss my eyelids down."

Chapter 27

The morning of December 31st, 1862 arrived with a cold gray mist as it started to get light. Everything was frozen or wet. Thomas poked Joseph awake. Joseph stretched and poked John to wake up. Thomas had coffee ready and each brother swallowed large gulps to try to warm up. The 41st Ohio, Company C, along with the others under General Hazen, gathered nearby at an old farmhouse, the Smith house. Other soldiers were in various states of getting their breakfast together. Both the Union officers and enlisted men assumed the battle would take place in the early afternoon and thought they had time to organize and prepare.

Joseph blew on his coffee to cool it just a bit and confirmed it was New Year's Eve. The last day of 1862. A new year would start at midnight. He asked John what time it was. John replied 6:22 am. Suddenly, they could hear shooting and yelling in the direction of the woods on the other side of a cotton field. Ohio soldiers under General Willich and Indiana soldiers under General Kirk had early orders to form picket lines in the forest. The Union commanders wanted to avoid a total surprise attack from the Confederates but expected a battle later in the day. The McGonagle brothers and other soldiers from the 41st Ohio around the Smith house assumed what they were hearing at this early hour was probably just a small skirmish. They had received no orders to get their guns and march to form their picket line. The Union soldiers continued to make coffee and forage some breakfast.

Five minutes after the first sounds of rifle fire, there were a few cannon volleys. Thomas realized that maybe this was more than a little skirmish. Soon the cannon fire increased even more. He advised John and Joseph to gather their rifles, canteens, and haversacks so they would be ready to go if an order was issued.

Suddenly, Union soldiers were running through the camp, away from the direction of the shooting. More and more soldiers in blue uniforms were panicked and running scared, not even slowing down as they wildly ran past the 41st Ohio. Some were wounded, holding an arm or a leg as they ran. In moments, it was total confusion. Union soldiers, like the McGonagle's, had camped near the Smith house and attempted to find something to eat other than hardtack. Only a few soldiers had gathered their weapons for a battle. Soon it became impossible to do anything because of the ferocious, total mayhem. More Union soldiers, some on foot, and some on horseback from the other regiments, ran through the camp. Horses without riders knocked over campfires, coffee pots, and slammed into soldiers.

John stopped a wild-eyed soldier with Indiana regiment markings on his uniform. He grabbed him by the shoulders and forced him to stop. The soldier struggled to get out of John's grasp and wanted to keep running but John would not release him until he got some kind of an explanation. Thomas and Joseph listened as the Indiana soldier breathed heavily and talked excitedly to John. He told them he was in General Kirk's picket line. It had crumbled as the Confederates had unexpectedly overrun them in a surprise morning attack, just as the sun came up.

The panicked soldier quickly told John that some of their rifles had been in a large stack in a tent to keep them out of the mist and rain. They had no time to get them and had no choice but to retreat. They were so outnumbered by the rebels that they were forced to run for their lives. The rebels screamed like demons in a fury of bayonet charges and collapsed the Union picket line. The panicked Indiana soldier talked fast as he described a vicious storm of fighting and dying. He had witnessed a huge number of Union soldiers fall in the unrelenting rifle fire

and bayonet charge. He even saw General Kirk get shot, which knocked him from his horse. The General was then captured. John released his grip on the soldier, who immediately started to run again, without any hesitation.

27.1

Thomas grabbed his hat from his head and slapped his leg several times in frustration. He couldn't remember being so angry. The Johnny Rebs had surprised the Billy Yanks once again. The Union troops were again surprised and unprepared.

"This is just what happened at Shiloh. The Confederates pulled a surprise attack on us at that battle too," Thomas said in frustration.

A horse without a rider charged through the camp, foaming at the mouth, running at full speed. It ran right at the McGonagle brothers. John grabbed Joseph and pulled him back as the horse glanced off Joseph's back, knocking John and Joseph both on the ground. Joseph's rifle flew through the air, hitting a tree, and landed thirty feet away. As John and Joseph helped each other up, Thomas retrieved the rifle and yelled for the brothers to come where he was positioned.

"Just stand here behind this tree until things settle down or we get some orders to move into position. This battle has started and the rebels certainly have the upper hand early in the day. I heard someone say that the Confederate picket lines were six lines deep."

After about twenty more minutes of confusion, soldiers started to gather in groups. There was a loud, deep almost continuous sound that was coming from the Confederate position.

"It sounds like a giant wind that comes before a furious thunderstorm," Joseph said.

The sound was incredibly loud. It occasionally decreased, then increased in intensity again. It was a storm – a massive Confederate storm. The 41st Ohio bugle sounded for picket formation.

"That's for us Joseph."

Thomas and Joseph started in the direction of the bugle call. John was a substitute, his call to formation had not yet been ordered. He waited and watched his brothers walk away. After a few steps, they both stopped and looked at John. The

27.2

brothers didn't like being separated. Each brother knew what they all wished – to fight together. Other regiments sounded their bugles, directing the soldiers for those regiments to report.

"That was a great talk last night, brothers. I will catch up with you when all the shooting stops later today," John yelled.

Soldiers ran to report to their regiments. In moments, Thomas and Joseph were in the infantry picket line with Company C, 41st Ohio regiment. John was in the infantry picket line with Company C, 62nd Ohio regiment. The 62nd Ohio infantry orders were to defend the Union cannons. The 41st Ohio was ordered to defend a 4-acre clump of cedar trees that were surrounded by cotton fields. The locals called this clump of trees the Round Forest. It was the strongest defensive position on the battlefield. General Palmer's division, commanded by Colonel Hazen, was ordered to hold the Round Forest with his troops.

The orders were to not just hold their position but not retreat an inch. A quick assessment determined that this patch of trees held the high ground. Railroad tracks ran through the southwest corner of the trees. The Army of the Cumberland or the Army of the Mississippi that controlled this railroad would have the advantage of bringing supplies when needed. The outcome of the battle would be decided by either the Union Army defending the Round Forest or the Confederate Army taking it away. The Confederates would fight fiercely with everything they had to force the Union from this strategic location

By 9:00 am Colonel Hazen held the Round Forest with four regiments: The 41st Ohio, the 110th Illinois, the 9th Indiana, and the 6th Kentucky. The Battle of Stones River accelerated. General Bragg commanded the Confederate Army and surprised the Union troops by attacking their left flank at dawn. General Rosecrans commanded the Union Army and after being initially caught off guard, attacked the Confederate left flank. Attacking each other's left flank caused the battle to take on a counter-clockwise movement of both Armies.

General Bragg ordered charge after charge of his Confederate soldiers across the open cotton fields that surrounded the Round Forest. The Confederate cannons pummeled the area, sending shrapnel, bullets, and tree limbs flying in every direction. The four Union regiments fired their rifles relentlessly. The Confederate attacks forced the Billy Yanks behind trees for cover. The artillery fire from the Confederates reached a crescendo. The firing of the guns and artillery was so intense that bushes exploded, large stones heaved and trees crashed among the Ohio, Illinois, Indiana, and Kentucky soldiers.

Thomas, Joseph, and the other Union soldiers struggled to defend the Round Forest. Showers of bullets arrived like thousands of frenzied geese taking flight. It was more intense than if twenty thousand snarling, snapping wolves were attacking the Union regiments that were entrenched on the knoll in the woods. A cannonball made a direct hit at the top of the Virginia pine tree Joseph was standing behind. A large branch fell, knocked him down, and pinned him under the limbs. Another private from the 41st helped lift the branch off and Joseph wriggled out from under the branches.

"It's like thousands of deranged woodpeckers in a hailstorm, during a continuous pounding of thousands of anvils!" Joseph yelled at Thomas.

"I can't believe they keep coming across that open cotton field. There's no cover. They must be willing to ---," Thomas started to yell back.

Thomas stopped mid-sentence as the horse Colonel Hazen was riding forcefully was thrown into the air from artillery fire. The horse landed in a heap, the Colonel's leg partially trapped beneath the dying animal. Thomas and Joseph both started towards the Colonel to lift the horse away. Bullets and shrapnel zinged around them. Amazingly, before Thomas and Joseph had taken many steps, the Colonel pushed out from under the horse. He calmly stood up, brushed himself off, then set off to find another horse. The brothers nodded at each other, knowing they needed to give Colonel Hazen cover. They swung around, raised their rifles together, and fired into the advancing Confederate picket line.

By 1:00 pm, Colonel Hazen's regiments had been battered for four hours from the continuous bullets and shelling from the Confederate cannons. The 41st Ohio and the other regiments suffered many casualties and wounded. But they held the ground in the Round Forest and had fully obeyed their orders. They had not given an inch.

Word was passed that a Confederate soldier had been captured. He informed the Union soldiers that General Hardee's and General

Polk's rebels from Alabama, North Carolina, Louisiana, and Georgia had lost almost half of their entire armies killed in their charges across the cotton field. The murderous storm of shot and shell from all directions into the Round Forest continued into the afternoon. General Bragg ordered his Confederates to reduce firing at 4:00 pm to reassess his strategy. There was a decrease in intensity that settled over the battlefield.

General Rosecrans, in his assessment of the battle, determined that at this point the Battle of Stones River was a draw. Rosecrans, as commander of the Union troops, knew the supreme importance of a victory. The victor of this battle could claim a victory for the state of Tennessee and the nation. General Bragg, as commander of the Confederate troops, also knew a victory here would give the Confederacy the momentum needed for permanent secession from the northern states. Both Generals assessed that the Army that had control of the Round Forest at the end of this day would win the Battle of Stones River. General Rosecrans decided to use this lull to firm up his defense of the Round Forest. General Bragg needed to gather his troops for one last offensive strike at the clump of cedar trees that the Union troops occupied.

While he gathered his officers for the plan of attack, General Bragg ordered more cannon and artillery fire at the four-acre clump of trees. This would certainly cause casualties and take out some trees that were giving them cover. General Rosecrans urgently needed to speak with Colonel Hazen face to face to impress on him the need to hold the Round Forest at all costs. General Rosecrans, with his Chief of Staff, Colonel Garesche, always by his side, galloped their horses hard towards the Round Forest. The Colonel and the General both charged to the forest with their horses stride for stride.

In addition to being Rosecrans Chief of Staff, Colonel Garesche had an additional reason to ride to the Round Forest. He wanted to check on his best friend - Colonel Hazen. Rosecrans and Garesche spurred their horses over an open cotton field. The fragile cotton stalks crackled and flew into the wind as the horses raced across the field. The two Union officers were surrounded by heavy Confederate fire. Rebel bullets zing past in massive swarms. Onward they rode. A cannonball exploded just in front of them, throwing shrapnel and huge plumes of dirt. Their horses reared up, too panicked to continue. A cannonball hit Colonel Garesche, killing him instantly. General Rosecrans halts his horse, sees there is nothing he can do for his Chief of Staff, and races to the Round Forest. General Rosecrans confers with Colonel Hazen. There is not much time to prepare for the final Confederate charge. He informs Colonel Hazen of the death of Colonel Garesche. There is no time for Colonel Hazen to grieve for his friend.

General Rosecrans commended Colonel Hazen for the valiant stand of his regiments. Colonel Hazen has ensured that the Round Forest has so far remained in Union control. The General impressed upon the Colonel that under no circumstance is he to order a retreat as the rebels make their final assault. The Union troops are ordered to fight to the last man. Colonel Hazen orders his battered soldiers to find a deep-down inner strength. The fate of the Union could be in their hands. The Colonel repositioned his brigades for a last defensive stand.

The 41st Ohio infantry is running very low on ammunition. Colonel Hazen's orders are to "fix bayonets and hold your ground" when the ammunition is depleted. The 110th Illinois is also almost out of ammunition and has no bayonets. They are ordered to "use your musket as a club and not give an inch". Colonel Hazen's orders are to not shoot until the expected final Confederate charge of the day is in very close range.

General Bragg consulted with his Confederate officers and decided to let General Breckenridge organize the final assault using four brigades. They will charge the Union position with all four of the brigades at the same time. There will be a single momentous rush at the Round Forest before darkness sets in. The plan involves Brigadier Generals Daniel Adams, John Jackson, William Preston, and Colonel Joseph Palmer to lead their brigades in the all-out final assault.

Chapter 28

Brigadier-Generals Adams and Jackson positioned their brigades for the charge. The other two brigades under Preston and Palmer are still being organized. Adams and Jackson determine that the other two brigades can join the fight when they're ready. They assume that General Breckenridge would agree that four brigades charging all at the same time can't be any different than two brigades attacking now and then two later. Adams and Jackson order an immediate charge towards the Round Forest.

Four Thousand Confederate cavalry and infantrymen charge, producing a swarm of gray uniforms across the cotton field, raining destruction at the soldiers in blue

The Union soldiers aim their rifles and anxiously wait for the order to fire. The Confederate troops rage towards the wooded knoll. Their flag bearers carry the flags proudly, waving them as high as possible. Time seems to stop for Thomas, Joseph, and every Union soldier watching the Confederate storm coming at them. The mass of gray seems to gather strength and confidence as they are directed right at the forest. The rebels charge past a rock that Colonel Hazen has chosen as a spot to give his order.

"Fire! Fire! Give it everything you've got boys!"

A single tremendous volley of rifle fire shakes the ground to the core of the earth. The raging storm of gray is mowed down as if a giant scythe had come out of the sky in a giant swoop. The first Breckenridge rebel charge is repulsed. Hundreds of soldiers in blue and in gray are lying dead or wounded in the forest or the cotton field. The smoke is as thick as fog, the large cedar trees in the Round Forest only a few yards away are barely visible. Colonel Hazen orders a cease-fire.

Joseph and Thomas and the 41st Ohio hear again what sounds like thousands of lumber wagons headed directly at the Round Forest. The smoke begins to clear. They see the other swarming Confederate charge. The offensive assault crosses the cotton field once more, with even more cavalry. Confederate soldiers on horses are yelling a blood-curling rebel yell, swords raised and whipping the air. A Confederate Captain on a galloping horse is firing a revolver in each hand, with the reins tightly clenched in his mouth. He fires one revolver, then the other, as fast as he can, riding at breakneck speed towards the clump of trees. Joseph steadies his stance, aims down the rifle sight, ready to pull the trigger. Colonel Hazen again gives the order to fire. Joseph squeezes the trigger.

His rifle doesn't fire. He is out of ammunition. The Confederate officer is now out of sight in the smoke. Joseph glances to each side to see where Thomas is standing. Maybe Thomas could hand him some of his ammunition. Joseph doesn't see him but he knows Thomas was there beside him as they watched the last charge. Maybe the smoke had separated them. There is only one thing for Joseph to do, as he is out of ammunition. He readied his stance with his bayonet, posed to fight hand to hand. Over the whirlwind of war, Joseph hears a strong, determined voice. It's Thomas.

"He has sounded forth the trumpet that shall never call retreat."

Before Joseph can answer Thomas, the earth shakes thunderously one last time, as the storm of gray attempts to overcome the Union soldiers. More men on both sides fall. The rebels grudgingly fall back. Colonel Hazen and the 41st Ohio have prevailed. The Round Forest belongs yet to The Army of the Cumberland. It is the last gasp of the rebels to gain control of the Round Forest. The shooting is now over, except for the sound of a

28.2

stray shot here and there. Still, Joseph maintained his stance with his bayonet ready. He noticed it getting darker. The end of the day. The end of the battle. There is an eerie silence. Joseph struggled with the words that described the sensation that washed over him.

"December 31, 1862 – a day I never will forget. The day that the gates of Hades opened wide and Lucifer himself was there to greet us. We sure gave those Rebs a big Ohio hello," Joseph said.

Joseph lowered his bayonet, still holding onto his empty rifle. He looked at the carnage that engulfed him. He wiped the sweat off his forehead. The smoke remained thick in the air and his eyes are stinging. There are trees, branches, horses, and Union soldiers lying all around.

Joseph gasped as he finds Thomas laying on the ground. Thomas is on his back. Motionless. Joseph leaned over, his knees buckled. He kneeled beside Thomas, grasped his hand, and confirmed his fears. Joseph bowed his head.

Death had found Thomas McGonagle.

Joseph McGonagle collapsed on the ground, exhausted, unbelieving that Thomas was gone. The battle was over for the day, tomorrow would more than likely be a repeat and Thomas would not be at his side. Joseph sat next to Thomas and the tears came fast. The winter night turned blustery, the wind whipped through the cedars and a drenching rain began again. It was turning dark very fast. Tears stung Joseph's eyes. It rained even harder. The tears that ran down his cheeks kept his face as wet as the rain that fell.

"Your Mission"

"If you cannot on the ocean, sail among the swiftest fleet,
 Rocking on the highest billows, laughing at the storms you meet.
You can stand among the sailors, anchored yet within the bay,
 You can lend a hand to help them, as they launch their boats
      away.
If you cannot in the conflict, prove yourself a soldier true.
 If, where fire and smoke are thickest, there's no work for you to do.
When the battlefield is silent, you can go with careful tread,
 You can bear away the wounded. You can cover up the dead."

28.3

28.4

Orders were issued. Soldiers that survived the assault on the Round Forest would walk back to a camp two miles back, along the railroad track. General Rosecrans Union Army would gather there, rest, have some food, and organize to fight tomorrow. Joseph requested that he stay behind to bury his brother. The request was denied. The major in charge said that the dead would be buried in a few days. Thousands of soldiers lay dead all over the battlefield. Thousands more were wounded. The wounded needed to be helped before they would be buried. Joseph had no choice. He walked to where Thomas lay on the ground. Joseph took one of Thomas's hands and folded it over the other.

"Thomas – I will be back to take care of you."

Joseph obeyed the order to go back to camp. He went with the other soldiers. It was a dark, cold, long, lonely walk in the rain.

John McGonagle had arrived at the camp and gathered some food and ammunition for his brothers to share. He had some coffee going on a small fire. He was on his second cup when he saw Joseph walking towards him. Just Joseph, not Thomas. John stood up and the coffee cup fell to the ground. Without a word being spoken, he knew Thomas was lying dead on the battlefield.

"John - I didn't want to leave him," Joseph said.

"I know. You obeyed orders, Joseph."

John put his arms around Joseph and hugged him. Tears cascaded down both of their faces.

"You had to obey orders," John said again.

"I know but I didn't want to leave Thomas like that. I told him I'd be back to take care of him. What are we going to do, John?" Joseph pleaded.

"Well, I think the two of us should find him and take care of him."

"The only thing we can do, if anything, is to bury him where he fell," Joseph agreed.

"Can you find him again?" John asked.

"I think so. The rain has eased off and the moon could help us find the Round Forest again," Joseph said.

"Have some coffee and some of the food I've got cooking. We'll make a plan," John said.

Joseph sat on a log near the fire. John handed him some coffee and a warm plate. Joseph just stared at the fire.

"It doesn't feel right without Thomas here. I can't eat anything. I just want to go right now and take care of him. Let's go, John."

"I agree we need to take care of him but we need to get permission to leave camp or they could shoot us for desertion," John said.

"Permission, or not – it's the right thing to do,"

"Let's just see if we can get permission first. If we can't then we'll come up with another plan."

"Well, we can try to get permission. I know other soldiers though that have asked to leave camp for some request or another. The answer is always the same. No. No. And No," Joseph said.

John drank sips of coffee while he studied Joseph's face. He knew that look. It was a recognizable Scottish expression that he could read, even without Joseph speaking the words. That face said, 'I'm going to find Thomas and take care of him all by myself if I have to. Nobody is going to talk me out of it'.

John thought about what he should say or what they should do. He was taking too long to say what Joseph wanted to hear, so Joseph spoke again.

"Just so you know, I am going to find Thomas and bury him tonight, permission or not."

John swallowed the last of his coffee. He thought of the sergeants and officers that they could ask permission to leave. What a terrible situation they faced. Desertion from the Army. Or desertion of Thomas. John knew if he deserted caring for his brother properly that guilt would follow him the rest of his life. He would have to find a way for them to bury Thomas.

"Just so you know Joseph, I feel the same. This is serious though. If we leave on our own without telling someone---"

"You don't have to say it. I know what happens to deserters, no matter their intentions," Joseph interrupted.

"We both know that Thomas would take care of us if need be," Joseph added.

"Aye, laddie. He would," John agreed.

"Well, just who do we ask for permission? Captain Opdyke?" asked Joseph.

"Maybe. What about that Lieutenant from Nebraska?" John asked.

"Who?"

"The one from Maple Grove, Nebraska – Lieutenant Peck," John wondered.

"Maybe."

The brothers thought for a while, different officers going through their minds.

"We have to be careful and really think about this. We need to come up with the name of an officer that won't say no without giving it some consideration," Joseph said.

"It has to be an officer that has the integrity to back us up if someone asks him if he gave us permission," John added.

"What about Major -----,"

"I just had a thought, Joseph. Why don't we go right to the top and ask our brigade commander – Colonel Hazen," John interrupted.

"Colonel Hazen. I like it. If we get permission from the Colonel, no other sergeant, lieutenant, captain, or major can question what we're doing away from camp," Joseph agreed.

The brothers were silent as each one thought about the best way to approach Colonel Hazen with their request.

"Colonel Hazen is a man of his word. You can take that to the bank," John said.

"The question is – will he say yes?" Joseph asked.

Joseph answered his own question.

"One reason that he might honor our request is that Thomas is in the 41st Ohio, which has been under Colonel Hazen's command since his beginning in the Union Army,"

"I heard some officers talking while I was waiting for you to come into the camp. They were saying that Colonel Hazen saved the day for the Union. They said we would not have won the Battle of Stones River without his leadership of the 41st Ohio to keep the Confederates from taking the Round Forest. Is that right Joseph?" John asked.

"Colonel Hazen was fearless," Joseph said.

"Also, Colonel Hazen lost his best friend today too – Colonel Garesche. Maybe he will better understand how we feel about losing a brother."

"Well, let's go find out one way or the other"

Chapter 29

John and Joseph walked to the tent area where the officers were quartered. They hoped they could find Colonel Hazen there. They found him as he conferred and planned for tomorrow with a group of junior officers. Some of the officers were the same ones that they had discussed approaching with their request to leave camp. That was before they had decided to go the head of the command chain. After a few minutes, almost all of the officers walked away from where Colonel Hazen was standing. Two other officers, Captain James Cole and Lieutenant Ezra Dunham remained by his side, pointing to a map. The brothers waited until the officers folded the map and also left. Remarkably, Colonel Hazen was now by himself. Joseph and Thomas watched as the Colonel walked over to a campfire and rubbed his hands over the flames to warm his hands. Then he sat down on a large fallen tree beside the fire.

"Well, here goes. It's now or never, Joseph," John said.

The brothers approached the Colonel. John decided to get right to the point and quickly make their request.

"Colonel Hazen, sir. My name is John McGonagle and this is my brother Joseph McGonagle. Our brother, Thomas, was killed in the battle today. We would like your permission to leave the camp tonight so we can bury him on the battlefield."

John was anxious and aware that he had a large lump in his throat as he spoke to the Colonel. His voice had been determined and steady though.

Colonel Hazen looked at John and studied his eyes. Then he looked directly into Joseph's eyes and studied his face. He could tell a lot about a soldier's character by doing that. He was always able to evaluate a man by looking into his eyes. What Colonel Hazen saw in the eyes of John and Joseph told him everything he needed to know. He saw that they indeed were willing to die fighting for their country. Soldiers in his command died every day. The Colonel knew though, that etched in their eyes, there was something deeper. Warriors, brothers. Brothers that lived by an unspoken code that they would die for their country and they would die for each other. Brothers that answered to a higher code. Their eyes told Colonel Hazen that John and Joseph believed they had a sacred duty to take care of Thomas.

Joseph and John could hardly breathe. Colonel Hazen's response seemed to take forever. John thought about saying something else but there was no use to say anything more. He had stated clearly what their request was. They both steadily held the Colonel's gaze.

Colonel Hazen reached into a pocket in his uniform and brought out a cigar. He bit off the tip of the cigar, spit it into the fire, and chomped it into his mouth. He sat with the unlit cigar in his mouth and didn't move. The brothers were beginning to wonder if he would say anything at all. Joseph thought maybe they should just move on and not take up any more of the Colonels time. No response at all from the Colonel was as clear as a loud no.

Then, Colonel Hazen took the cigar out of his mouth. He looked again intently into the eyes of John and Joseph.

"I can't give you permission to do that boys. But ---,"

The Colonel found a branch in the fire, lit the cigar, inhaled deeply, held the smoke for a moment, then blew it out over the fire.

"But ---- I'm going to have a smoke and what you boys chose to do between now and tomorrow morning is up to you."

John and Joseph looked at each other, astonished at the words they had just heard. John started to open his mouth to say something but no words came out. Time seemed frozen. The brothers were so certain the Colonel would say no. Now that he had not declined their request, they needed their feet to move but they seemed to be frozen in place

'Yes, sir," John finally said.

The brothers backed away from the campfire into the trees. They both wanted to just observe Colonel Hazen for a while. They admired him at this moment more than any other time they had been with him. Usually, Joseph would ask a question about this time. He didn't have to ask John a question about what they heard Colonel Hazen say. Joseph heard the words and he knew what the Colonel intended.

"The Colonel said what we do until tomorrow morning is up to us."

"Aye, Joseph. Colonel Hazen is a giant of a man. We will have to think of something to honor him for allowing us a way to bury our brother."

"Let's get going,"

Joseph and John hurried back to their campsite to gather the things they needed for their task ahead. Colonel Hazen placed the cigar in his mouth and inhaled deeply again. He turned to watch as the boys hurried away.

Colonel Hazen thought about the McGonagle brothers. It took a lot of courage for them to ask me for permission to bury their brother. Their brother must have meant a lot to them. That is some family loyalty. A bond between brothers. A bond between brothers was like a bond between friends, only deeper. The Colonel was going to miss his close friend, Julius Garesche, terribly. They had been friends since the Indian and Mexican wars that they had fought together. They were both graduates of West Point. He remembered Julius had told him that he had been born in Havana, Cuba. Also, Major Garesche was a Catholic scholar and had even been decorated by Pope Pius IX. Colonel Hazen took comfort in knowing that his friend Colonel Garesche had

mass with General Rosecrans early this morning before the battle started. He would miss discussing religion with him and having a drink after a battle. Colonel Hazen knew General Rosecrans was probably also thinking about Colonel Garesche. They both knew he was very capable and would be almost impossible to replace. It would certainly be impossible to replace him as a friend.

29.1

"Colonel Julius Garesche – I smoke this cigar in honor of you, my friend. I will miss you. I hate this war, now more than ever."

His words were heard only by the cedar trees and large stones that listened.

As Colonel Hazen thought about the battle, he was proud of his regiments. The 41st Ohio had displayed unflinching fighting ability at the Round Forest. Those boys said their brother's name was Thomas. Thomas McGonagle. Ancestors probably from Scotland. He was probably one of the soldiers whose ammo was depleted. Then I had to give the order to fix bayonets and hold our positions. How incredibly brave they were to fight until their last cartridge was expended. The Colonel was proud that the 41st Ohio under his command had a reputation of perfect discipline, dauntless courage, and fighting abilities. All on display today. He wished he had more soldiers like Thomas McGonagle.

Colonel Hazen smoked his cigar, honoring his friend. The cigar was a reminder to appreciate surviving the bloody battle and carnage of the Battle of Stones River. Death had come close to calling his name today when his horse was shot out from under him. I really liked that horse. Named him Buchanan, not necessarily in honor of President Buchanan. He had disliked Buchanan and his Democrat party so much that he enjoyed jabbing his spurs into that horse's side as if he was spurring Buchanan for real. Anyway, the horse can be replaced, unlike Colonel Garesche.

Colonel Hazen understood why John and Thomas wanted to bury their brother. Just an hour before the McGonagle's came to talk to him, he had given orders to find Colonel Garesche's body and bury him. He felt it would be a tribute to a great friend and soldier. Colonel Garesche had given his life for his country, just as Thomas McGonagle had fought hard and to his last breath. Dying to end the scourge of slavery and end the secession of the southern states.

Chapter 30

Joseph and John walked towards the Round Forest, using the surrounding trees and rocks to avoid being in the open as much as they could. There was a full moon but quite often it wasn't shining too bright due to the cloud cover. At times the moon disappeared into the darkness and a cold rain would follow. They tried to step quietly and whispered to each other as they made their way. The devastation of war enveloped them, the horrors of war unimaginable. Joseph and John were committed to the dreadful task that they had to face and live with for the rest of their lives. They proceeded silently, carefully. Although the distance wasn't great, just a couple of miles, they walked cautiously, stopping every few steps to ensure they were not detected. They did not want anything to affect their mission.

The open cotton field now needed to be crossed. The cedar trees of the knoll in the forest beckoned to them. They waited until the moon disappeared behind a cloud. Many of the cotton stalks had been pulverized when the Confederates charged towards the Round Forest. The field was littered with blue and gray uniforms of those that gave their last full measure. Joseph stopped John and pointed at a soldier. An overpowering question nagged at him. John looked and saw a large wad of cotton in the soldier's ears. John quietly whispered to Joseph. The cotton had been placed there to dull the intense battle noise. The brothers tried to be careful and quiet. They did not want to start a skirmish with some rebels wandering around. The night continued to be silent and cold. Joseph stepped, taking too large a stride, snapping a cotton stalk. The sound was like a whip being cracked. They both froze in place just as the moon appeared again. The moonlight cast their shadows over the field. Feeling exposed, they quickly did double time over the remaining field until they reached the trees of the Round Forest.

Joseph knew where Thomas had fallen. They found him once they were in among the cedar trees. Branches scattered the ground, torn from the trees by the fury of war. Some branches hung down, barely clinging on, ready for the wind to take them away. The brothers discussed and whispered a plan while they walked. Now it was time to put their plan into action. Joseph surveyed the best spot and began to dig a shallow grave. He would also need to gather some stones. John used an axe and a knife and selected some of the tree branches to create a headstone out of a cedar plank.

The wind whipped at their coats and swayed the cedar branches as they worked to accomplish a final resting place for Thomas. John and Joseph reminisced in their minds about memories of their brother as they completed their task.

John thought about the lengthy discussion they all three had enjoyed the night before. It seemed so much longer ago. He thought about Maggie playing the piano. She had probably played it earlier today even. He thought about what songs she would have played. What songs would she be playing if she was aware of the death of Thomas? She would take his passing harder than most. John lamented that there would not be any music for some of their favorite melodies in honor of Thomas.

He dreaded thinking of how to find the words to write a letter to his mother. John worked on the headstone. The cedar was being transformed, with curl after curl of wood shaving giving way to form Thomas's name and the date. John quietly hummed one of Thomas's favorite Scottish songs, 'Mary of Argyle'. As John recalled the words to the song, he stopped carving the headstone when he remembered that Thomas liked to tease Maggie by substituting the words 'Mary of Argyle' for 'Maggie of Argyle'. John brushed away his tears and the wood shavings from the cedar plank, then started to carve again.

"Mary Of Argyle"

"I have heard the mavis singing, his love song to the moon. I have seen the dewdrop clinging to the rose just nearly born.
But a sweeter song has cheered me. At the evening's gentle close.
And I've seen an eye still brighter, than the dewdrop on the rose.
T'was thy voice, my gentle Mary, and thine artless winning smile.
That made this world an Eden, Bonny Mary of Argyle!"

30.1

Joseph thought about the family history and stories they had all shared last night. He was grateful to have learned so much about his family. Thomas had contributed so much. Now that Thomas was gone, Joseph would have to hold onto the family stories and pass them along. Joseph appreciated that family history was important because actually, it helped him understand himself. Joseph grasped that his life experience was based on what his ancestor's lives had been. The Scottish warrior part of him made him able to fight and stand his ground for what he believed in. Scottish warriors did not go through the world as if in a perpetual barroom fight. It was fighting for a cause. Like preservation of the Union and freedom for everyone, regardless of the color of their skin. Joseph pledged to himself that, just as in a battle, when it came to standing up for what was right, that he would not give an inch. The Quaker legacy that had been passed down from his mother's ancestors had everything to do with taking care of family. That is why he was so adamant about caring for Thomas. It was just who he was. Joseph wanted this night to be a memorial for Thomas.

"Thank you, Thomas, for not allowing all those wonderful family stories you told me to be buried with you," Joseph whispered.

As Joseph dug into the cold hard ground, he was grateful for Colonel Hazen's permission to bury their brother. He considered bestowing an honor for Colonel Hazen by naming a son, if he ever had one, the name of Hazen. Joseph cared enough to provide a final resting place for Thomas and he cared enough to honor Colonel Hazen in some way.

When everything was ready, Joseph removed the quilt from his knapsack. The brothers wrapped Thomas in the quilt and lowered him into the grave. The quilt represented a loving tribute to their brother. They knew their mother would be touched that Thomas had something she had made to carry him into his next journey. Just as a bear's paw quilt guided those to freedom, the quilt would now guide Thomas into the next world. John and Joseph placed stones over the grave and secured the engraved headstone. The brothers stood side by side.

John read the words he had carved. "T. McGonagle 12-31-1862".

Shafts of moonlight beamed onto the grave. A few moments later, the moon disappeared into the darkness. The brothers could see Stones River in the distance when the moon came out of the clouds.

The wind mostly obscured any sound from the river but when the wind settled down, they could hear the gentle cascading of the river over the rocks. It added a sense of serenity and peace for them.

A lull in the wind prompted John to find a Bible verse to read. He retrieved a small Bible from the haversack that Thomas carried. It seemed fitting to John that you should read a Bible verse when you buried a brother. John held the Bible, unsure of what verse he would read. He noticed a piece of paper that had been inserted to mark a place in the Bible. John opened the page that was marked. The moon appeared again and there was just enough light for him to see, as the wind fluttered the pages of the Bible. The marker in the Bible was placed into a chapter on Amos. John's eyes focused on a verse. He had the sensation that an unknown power in the wind had helped him to find the verse, which he read aloud.

"Amos 5:24: 'Let justice roll on like a river, righteousness like a never-ending stream'."

John handed the Bible to Joseph and he gently thumbed the pages in his hands. As he opened the Bible to find a chapter, the wind again seemed to whisper over the brothers. Joseph saw that he had stopped on Psalms, the book in the Bible that he liked the most. His eyes went to verse 95, which he read aloud.

"Psalm 95:14: 'He shall call upon me and I will answer him. I will be with him in trouble. I will deliver him and honor him',"

The moon drifted back into the clouds and the wind swayed the upper branches of the cedar trees. Joseph and John had worked quickly to care for their brother. Even though the wind was raw and the cold nipped at them, they had worked hard enough to keep from shivering. There had been a bond between the three McGonagle brothers. The bond was still there, just between two of them now.

Old habits and patterns never changed. Joseph still was the brother to ask a question.

"John?"

"Yes, Joseph?"

"Can you do one other thing before we go?"

"What's that?"

"I know how much you and Thomas enjoyed Shakespeare. You have memorized a lot of poems. There's one I like that you may be able to remember. I don't know what sonnet it is but it begins 'like the waves'. Can you recite it?"

John thought for a moment. Joseph had asked about a specific Shakespeare sonnet. He knew the sonnet that Joseph requested. He recalled how the sonnet started. John practiced the words in his head, "I'll give it a try."

"Sonnet 60"

"Like as the waves make towards the pebbled shore,
So, do our minutes hasten to their end.
Each changing place with that which goes before,
In sequent toil, all forwards do contend." **30.3**

John had not thought about Sonnet Sixty in quite a while. He was grateful that he remembered the words. It was a fitting tribute to Thomas. Now that they were standing still, the cold and exhaustion started to take a toll. Joseph shivered. John buttoned the top of his coat. Neither brother wanted to leave. Neither knew what else to do. Or say. Joseph shivered again

30.4

and repeated part of the sonnet.

"Like as the waves make towards the pebbled shore, so, do our minutes hasten to their end. Thanks, John. We can go now."

John and Joseph started to walk away, just as the moon came out of the clouds again. A single moonbeam cast its glory on the grave. Joseph stopped for one last look.

"Goodbye, Thomas."

John joined Joseph as he also had one last look.

"Goodbye, Thomas."

Chapter 31

By now, it was several hours after midnight. A new year had begun, January 1, 1863. John and Joseph retraced their steps back to camp. Thomas had given his life to defend the Union. Thomas believed in his heart and soul, as did John and Joseph, that this war was being fought to keep the Union together. When the war was over, slavery would be over. It was past time that the inhumanity of slavery should end.

John and Joseph arrived back in camp, just as the morning light filtered through the pines and cedars. They succeeded in keeping with Colonel Hazen's 'permission'. They both prepared for another day, more than likely another day of fighting. The Battle of Stones River wasn't over. They knew it was possible that they could be joining Thomas. John stopped cleaning his rifle as he realized the significance of today's date.

"Joseph – I just remembered something. It is on this date, January 1, 1863, that the Emancipation Proclamation, that Abraham Lincoln issued, goes into effect," John said.

"That's right. Thomas died to help ensure that the proclamation went into effect," Joseph said.

"It declares that as of today all persons held as slaves within the rebellious states are free'."

"It was just a few hours ago that the three of us were talking about our family history," Joseph said.

"I'm sure glad we did that. Hopefully, one of us will survive this terrible war and be able to pass on all the things we talked about," John said.

An officer mounted on a Morgan thoroughbred stopped a few feet away from John and Joseph. They recognized Major Wiley. The Major studied each of them for a moment, then drew his sword and held it erect. Without a word being spoken, John and Joseph knew the Major was extending his sympathy to them for the loss of Thomas. The brothers nodded their acknowledgment. After a few moments, the Major placed the sword to his shoulder.

"Okay boys, let's go. It's time to show those rebels our terrible swift swords," Major Wiley yelled.

The Major spurred his horse around to organize the picket lines being formed.

John shook his head, then looked at Joseph and was surprised to see the look on Joseph's face.

"What?" asked John.

"I just realized something when the Major said 'terrible swift sword," Joseph said.

"It's part of a verse from 'The Battle Hymn of the Republic'. 'He has loosed the fateful lightning of His terrible swift sword'," John said.

"Aye. It jogged my memory. I remember the last words that I heard Thomas say," Joseph said.

"Tell me before the opening of the ball," John said.

"I didn't realize it until just now. Thomas was repeating a verse from 'The Battle Hymn of the Republic'."

I heard Thomas say, "He hath sounded forth the trumpet that shall never call retreat."

"Sounds like the last words from a Scottish warrior," John said.

"A Scottish warrior. And a brother."

"I can't wait to get out of Tennessee and get back to Ohio. But not until the Confederacy is defeated," John said.

"I'm with you brother."

John picked up his rifle and made a few steps towards the 62nd Ohio Infantry picket line. Joseph watched John walk away, then swung his rifle over his shoulder and started in the direction of the 41st Ohio Infantry picket line. Joseph stopped, then turned to look at John. He wanted one more look. When he turned around, he was surprised that John had stopped walking and was also looking at Joseph. One more look.

"What is it, John?" Joseph asked.

"I just couldn't walk away without hearing you ask one more question, Joseph," John said.

John knew he could get Joseph to ask one more question. He smiled at Joseph.

Joseph knew too. John could get Joseph to ask a question just by giving him a certain look. He smiled back at John.

"Also, I wanted to thank you for sharing the last words Thomas spoke. It reminded me of another verse from 'The Battle Hymn of the Republic'," John said.

"What verse is that?"

"As He died to make men holy, let us die to keep men free."

Joseph thought for a moment about the verse. He nodded to John. John nodded back.

They both started walking towards the formation of each of their picket lines. That last verse played over and over in Joseph's head. And the last verse repeated over and over in John's head. 'Let us die to keep men free'.

Another thought was also in Joseph's head. Amazingly at the same time, it was also in John's thoughts. 'If that's what it takes, then that's what it takes'.

After all, they were brothers.

Chapter 32

32.1

The Battle of Stones River continued. The bloodshed and carnage on January 1, 2, and 3 of this new year, 1863, was unimaginable. When the battle was finished, out of 310 soldiers in the 41st Ohio, 73 men died and 39 were wounded. The North named battles after places. They called it ''The Battle of Stones River'. The Union totaled 13,000 dead. The South named their battles after towns. They called it 'The Battle of Murfreesboro', The Confederacy totaled 10,000 dead.

Joseph and John McGonagle grieved for their brother Thomas. His death on a battlefield in Tennessee invigorated their passion, even more than it did before. They were dedicated to keeping the Union together. The McGonagle brothers were Scottish warriors though. They didn't take a day off, they didn't pack up and go home. They didn't let their mourning for their brother prevent them from honoring the oath they took to defend their country.

Their courage and spirit were infectious to the other soldiers around them. They influenced and inspired the other Union soldiers by their courage. John and Joseph were as committed to the Union cause as much as Thomas. Just as Thomas willingly 'gave the last full measure, John and Joseph were committed 'to die to keep men free'. The

Confederates withdrew a few days later. John and Joseph could be content that the Battle of Stones River was a victory for the Union and their brother. Thomas gave his life to help ensure this victory.

After the battle of Stones River, the regiments of the Ohio infantry received orders for different areas of the country.

John McGonagle was transferred to the 27th Ohio Infantry where he joined the Army of the Mississippi. John fought in the October 1863 Battle of Iuka, Mississippi and the Battle of Corinth, Mississippi. He wrote this letter to his mother while in Mississippi.

32.3

32.2

Iuka, Miss.   October 28, 1863

Dear Mother,

You will no doubt be surprised to know of me being at this place but never the less, I am here and in great health and ready for another tramp whenever.

"Old Johnny" gives the command forward. We left Memphis on the 18th enroute for Corinth where we arrived on the 24th with the exception of one that we left asleep on the road but no earthly power can wake him. Shortly after leaving Camp at Germantown, we struck the Mississippi R.R. and the cars overtaking our wagon train, frightened the mules that one of our boys was driving, causing him to be thrown off and then run over him which killed him instantly. He died one of our best men, one that was loved by all. We carried him in an ambulance to Lafayette where we camped that night & buried him in honors of war. I had charge of the scout that followed him to the grave & I hope that I may never be called on to perform the same duty again.

I received a letter from Joseph that same evening but could not answer it til I got here. I extended to him ten dollars as soon as I received the letter & would have sent the rest of this months pay home but I thought I would wait till I could write at the same time but as there is no express office here. I can't send it, unless I send it by mail. We started from Cornith on last Sabbath evening & camped about 2 miles from Camp Davis, where Thomas Lisle is, but I could not go to see him because I was on duty that night. We arrived here yesterday morning and I went into camp on the same ground that we occupied, a little more than one year ago but how long we will stay here, no one knows. I received the letter that Lib wrote on the 13th, yesterday evening. I was greatly surprised for I only thought that she did not intend to write at all.

It has been about three months since I heard direct from home & did not hear whether you had received that check that I sent until Joseph wrote to me. I would like to hear from home at least once a month. You wished to know whether Millford sent any money home but I can't tell you, he said that he sent $30. He paid me all that he owed me. Give my compliments to Van & ask her how her &

Lib settled the photo question. I intended to have some taken before we left Memphis but we left so sudden that I had not time.

Tell Robert to be a good boy & help you all he can & I will send him a present in a few days.

I have nothing more to write. I will close with my best wishes for your well fare.

John McGonagle

P.S. Direct to Corinth.

I will enclose a photo of Col. Fuller & Staff, they stand thus:

Lieuten. Orr   Lieuten. Ells

Col. Fuller   Capt. Dustan

32.4

Chapter 33

In December of 1863, the 27th Ohio fought in The Battle of Parkers Cross Road, where Union forces battled against Confederate General Nathan Bedford Forrest. In March of 1864, the 27th Ohio captured the city of Decatur, Alabama. In July of 1864, John was at the Battle of Atlanta, where he was wounded. Discharged from Army service on August 17, 1864, John was in and out of Army hospitals. John died from peritonitis on March 21, 1865 at the Todd Military Barracks in Columbus, Ohio, just two weeks before the end of the Civil War on April 9, 1865. His cousins, Thomas and Maggie Lisle brought him home to Lima, Ohio for internment.

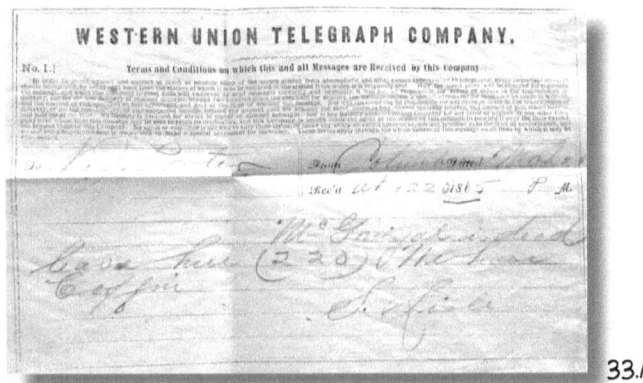

33./

WESTERN UNION TELEGRAPH COMPANY

To: *N. Porter* **From:** *Columbus* **Dated:** *March 22*

Rec'd: *at 12:20   1865   P.M.*

McGonigal is dead

leave here   (2:20)   We have Coffin.

T. Lisle

J McGonigal
Registers of Deaths of Volunteers, 1861-1865

Name:	J McGonigal
Death Date:	24 Mar 1865
Death Place:	Todd Barracks Columbus, Ohio
Enlistment State:	Ohio
Rank:	Private
Regiment:	Substitute

Lisle, a cousin of John McGonagle, acted as spokesman for the family and settled his estate on April 10, 1865.

33.2   After the Battle of Stones River, Joseph McGonagle and the 41st Ohio were ordered east to Ft. Woodbury, Virginia, then back to middle Tennessee. In September of 1863 they fought at Chickamauga. In November of 1863, they battled at Missionary Ridge near Chattanooga, Tennessee. They fought at Pickett's Mill in Paulding County, Georgia, in May of 1864. The last major battle for Joseph, before his three-year enlistment obligation was over, was the Battle of Atlanta in DeKalb County, Georgia, part of Sherman's march to the sea. Joseph was discharged on September 29, 1864.

33.3   Joseph returned to Ohio to visit his mother and family for a few months. The Civil War continued. Joseph re-enlisted in the Army because he was so adamant about the preservation of the Union. He was assigned to the 192nd Ohio Infantry on January 23, 1865. He remained in the Army for seven more months, until his discharge on September 1, 1865. Joseph returned to Ohio to become a shoemaker and married Caroline "Callie" Rodabaugh on December 25, 1867. They had three children, Edgar on November 13, 1869, Charlie on June 22, 1872 and Gertrude on August 8, 1874. Joseph and Callie moved to Indiana, where Callie McGonagle died July 5, 1877.

33.4

THE STATE OF OHIO,
PUTNAM COUNTY, ss.

I do hereby Certify, that

M. *Joseph M M Emagh*

AND

M. *Caroline Radabaugh*

*were joined in Marriage by me, on—
the Twenty fifth   day of
December   A. D. 1867
J A Smith M G
I Certify the above Return was
filed in the Probate Office, the 27
day of December   A. D. 1867
Attest: John Treadway
                                    Probate Judge.*

33.5

Joseph married Anna Villa Reece May 16, 1878 in Huntington, Indiana.

33.6

33.7

Joseph Mcgonigal
in the 1870 United States Federal Census

Name:	Joseph Mcgonigal
Age in 1870:	28
Birth Year:	abt 1842
Birthplace:	Ohio
Dwelling Number:	41
Home in 1870:	Pierceton, Kosciusko, Indiana
Race:	White
Gender:	Male
Post Office:	Pierceton
Occupation:	Shoemaker
Male Citizen over 21:	Y
Personal Estate Value:	100
Inferred Spouse:	Caroline Mcgonigal
Inferred Children:	Robert E Mcgonigal

Household Members:	Name	Age
	Joseph Mcgonigal	28
	Caroline Mcgonigal	21
	Robert E Mcgonigal	6/12

33.8

J. Mcgonegal
in the 1880 United States Federal Census

Name:	J. Mcgonegal
Age:	38
Birth Date:	Abt 1842
Birthplace:	Ohio
Home in 1880:	Pierceton, Kosciusko, Indiana, USA
Dwelling Number:	91
Race:	White
Gender:	Male
Relation to Head of House:	Self (Head)
Marital status:	Married
Spouse's name:	Anna Mcgonegal
Father's Birthplace:	Ohio
Mother's Birthplace:	Ohio
Occupation:	Shoe Maker
Neighbors:	View others on page

Household Members:	Name	Age
	J. Mcgonegal	38
	Anna Mcgonegal	27
	Edgar Mcgonegal	10
	Charles Mcgonegal	8
	Gertrude Mcgonegal	6
	Mable Mcgonegal	1

33.9

Joseph continued to work as a shoemaker and also became involved in politics. He was a delegate from Kosciusko County, Indiana to the 1880 Republican Convention and supported James Garfield for President. The Garfield/Arthur ticket was a natural for Joseph to support, as Garfield was born in Moreland Hills, Ohio, which is sixty miles from Joseph McGonagle's hometown of Wooster, Ohio. Joseph and James

33.10

Garfield also had several Civil War connections. Garfield was in the 42nd Ohio Infantry and they had both fought at the Battle of Shiloh. James Garfield was a Major and chief of staff under General Rosecrans. Garfield, Rosecrans, and Joseph McGonagle all fought at the Battle of Chickamuga.

33.12

33.11

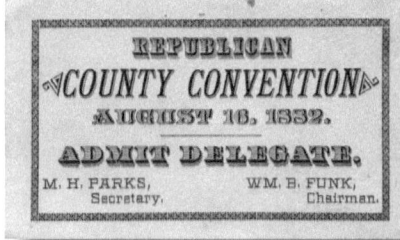

33.13

Anna Reece McGonagle was also involved in politics. She campaigned for the women's right to vote as part of the suffrage movement. Anna also was a member of the Temperance Legion and worked to rid the country of alcohol consumption. She pledged allegiance to the American Flag, the Christian Flag, and the Temperance Flag.

PLEDGES OF ALLEGIANCE

American Flag: I pledge allegiance to the Flag of the United States of America and to the Republic for which it stands; one Nation, indivisible, with Liberty and Justice for all.

Christian Flag: I pledge allegiance to the Christian Flag, and to the Saviour for Whose Kingdom it stands. One brotherhood, uniting all man-kind in service and love.

Temperance Flag: I pledge allegiance to the Temperance flag, the emblem of temperance, self-control, pure thoughts, clean habits; the white flag that surrenders to nothing but purity and truth, and to none but God whose temples we are.

33.14   33.15

33.16

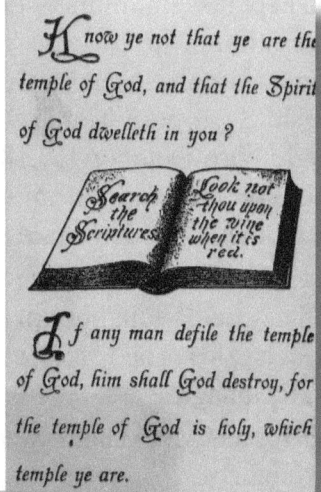

Know ye not that ye are the temple of God, and that the Spirit of God dwelleth in you?

Search the Scriptures

Look not thou upon the wine when it is red.

If any man defile the temple of God, him shall God destroy, for the temple of God is holy, which temple ye are.

I. Cor. iii. 16, 17.

33.17

--PLEDGE--

Trusting in God's help, I solemnly promise to abstain from the use of alcoholic drinks, including wine, beer and cider; from the use of tobacco in any form and from profanity.

*   *   *

May God help you to keep this Pledge, which makes you a Member of

The Loyal Temperance Legion of

33.18

33.19

Joseph and Anna McGonagle's first child was named Mabel, born on March 10, 1879.

Twin daughters, Ardella Launa and Estella Laona, were born September 1, 1886.

Joseph kept his commitment to honor Colonel Hazen, who allowed Joseph permission to bury his brother Thomas. Joseph named his firstborn son Joseph Hazen McGonagle, born May 22, 1882. A second son, Donald Scott born March 9, 1884. Another son, Thomas Lisle McGonagle born October 12, 1892, whose first name was a tribute to Joseph's brother and the middle name of Lisle, was a tribute to Joseph's mother's maiden name.

Joseph and Anna's first born son, Joseph Hazen, married Luella Fankell. They had a son, born in 1911, and also gave him the name of Joseph Hazen (Jr.) The Hazen middle name was used in two generations of McGonagles.

Joseph Hazen McGonagle was a partner in a mercantile store in Palmer, Nebraska.

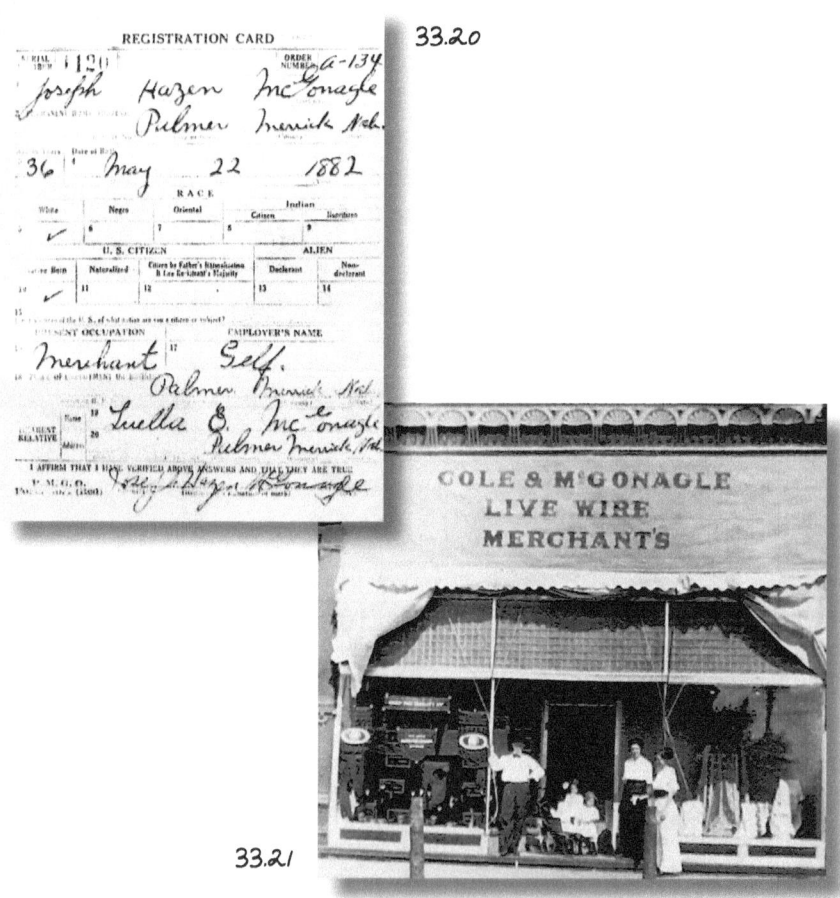

33.20

33.21

Joseph A. McGonagle was an 1880 census taker for Kosciusko County, Indiana. As a veteran, Joseph took advantage of the Nebraska Homestead Act, which had been signed by President Lincoln in May of 1862. Possibly inspired by the tales of A.J. Camblein, Joseph and Anna loaded a wagon and headed to Nebraska Territory in1884. He homesteaded three miles north and two miles east of Palmer, Nebraska. Veterans were given special consideration and were allowed to subtract their time in military service from the time required to settle their land.

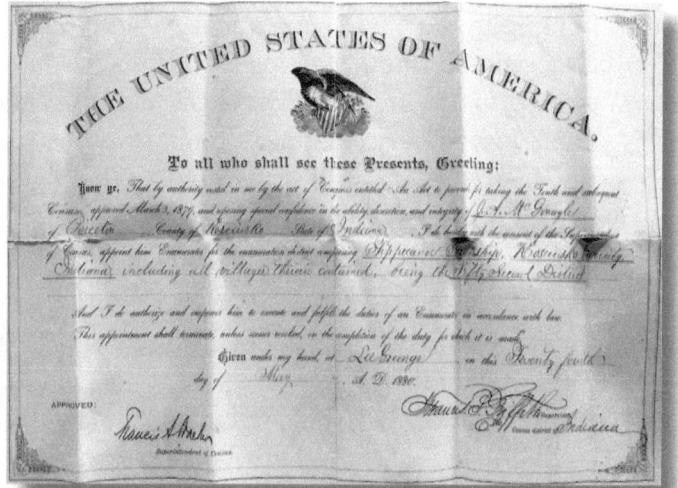

33.22

Joseph McGonagle became the Postmaster of Palmer, Nebraska in 1889, and every day, as part of his duties, he raised the flag at the post office. He would take a moment to admire the flag waving in the wind and know he had helped to ensure those stars and stripes would continue to wave.

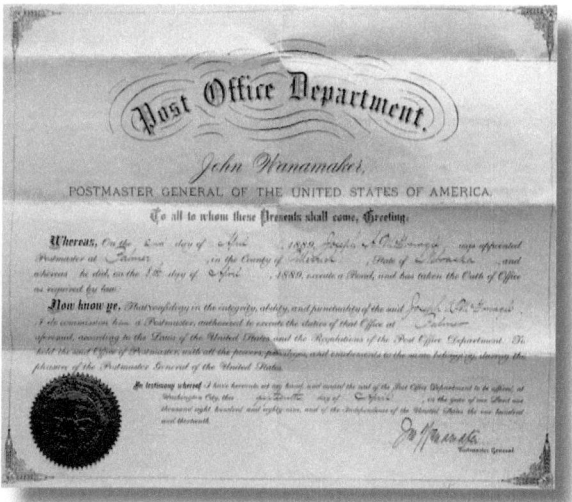

33.23

Joseph survived many battles of the civil war, however, as was very common, soldiers were very susceptible to infectious diseases. More soldiers died from infectious diseases than from gunfire. The unsanitary conditions of the war caused many casualties from dysentery, typhoid, pneumonia, malaria, and tuberculosis. Three out of five Union soldiers and two out of three Confederate soldiers died of disease.

Joseph contracted tuberculosis during his service in the Army and fought a persistent cough and shortness of breath for twenty-eight years after the end of the Civil War. People would often ask him if it was worth fighting in the Civil War. Was it worth having a brother killed in battle, another brother dying from infection after being wounded? Was it worth contracting tuberculosis and suffering from it for so many years? Joseph never hesitated in his answer.

"War is terrible and only worth it if you are fighting for freedom, peace, and equality. War is only worth it if you are willing to die for your country and your belief to help others gain their freedom."

Throughout his life, people would ask him about his experiences in the Civil War. Joseph would tell them about the discussion he had with his brothers around a campfire by Stone's River on a cold Tennessee night on December 31, 1862. He would tell them how grateful he was for Colonel Hazen allowing them to bury Thomas. Joseph would tell them about two things he remembered that Thomas had told him.

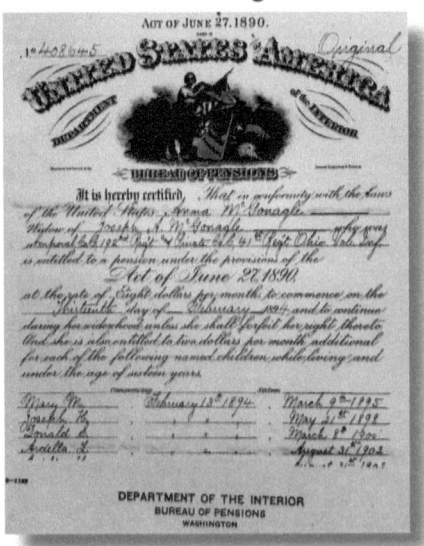

33.24

"It's better to be a lion for a day than a sheep for the rest of your life."

"Life is like riding a stampeding two-ton Scottish Highland dragon. It will buck furiously, breathe fire, and drag you through the most demented, atrocious, dreadful situations in this world. The knack is to hang on tight and that dragon will give you the ride of your life."

Joseph attended several Civil War soldier reunions. He remained proud of his service and the sacrifices of his family. He died from complications of tuberculosis on September 18, 1893 in Palmer, Nebraska at age 51.

The McGonagle brothers who defended the Union in the civil war are heroes that fought to give us our country, our freedom, our very lives. They ensured that America would remain a union of all the states and their families would forever be beneficiaries of their sacrifice. Their love of country, their bravery, and devotion to family ensured that generations later, we still have 'Home, Sweet Home'.

The devotion to family and how much they cherished their friendship is evident in these two beautiful poems, composed by Maggie Lisle, written to celebrate the life of John McGonagle.

33.25

Written in Memory of John McGonagle
Who died March the 24th of 1865

He slept as calm and peaceful,
As lingering in life's breath.
While less his life story proclaimed,
But tho' he slept in death.
His coffin stood upon the biers,
And as we passed him by,
We wept that one so kind and good
And beautiful should die.

The brightest flower that for me bloomed,
Had took its lasting flight.
'Twas Morn upon the sky – But Oh
Within ours 'twas Night.
And as we stood beside the grave,
The light breeze seemed to sigh,
Oh, heaven that one so kind and good
And beautiful should die.

We wept the tears of sorrow,
But 'twas in poor relief,
That welled up from one stricken heart,
Or charged with bitterest grief.
And as they sadly hid his form
From many a tearful Eye,
We wept that one so young and loved
And beautiful should die.

But whilst we mourned for the love and
With hearts bowed down with grief,
And felt that no earthly comfort
Could bring to me relief.
We cast our eyes to heaven
With faith and humble prayer,
There's more beautiful in that world of bliss,
We should meet that loved one there.

Lined Feb. the 13th of '66
Maggie

33.26

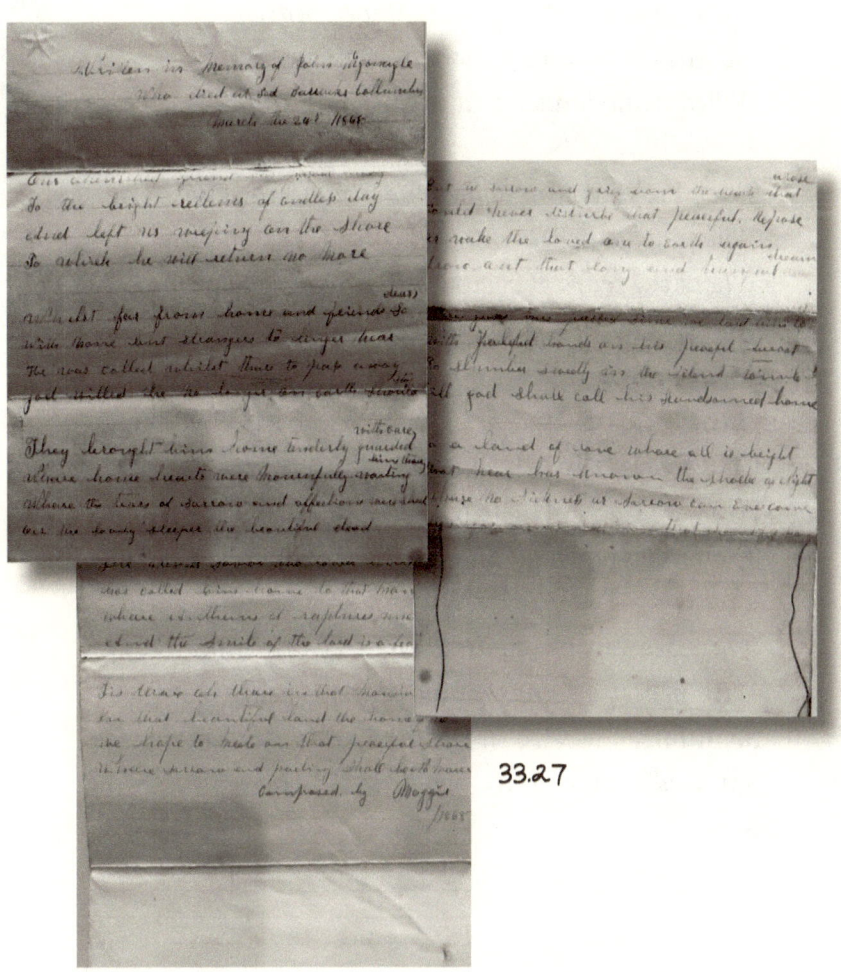

33.27

Written in Memory of John McGonagle
Who died at Tod Barracks, Columbus
March the 24th 1865

Our cherished friend has passed away,
To the bright release of another day,
And left us weeping on the shore,
To which he will return no more.

Whilst far from home and friends so dear,
With none but strangers to linger near,
He was called whilst there to pack away,
Willed he no longer and with should stay.

They brought him home tenderly guarded with care,
Where home hearts are mournfully waiting him there.
Where the tears of sorrow and affection were shed,
And the lovely sleeper, the beautiful death.

But the sorrow and grief from the hearts that arose,
Could never disturb that peaceful repose.
As make the loved one to Earth again,
From out that long and tearful dream.

Three seasons have passed since we laid him to rest,
With peaceful hands on his peaceful heart,
So, slumber sweetly in the land,
Till God shall call his own dear to home.

In a land of love where all is bright,
That never has known the shadow of light,
Where no sickness or sorrow can ever come,
He's forever safe in that beautiful home.

The blessed savior who loved him best,
Has called him home to that mansion of rest.
Where anthems of rapture uncessingly roll,
 And the smile of the Lord is a feast for the soul.

Tis there oh there in that mansion of rest,
For in that beautiful land, the home of the blest,
The hope to meet on that peaceful shore,
Where sorrow and parting shall be no more.

Composed by Maggie
1865   33.28

Origin of the letters in this book:

The family story of the events at the Battle of Stones River had been told to me when I became part of the family and married a great grand-daughter of Joseph McGonagle.

The letters and memorabilia in the book were given to us from her Uncle Virgil Iler, a grandson of Joseph McGonagle. Uncle 'Virge' lived in the same house in Nebraska that his parents owned when they were first married. His mother, Stella was one of the twin daughters born to Joseph and Anna McGonagle.

The letters were folded and stored in two cigar boxes. A wooden 'Diamond' cigar box contained the letters, which fit snugly into a cardboard Benson & Hedges Habana Cigar box. Other papers, photos, and documents were also placed into the cigar boxes. My wife and I were told by her uncle that there were letters in the cigar box from the civil war. We were excited and very interested to be entrusted with these family heirlooms. Being young and busy with careers, we gave the box a cursory look, thinking we would spend more time analyzing the information 'someday.'

That 'someday' arrived years later, when we were forced into retirement and sheltering in place by the coronavirus pandemic. Now that we read the letters, we realized the Connellsville letter had no envelope to whom it was mailed, no signature from whom the letter was written, and only addressed to Dear Brother. The New Cumberland letter was signed by M. McGonagle, mailed to R. McGonagle, and addressed to Dear Brother. The Ft. Kearney letter was signed by A.J. Camblein, a surname that was nowhere in the family tree. There were no longer any older relatives to give us any clues about the letters and many questions to be answered.

I became determined to find out as much as I could about the significance of the letters, why they remained in the family and who wrote and received them. It became a mission to find out as much as I could before the contents of the cigar boxes were passed down to another generation. I became a history detective. With the help of Ancestry. com, stacks of reference books, and the internet, I pieced together much information about the letters. It was not a straight forward path to uncover the information. There were many hours logged on my computer, with chasing down many different paths before arriving at the correct conclusions. It is a family story that spans six generations of United States history. It is America's story.

The letters are over 170 years old. They were read, reread, folded, and refolded many times before they were given to us. The paper the letters are written on is fragile and thin. I have included a scan of the original letters in the book, with the premise that I did not want to do any further damage to the letters by flattening them to make the folds disappear. I provided a transcription of each letter after the scan of the original. The letters have many family connections from Scotland, Pennsylvania, Ohio, Indiana, and Nebraska. It truly is like blocks in a quilt.

New Cumberland Letter Authentication:

The New Cumberland letter is signed by M. McGonagle, This is McCaslin McGonagle. The letter is mailed to R. McGonagle. This is Robert McGonagle, McCaslin's older brother. McCaslin mailed the letter from New Cumberland, Ohio to Wooster, Ohio, which is where Robert McGonagle lived. The letter also mentions his other brothers, Alexander, Thomas, and Joseph. McCaslin has a reference to his cousin, Ellen McGonagle in the letter, who is the daughter of another brother, John.

The 1850 Census lists the home of M. McGonigal as New Cumberland, Ohio, and his occupation as a cabinet maker, in the furniture industry. The letter is dated 1851 and mentions a shop in town, probably a furniture store. The dates and names in the census all correspond.

I believe this letter was sent to Robert McGonagle, then entrusted to his son, Joseph McGonagle, then to his daughter Stella, who eventually placed it in the cigar box.

Connellsville, Pennsylvania Letter Authentication:

The letter is not signed. It is being sent from Connellsville, Pennsylvania, and is addressed Dear Brother. I have determined that the person writing the letter is John Reece. He lists his ten children and their birthdates. The name of the youngest daughter is Harriet. Harriet's death certificate lists her father, John Reece, and her mother, Martha Shallenberger. I have concluded that John Reece is writing the letter to his brother, Jacob Reece, to inform him of the death of Martha. The date of the letter is 1847. The 1850 Census lists John Reece living in Fayette County, Pennsylvania, He is a widower and there is a list of most of the children that he references in the letter.

I have concluded that the 'Dear Brother', to whom the letter is addressed, is Jacob Reece. The 1850 Census lists Jacob and Sophiah Reece residence in Ohio, with their children. Jacob Reece has a daughter, Anna (Arville) Reece who eventually marries Joseph McGonagle. The letter also references several other brothers: Wallace, Nathan, and Andrew, who all live in Pennsylvania. The letter mentions sending regards from the Weever family, a reference to Sophiah (Weaver) Reece, who is married to Jacob. The pieces of this puzzle were finally solved.

I believe this letter to Jacob Reece was entrusted to his daughter, Anna (Reece) McGonagle, then to her daughter Stella and subsequently stored in the cigar box.

There were no living family members to give me a hint about who wrote and who received the Connellsville letter. After many hours of research on ancestry.com, I was able to confirm that John Reece sent the letter to Jacob Reece. As I was putting the final touches on my story and adding information to confirm that I had the correct names and people, my wife found an 'Auld Lang Syne Birthday Book' tucked away in a seldom opened drawer. Inside the small book was a hand-written note signed by Stella McGonagle Iler. If I had discovered the note earlier, it would have saved me many hours of research. However, I would not then have enjoyed the thrill of being a history detective. It was gratifying to confirm I had arrived at the correct information.

33.29

A.J. Camblein Ft. Kearney Letter Authentication:

The letter from Ft. Kearney, Nebraska was folded into a 3x3 inch square and mailed to Robert McGonagle in Ohio. It is signed by A.J. Camblein. There are a number of Camblein families listed in the 1850 and 1860 Census information that live in or close to Wooster, Ohio. Genealogy research shows Camblein families living in Ohio, where the McGonagle families also reside. The 1860 Van Buren County, Iowa Census lists A. J. Camblein as female, head of the house, occupation farmer.

There is a David Camblein, recorded as married in Wooster, Ohio. I believe A.J. is a cousin to David. David Camblein's mother is Sidonia Evans. The Evans family is referenced in the letter. A Searight family is referenced in the Ft. Kearney letter and there is a record of this family residing in Wayne County, Ohio. A man by the name of Israel Evans, from Hanover County, Ohio is recorded to be an original member of the Mormon Battalion. David Camblein also has a homestead deed recorded in Merrick County, Nebraska in 1890.

The letter states that the battalion is headed to Oregon or California. Records show that

A.J. Camblein died in Trinity County, California. I have concluded that her battalion probably arrived in California and unfortunately, A.J. Camblein died at the age of 33. Her cause of death is listed as 'froze to death'.

I believe the McGonagle and Camblein families were neighbors and friends. Their family names can both be traced from Scotland to Pennsylvania to Ohio. The Ft. Kearney letter was mailed from A.J. Camblein to Robert McGonagle, who entrusted the letter to his son Joseph, who entrusted it his daughter Stella, who subsequently placed it in the cigar box.

Poem by Maggie Authentication:

There is not a person with the first name of Maggie in the family tree. Maggie is often a nickname for Margaret and I have concluded that Maggie is actually Margaret Lisle, born in Ohio in 1832. Her parents are Robert and Nancy Lisle. Robert Lisle's sister is Isabella

(Lisle) McGonagle, who is Joseph McGonagle's mother. The birth dates of Margaret Lisle and her brothers, Slemmons and Thomas, correspond well with the birth dates of Thomas, John, and Joseph McGonagle. The McGonagle and Lisle families lived in the same Ohio county and I have concluded the families must have been very close. Thomas Lisle brought John McGonagle home to Ohio to be buried. Slemmons Lisle was the appointed representative to settle the John McGonagle estate.

The 1860 Census lists Margaret Lisle as having the married name of Kilgore. Margaret (Maggie) and her husband lived in Wayne County, Ohio with Wooster as their post office. It is probable that Margaret Lisle was called Maggie and was the author of the poems written in memory of John McGonagle.

I believe that Margaret (Maggie) Lisle wrote the poem and gave it to Anna McGonagle, the mother of John McGonagle, who then entrusted it to her son, Joseph McGonagle who entrusted it to his daughter Stella, who eventually placed it in the cigar box.

A final 'Rest of the Story'

The family story of the events at the Battle of Stones River was explained to me when I became part of the family in 1968 and married a great grand-daughter to Joseph McGonagle. In December of 1990, I was at a continuing education conference in Nashville, Tennessee. One afternoon I rented a car and drove to the Stones River battlefield. After wandering through the battlefield, I talked to a ranger just as I was leaving and relayed the family story of the McGonagle brothers burying their brother on the battlefield. The ranger looked in a reference book and told me Thomas McGonagle had been reinterred in the soldier's cemetery, complete with a headstone. This was news to me and information to tell the family when I returned from my trip. I asked the ranger where the headstone was located among the 20,000 headstones lined up in row after row. He gave me a general description but said I had to hurry, the grounds were closing in about 20 minutes. I quickly purchased a disposable camera and hurried to rows of headstones. Where to start looking? Time was quickly running out. It was an overcast day but just then, a beam from the sun appeared over an area of the cemetery. I decided that would be as good a place as any to begin a hurried search. Amazingly, that beam of sunlight was shining on the headstone with Thos. McGonagle inscribed. It gave me a chill and I could feel the hair standing up on the back of my neck. Gratefully, I clicked several photographs and drove away just as the gates to the battlefield closed behind me.

Chapter Notes .

The documentation for each image is listed in order by each chapter with a corresponding number.

The letters, photographs, documents, and memorabilia found in the cigar boxes are noted as being 'From the M. Iler Family Collection'.

Photographs and other items from the family are noted as being 'From personal item of M. Iler'.

Cover:

'Dear Brother' Enlargement – From Connellsville, Pennsylvania letter – August 13, 1847 – From M. Iler Collection

Envelope addressed to Mr. Thomas McGonagle with Kentucky Seal – 1862 - From the M. Iler Collection

Chapter 1:

1. "Home Sweet Home" Sheet Music Cover- Composed by H.R. Bishop, Instrumental Arrangements   F.A. North & Co. 1308 Chestnut St. Philadelphia 1849
2. "Home Sweet Home" – Music Stanza – by H.R. Bishop (1849) – Will Rossiter Publisher Chicago & New York - 1899
3. "Yankee Doodle" Sheet Music Cover – by Edward L. White – Russell & Techam Publisher – Boston, Massachusetts - 1857
4. Bromo-Seltzer headache ad – From Song Lyric Page - "Home Sweet Home" – Bromo-Seltzer Collection - by G.J. Webb – Prepared by Emerson Drug Co. – Baltimore, Maryland – (circa 1850)
5. 'General View of Cumberland Gap, Tennessee' – From "Harpers Weekly" Newspaper – July 5, 1862
6. 'Dear Brother' – Word Enlargement – From New Cumberland 1851 letter – From the M. Iler Collection

7. New Cumberland Letter – August 15, 1851 – From the M. Iler Collection
8. Transcription of New Cumberland Letter –provided by Author
9. "Hail Columbia" – Sheet Music Cover & Song Lyrics –Bromo-Seltzer Collection - by F. Hopkinson, (1798) – Prepared by Emerson Drug Co. – Baltimore, Maryland – (circa 1850)
10. "Bonnie Blue Flag" – Sheet Music Cover & Song Lyrics - by Harry McCarthy – Published by A.L. Blackman & Bro. – New Orleans, Louisiana - 1861
11. Bonnie Blue Flag with Single Star - Drawing by Owen Kane
12. "Home Sweet Home" – Song Lyrics – by H.R. Bishop (1849) – Will Rossiter Publisher - Chicago & New York - 1899
13. "Home Sweet Home" – Sheet Music Cover – Bromo-Seltzer Collection - by G.J. Webb – Prepared by Emerson Drug Co. – Baltimore, Maryland – (circa 1850)
14. Adjutant Generals Office Document – Joseph McGonigal - May 29, 1883 – From M. Iler Collection

Chapter 2:

1. Photograph –Joseph McGonagle (1842-1893– Taken at the D.F. Shoemaker Photographic Studio - Warsaw, Indiana – Circa 1870 - From the M. Iler Family Collection
2. Shoemaker Photographic Studio – Printed on the back of Photograph –Joseph McGonagle (1842-1893– Taken at the D.F. Shoemaker Photographic Studio - Warsaw, Indiana – Circa 1870 - From the M. Iler Family Collection
3. "Beautiful Dreamer" – Sheet Music Cover & Song Lyrics – Composed by Stephen C. Foster – Published by Wm. A. Pond & Co. – New York – 1864
4. J.A. McGonagle (1842-1893) Metal Civil War Reunion Badge – Company C, 41st Ohio Volunteer Infantry – From the M. Iler Family Collection
5. "Mary Bell" – Song Lyrics – Poetry by Thomas FitzGerald – Composed by George F. Benkert – Published by Edward L. Walker – Philadelphia, Pennsylbania - 1849

6. "Molly Bawn" – Song Lyrics – From 'Songs of Erin, Irish Ballads – Composed by S. Lover - Published by W.C. Peters & Son – Cincinnati, Ohio – Circa 1850

7. Volunteer Enlistment Document – Thomas McGonagle, Lima, Ohio - August 14, 1862 - From M. Iler Family Collection

Chapter 3:

1. Declaration of Recruit – Thomas McGonagle, Lima, Ohio – August 14, 1862 - From M. Iler Family Collection

2. "Let Us Haste to Kevlin Grove" – Song Lyrics – by M. Braham – Published by Firth & Hall – New York, New York – Circa 1830

3. "Corporal" – Poem by Ambrose Bierce (1842-1914) – Written in 1862 - From PoetryFoundation.org

4. Envelope addressed to Nancy McGonagle Porter from John McGonagle – Circa 1862 - From the M. Iler Family Collection

5. George Porter – Company B 128th Indiana Infantry – From Civil War Pension Records - Ancestry.com

Chapter 4:

1. Ohio Ribbon – Purchased at Stones River National Battlefield – U.S. National Park Service –From M. Iler Collection

2. "Camptown Races" – Song Lyrics – Composed by Stephen Foster – 1849

3. Hummingbird Quilt - Drawing by Zoe Kane

4. Bears Paw Quilt - Drawing by Zoe Kane

Chapter 5:

1. American Flag With 33 Stars - Drawing by Owen Kane

Chapter 6:

1. Envelope addressed to Mr. Thomas McGonagle with Kentucky Seal – 1862 - From the M. Iler Collection

2. 'Fruitless Attempt of The Army of The Potomac' - From "Harpers Weekly" Newspaper – February 14, 1863
3. "To A Mouse" – Poem by Robert Burns in 1785 – PoetryFoundation.org
4. Bride and Groom – Drawing by Zoe Kane
5. "A Red, Red Rose" – Poem by Robert Burns in 1794 – PoetryFoundation.org

Chapter 7:

1. Black Watch Soldier - Drawing by Owen Kane
2. 'Gems of Scotland –Sheet Music Cover – From "A Beautiful Collection of Scotch Songs" – Published by Lee & Walker, Philadelphia, Pennsylvania - Circa 1850
3. 'Dalley's Magical Pain Extractor' Ad – From "Harpers Weekly" Newspaper – April 29, 1865
4. Bromo-Seltzer Advertisement – Back page of "The Bromo-Seltzer Collection of 83 Popular Songs"- "Hail Columbia" – Emerson Drug CO. Baltimore, Maryland – Circa 1850
5. Lady playing upright piano – Image from sheet music cover of "The Bromo-Seltzer Collection of 54 Popular Songs" – "Home Sweet Home" - - by G.J. Webb – Prepared by Emerson Drug Co. – Baltimore, Maryland – (circa 1850)
6. "The Merchant of Venice" – William Shakespeare – 1605 – Shakespeare.mit.edu
7. 'Faith and Hope" - Word Enlargement - "Faith and Hope" Sheet Music Cover – Words by Rembrant Peale - Music by H. Millard – Published by G. Schirmer Co. – New York, New York – 1860

Chapter 8:

1. "On Keeping the Sabbath" – Poem by Emily Dickinson – EmilyDickinsonMuseum.org
2. Quaker Woman – Drawing by Zoe Kane

Chapter 9:

1. "Patriotic Compositions" – Sheet Music Cover & Song Lyrics – Published by McKinley Music Co. - Chicago & New York – 1908
2. "Sweet Spirit, Hear My Prayer" – Sheet Music Cover & Song Lyrics – by W. Vincent Wallace – Published by Wm. Hall & Son – New York, New York – 1868
3. "Wings of a Dove" – Sheet Music Cover & Song Lyrics – Written by Charles Jefferys – Arranged by L. Devereaux – Published by G.E. Blake – Philadelphia, Pennsylvania – Circa 1850
4. "Roy's Wife Of Aldivalloch" – Sheet Music Cover & Song Lyrics – Arranged by Thomas Comer – Published by Oliver Ditson – Boston, Massachusetts – Circa 1830

Chapter 10:

1. Harper's Weekly Journal of Civilization – Newspaper Heading – Saturday December 27, 1862
2. Connellsville, Pennsylvania August 13, 1847 Letter – From the M. Iler Collection -Pages 1, 2, 3, and 4
3. Transcription of Connellsville Letter – Provided by the Author

Chapter 11:

1. Artificial Legs Advertisement – From "Harpers Weekly" Newspaper – January 9, 1864
2. Worcestershire Sause Advertisement – From "Harpers Weekly" Newspaper – August 3, 1861
3. Photograph – Dorothy Gibson – From the M. Iler Collection
4. Folded Envelope/Letter Addressed to Robert McGonagle – From Army Station at Ft. Kearney, Missouri Territory -1848 – From the M. Iler Collection
5. Transcription of Ft. Kearney Envelope – Provided by the Author
6. Letter to Robert McGonagle - From A.J. Camblein at Fort Kearney, Nebraska 1848 – From the M. Iler Collection – Page 1 and 2

7. Transcription of Ft. Kearney Letter – Provided by the Author

Chapter 12:

1. "Tittery-Trie-Aye" – Pioneer Folk Song – Circa 1840 – Sing-praises.net
2. "The Lonesome Roving Wolves" – Pioneer Folk Song by Levi Hancock – Circa 1840 – Fiddle-Sticks.com
3. "Come, Come Ye Saints: - Pioneer Folk Song by William Clayton – 1846 – TheTabernableChoir.com
4. "For Whom the Bell Tolls" – Poem by John Donne – published in 1624 as part of his 'Devotions on Emergent Questions' – Poetryofquotes.com

Chapter 13:

1. Thomas McGonagle War of 1812 Ohio Militia Registration Card – From Iler Family Tree-Ancestry.com
2. "The Tippecanoe Quick Step" Sheet Music Cover –Published by Sam Carusi – 1840 – Baltimore, Maryland
3. "Tip & Ty" - Song Music Lyrics – Words by Alexander Coffman Ross – Electtionsongs.com
4. Civil War Soldier Regiment Card – John McGonagle – 27th Ohio Regiment, Ohio Infantry - Ancestry.com

Chapter 14:

1. "Dearest Spot of Earth to Me is Home" – Sheet Music Cover & Lyrics – composed by W.T. Wrighton – Published by Beck & Lawton – Philadelphia, Pennsylvania - 1857
2. Robert McGonagle and Isabel Lisle Marriage Certificate – April 1833 – Ancestry.com
3. Lady watching ship in a storm – Drawing by Zoe Kane

Chapter 15:

1. 'Longstreet's Sharpshooters' – From "Harpers Weekly" Newspaper – January 9, 1864
2. Thomas Lisle – Civil War Records and Profiles – Sharp Shooter 3rd Ohio – Ancestry.com
3. Apple Tree Quilt Drawing – by Zoe Kane
4. Isabella McGonagle Drawing – by Zoe Kane
5. "La Priere Dune Vierge" (The Maidens Prayer) – Song Lyrics – by T. Badarzewska – Published by Oliver Ditson & Co. – Boston, Massachusetts – Circa 1850

Chapter 16:

1. Sacagawea Drawing – by Zoe Kane
2. Lewis and Clark Drawing – by Owen Kane
3. "When You and I Were Young Maggie" –Sheet Music Cover and Song Lyrics-
4. by George W. Johnson – Published by J.A. Butterfield – Chicago, Illinois – 1864 Sheet
5. Nine Square Welsh Quilt – Drawing by Zoe Kane

Chapter 17:

1. "Three Fishers Went Sailing" – Sheet Music Cover and Song Lyrics - by Charles Kingsley – Music by John Hullah – Published by Oliver Ditson & Co. –p New York, New York – 1851
2. "Under the Daisies Ballad" - Sheet Music Cover and Song Lyrics – by H. Millard – Published by S.T. Gordon – New York, New York – 1865
3. "National Beauties" – Sheet Music Cover – Published by Marsh – Philadelphia, Pennsylvania – Circa 1840
4. 'Kentucky Seal' – Image Enlargement - From Envelope addressed to Thomas McGonagle – From the M. Iler Collection

Chapter 18

1. Joseph McGonagle Enlistment Card – Company C 41ˢᵗ Ohio – Ancestry.com
2. The War for the Union Envelope – addressed to Mrs. Isabella McGonagle – From M. Iler Collection
3. 'Charge of Seventy-Eighth Pennsylvania & Twenty-First Ohio at Murfreesboro' – From "Harpers Weekly" Newspaper – January 26, 1863
4. American Flag – Tole Painting by Wood River Carver – From personal item of M. Iler
5. Flag with 31 Stars – Drawing by Owen Kane
6. "The Flag" –Poem by Julia Ward Howe – From Atlantic Magazine April 1863 – TheAtlantic.com
7. "We Are Coming Father Abraham" –Song Lyrics - by A.B. Irving – Published by H.M. Higgins – Chicago, Illinois – 1862 – Whatsoproudlywehail.com
8. 'The Picket Guard in The Army Of The Potomac' – "Harpers Weekly" Newspaper – February 14, 1863

Chapter 19:

1. J McGonigal Substitute - from Ohio - Service in U.S. Army Infantry in Civil War – Military Records – Ancestry.com
2. "Jeannette & Jeannot" – Sheet Music Cover & Song Lyrics – by Charles Jefferys – Composed by Charles W. Glover – Published by E. Ferrett & Co. – Philadelphia, Pennsylvania – Circa 1850
3. Roller Skates Advertisement – "Harpers Weekly" Newspaper – January 9, 1864
4. "Just After the Battle" – Sheet Music Cover and Song Lyrics – by George F. Root – Published by Root & Cady – Chicago, Illinois – 1863

Chapter 20:

1. Betsy Ross Oval Star Flag - 'The Flags of Freedom' Quilt –

From Quilt Under Construction by M. Iler - From personal item of M. Iler

2. "Battle Cry of Freedom" – Union Version –Song Lyrics - by George Root – Published by Root & Cady – Chicago, Illinois - 1862

3. Confederate Flag – 'The Flags of Freedom' Quilt – From Quilt Under Construction by M. Iler – From personal item of M Iler

4. "Battle Cry of Freedom" – Confederate Version – Lyrics re-written by William H. Barnes – Music modified by Hermann L. Scheiner – Circa 1862 – Whatsoproudlywehail.org

5. 'Your Mission' Verse – From "Your Mission" Poem by Ellen M. H. Gates – Circa 1850 EllenBailey.com

Chapter 21:

1. Eagle – Hand Stitched by M. Iler – From personal item of M. Iler

2. Kansas Union Envelope – Personal item of M. Iler

3. American Flag With 31 Stars - 'The Ft. Sumner Stars and Stripes Flag' – Thirty –Three Cent Commemorative Stamp issued by U.S. Postal Service – Personal item of M. Iler

Chapter 22:

1. "The Rainy Day" –Song Lyrics – Poetry by Henry Wadsworth Longfellow – Music by William R. Dempster – Published by Oliver Ditson Co. – Boston Massachusetts – 1847

Chapter 23:

1. 'Santa With Union Troops' – From 'Blue & Gray Magazine' – Published by Blue & Gray Enterprises – Galloway, Ohio – February 1989 – From a Thomas Nast sketch named 'Christmas in Camp'

Chapter 24:

1. Music in Camp" – Poem by John Reuben Thompson – Bartleby. com
2. 'Kentucky Seal' – Image Enlargement - From Envelope addressed to Thomas McGonagle – Circa 1862 - From the M. Iler Collection

Chapter 25:

1. 'A Cavalry Attack'– From "Harpers Weekly" – Saturday, May 30, 1863
2. Nine Square Block Quilt with Binding– Drawing by Zoe Kane
3. "I Lo'e Nae a Laddie But Ane" –Sheet Music Cover Enlargement & Song Lyrics – by John Parky – Published by E. Riley New York, New York – Circa 1840

Chapter 26:

1. Colonel William Babcock Hazen Photo – From personal item of M Iler
2. 'Fruitless Attempt of The Army Of The Potomac' –Image Enlargement- From "Harpers Weekly" Newspaper – February 14, 1863
3. "Darling Kiss My Eyelids Down" – Sheet Music Cover and Song Lyrics – Written by Mrs. Elizabeth Akers – Music by E.A. Hall – Published by G.D. Russell & Co. –Boston, Massachusetts – 1865

Chapter 27:

1. 'Decisive Charge of General Negley's Division across the river"–Image Enlargement- From "Harpers Weekly" Newspaper – February 14, 1863
2. 'Charge of Seventy-Eighth Pennsylvania & Twenty-First Ohio at Murfreesboro' – From "Harpers Weekly" Newspaper – January 26, 1863

Chapter 28:

1. 'The attack on Fredericksburg – The forlorn hope scaling the hill' – "Harpers Weekly" – December 27, 1862
2. 'Battle of Stones River" – Image Enlargement - From Kuta & Allen Art Publishers – 1891 – From personal item of M. Iler
3. "Your Mission" – Poem by Ellen M. H. Gates – Circa 1850 – EllenBailey.com
4. Soldier with Head Down – Zoe Kane Drawing

Chapter 29:

1. 'Night Burial of Colonel Garesche on the Battlefield of Stone River' – From "Harpers Weekly" Newspaper – February 28, 1863

Chapter 30:

1. "Mary Of Argyle" – Song Lyrics – by S. Nelson – From 'Heather Blossoms Collection of Scotch Songs' – Published by J. L. Peters – New York, New York – 1868
2. 'Moon In Cedar Trees' – Image Enlargement - From 'The Picket Guard In The Army Of The Potomac' – "Harpers Weekly" Newspaper –February 14,1863
3. 'Sonnet 60' – by William Shakespeare – Originally published in 1609 - Poetryfoundation.org
4. Lady Liberty Crying, Arm Over Flag – Drawing by Zoe Kane

Chapter 32:

1. Thomas McGonagle – Headstone at Stones River Battlefield Cemetery – From Civil War Records – Ancestry.com
2. John McGonagle Letter: Dear Mother – sent from Iuka, Mississippi October 28, 1863 – From M. Iler Collection – Pages 1, 2, 3, & 4
3. Envelope Addressed to Mrs. Nancy Porter with August 8, 1864 Nashville, Tennessee Postal Stamp - From M. Iler Collection
4. Transcription of Dear Mother Letter – Provided by the Author (Author note: No photo was found)

Chapter 33:

1. Western Union Company – Telegraph to Nancy Porter with information that John McGonigal is dead - From M. Iler Collection
2. Resister of Death for U.S. Army Private John McGonigal – Noting death at Todd Barracks in Columbus, Ohio – His Regiment listing is: Substitute – Ancestry.com
3. Civil War Service Record – Joseph A. McGonagle served in 41st Ohio, Sept 19, 1861-Sept 29, 1864 and then 192 Ohio Jan 23, 1865-Sept 1, 1865 – Ancestry.com
4. Photograph of Joseph McGonagle and Caroline 'Callie' Rodabaugh McGonagle– Circa 1867 - From the M. Iler Collection
5. Marriage License of Joseph McGonagle and Caroline Rodabaugh December 25, 1867 – Ancestry.com
6. Photograph Joseph McGonagle –Circa 1875 - From personal item of M. Iler
7. Photograph of Anna Reece McGonagle – Circa 1875 - From personal item of M. Iler
8. 1870 Federal Census listing Joseph and Caroline McGonagle – Ancestry.com
9. 1880 Federal Census listing Joseph and Anna McGonagle – Ancestry.com
10. Photograph of Joseph McGonagle – Circa 1885 – From the M. Iler Collection
11. U.S. Civil War Veteran Ribbon - Belonging to Joseph McGonagle attending the Garfield and Arthur President Campaign of 1880 – From the M. Iler Collection
12. Kusciusko County Republican Convention Ticket from Tuesday, April 20, 1880 – Belonging to Joseph McGonagle – From the M. Iler Collection
13. Republican County Convention Delegate Ticket – August 16, 1882 – Belonging to Joseph McGonagle – From the M. Iler Collection
14. Photograph of Anna Reese McGonagle – Circa 1910 – From the M. Iler Collection

15. Pledges of Allegiance –Newspaper Clipping - From the M. Iler Collection

16. Front Outside Cover of 'Temperance Legion Card' - From the M. Iler Collection

17. Back Outside Cover of 'Temperance Legion Card' - From the M. Iler Collection

18. Inside Wording of 'Temperance Legion Card' - From the M. Iler Collection

19. Photograph of oldest daughter, Mabel McGonagle with her baby, Kathleen and with her twin sisters Della and Stella McGonagle – Circa 1895 – From personal item of M. Iler

20. Joseph Hazen McGonagle WWI Registration Card – Ancestry.com

21. Photograph of Cole & McGonagle Mercantile in Palmer, Nebraska – Joseph Hazen McGonagle, Partner – Circa 1930 - From personal item of M. Iler.

22. United States Certificate appointing Joseph McGonagle Census Taker for Tippecanoe Township, Kosciusko County, Indiana on March 3, 1879 – From the M. Iler Collection

23. Post Office Certificate appointing Joseph McGonagle Postmaster of Palmer, Nebraska on April 8, 1889 by order of the Postmaster General – From the M. Iler Collection

24. Bureau of Pensions Document – Anna McGonagle, widow of Joseph McGonagle application – February 13, 1894 – Ancestry.com

25. Poem written in Memory of John McGonagle – 'who died March 24, 1865' - by Maggie – from M. Iler Collection – Page 1 and 2

26. Transcription of Poem 'who died March 24, 1865 - written by Maggie – Provided by Author

27. Poem written in Memory of John McGonagle – 'who died at Todd Barracks, Columbus' - by Maggie - From M. Iler Collection – Pages 1, 2, and 3

28. Transcription of Poem 'who died at Todd Barracks' – written by Maggie – Provided by Author

29. Hand Written Note – Signed by Stella McGonagle Iler – Dated February 8, 1955 – From Personal Item of M. Iler

Documentation used to verify people in the letters:

New Cumberland Letter Authentication:

Thomas McGonagle (1778-1815) Family Tree – Ancestry.com

McCaslin McGonagle (1811-1864) - 1850 Federal Census – Ancestry.com

Ellen McGonagle – Age 20 - 1850 Federal Census – Ancerstry.com

Connellsville, Pennsylvania Letter Authentication:

John Reece and Family 1850 Federal Census –From Census Ledger Fayette County, Pennsylvania – John is the brother who wrote the Connellsville letter - Ancestry.com

John Reece and Family 1850 Federal Census – Detailed Listing – Ancestry.com

Death Certificate for Harriet Reece – Listing Mother as Martha Schallenberger – Ancestry.com

Jacob Reese and Family 1850 Federal Census - From Census Ledger - Jacob is the brother the Connellsville letter was addressed to – Jacob is the father of Anna Reece McGonagle –Amcestry.com

Jacob Reese and Family 1850 Federal Census – Detailed Listing – Home in Ohio – Ancestry.com

Jacob Reese and Family 1860 Federal Census – Detailed Listing – Home in Indiana –Ancestry.com

Stella McGonagle Iler hand-written note dated 1955, referencing the Connellsville letter –From M. Iler personal item

Fort Kearney Letter Authentication:

A.J. Camblein, Head of Household, Occupation Farmer, 1860 Federal Census for Van Buren County, Iowa – From Census Ledger – Ancestry.com

A.J. Camblein Cemetery Record in Trinity County, California – Ancestry.com

David Camblein 1827 Marriage in Wayne County, Ohio – Father David Camblein and mother Sidonia Evans – Ancestry.com

Poem by Maggie Authentication:

Margaret (Maggie) Lisle – 1850 Federal Census - Father Robert Lisle, Brother Thomas Lisle – Home in Ohio –Ancestry.com

Margaret (Maggie) Lisle Kilgore – 1860 Census – Home still in Ohio – Ancestry.com

Margaret (Maggie) Lisle Kilgore Grave Information – York County, Nebraska – Ancestry.com

John McGonagle Estate in Allen County, Ohio – Slemmons Lisle, the Representative to settle the estate – Slemmons is Maggie's Brother – Ancestry.com

Civil War Era Slang and Terms – A Writer's Guide for the American Civil War

Absquatulate - to take leave, to disappear

Acknowledge the Corn - to admit the truth, to confess a lie, or acknowledge an obvious personal shortcoming

Arkansas Toothpick - a long, sharp knife

A.W.O.L. - Absent With Out Leave

Bad Egg - bad person, good for nothing

Balderdash - nonsense

Bark Juice, Red Eye, O Be Joyful - liquor

Beat the Dutch - if that don't beat all

Bluff - trick or deceive

Bragg's Body Guard - lice

Been Through the Mill - been through a lot, seen it all

Bellyache - complain

Big Bugs - big wigs, important people

Bivouac - to camp without formal shelter or in temporary circumstances

Blowhard - braggart, bully

Blue Mass - refers to men on sick call; named after blue pill.

Bread Bag - haversack

Bread Basket - stomach

Bully - exclamation meaning, 'terrific!' or 'hurrah!'

Bully for You - good for you

Bummer – malingerer, someone who deliberately lags behind to forage or steal

Bummer's Cap - regulation army cap with a high/deep crown, so-called because it could be filled with gathered foodstuffs

Bust Head / Pop Skull - cheap whiskey

Camp canard - tall tale circulating around camp as gossip

Cashier - to dismiss from the army dishonorably

Chief Cook and Bottle Washer - person in charge, or someone who can do anything

Chicken Guts - gold braid used to denote officer ranks

Company Q - fictitious unit designation for the sick list

Conniption Fit - hysterics, temper tantrum

Contraband - escaped slaves who sought refuge behind Union lines

Copperhead - Northern person with Southern, anti-Union sympathies

Cracker Line - supply line for troops on the move

Deadbeat - useless person, malingerer

Desecrated Vegetables - Union, dehydrated (desiccated) vegetables formed into yellowish squares

Dog Robber - soldier detailed from the ranks to act as cook

Dog Collar - cravat issued with uniforms, usually discarded

Duds - clothing

Embalmed Beef - canned meat

Essence of Coffee - early instant coffee, found in paste form

Forage - to hunt for food, live off the land; also came to mean plundering enemy property for sustenance

Fit as a fiddle - in good shape

Fit to be tied - angry

Forty Dead Men - a full cartridge box, which usually held forty rounds

French Leave - to go absent without leave

Fresh Fish - new recruits

Go Boil Your Shirt - take a hike, get lost, bug off

Grab a Root - eat a meal, especially a potato

Greenbacks - money

Grey Backs - lice, also derogatory term for Confederate soldiers

Grit - courage, toughness

Goobers - peanuts

Hanker - a strong wish or want

Hard Case - tough guy

Hard Knocks - hard times, ill use

Hardtack - unleavened bread in the form of ¼ inch thick crackers issued by the army

Haversack - canvas bag about one foot square, which was slung over the shoulder and used to carry a soldier's rations when on the march

High-falutin - highbrow, fancy

Horse Sense - common sense, good judgement

Hospital Rat - someone who fakes illness to get out of duty

Housewife - sewing kit

Huffy, In a Huff - angry, irritated

Humbug - nonsense, a sham, a hoax

Hunkey Dorey - very good, all is well

Jailbird - criminal

Jawing - talking

John Barleycorn - beer

Jonah - someone who is or brings bad luck

Knock into a Cocked Hat - to knock someone senseless or thoroughly shock him

Let 'er Rip - let it happen, bring it on

Let Drive - go ahead, do it

Likely - serviceable, able-bodied

Light Out - leave in haste

Long Sweetening - molasses

Lucifers - matches

Muggins - a scoundrel

Mule - meat, especially if of dubious quality

Mustered Out – wry term meaning killed in action

No Account - worthless

Not By a Jug Full - not by any means, no way

On His Own Hook - on one's own shrift, without orders

Opening the Ball - starting the battle

Opine - be of the opinion

Peacock About - strut around

Peaked - pronounced peak-ed; weak or sickly

Pie Eater - country boy, a rustic

Pig Sticker - knife or bayonet

Picket - sentries posted around a camp or bivouac to guard approaches

Play Old Soldier - pretend sickness to avoid combat

Played Out - worn out, exhausted

Pumpkin Rinds - gold lieutenant's bars

Quartermaster Hunter - shot or shell that goes long over the lines and into the rear.

Quick Step, Flux - diarrhea

Robber's Row - the place where sutlers set up to do business

Row - a fight

Salt Horse - salted meat

Sardine Box - cap box

Sawbones - surgeon

Scarce as Hen's Teeth - exceedingly rare or hard to find

Secesh - derogatory term for Confederates and Southerners: secessionists

See the Elephant - experience combat or other worldly events

Shakes - malaria

Shanks Mare - on foot

Sheet Iron Crackers - hard tack

Shoddy - an inferior weave of wool used to make uniforms early in the war; later came to mean any clothing or equipment of substandard quality

Sing Out - call out, yell

Skedaddle - run away, escape

Slouch Hat - a wide-brimmed felt hat

Snug as a Bug - very comfortable

Somebody's Darling - comment when observing a dead soldier

Sparking - courting a girl

Spondulix - money

Sunday Soldiers / Parlor Soldiers - derogatory terms for unsuitable soldiers

Take an Image - have a photograph taken

Tennessee or Virginia Quick Step - diarrhea

Tight - drunk

Toe the Mark - do as told, follow orders

Top Rail - first class, top quality

Traps - equipment, belongings

Tuckered Out - exhausted

Uppity - arrogant

Vidette - a sentry same as Picket but usually on horseback

Wallpapered - drunk

Whipped - beaten

Wrathy - angry

Zu Zu - Zouaves, soldiers whose units wore colorful uniforms in a flamboyant French style with baggy trousers, known for bravery and valor

Compiled by G. M. Atwater, March 2005
www.freepages.rootsweb.com

Bibliography:

Angle, Paul M. – "The Civil War Years" – Published by Doubleday & Company, Inc. – Garden City, New York – 1967. Book.

Barker, Lorenzo A. – "Birge's Western Sharpshooters" – Published by Big Byte Books – San Bernardino, California – 2016. Book.

Beyer, Jinny - "Patchwork Patterns" - EPM Publications – McLean, Virginia - 1979. Book.

Bernard, Kenneth A. – "Lincoln and the Music of th Civil War" – Published by Caxton Printers – Caldwell, Idaho – 1966. Book.

Blue & Gray Magazine – "The Battle of Stones River" – Published by Blue & Gray Enterprises, Inc. – February 1989. Magazine.

Bowers, John - "Chickamauga and Chattanooga" – Harper Collins Publishers -1928. Book.

Brackman, Barbara - "Unraveling the History of Quilts & Slavery" - Published by C & T Publishing, Inc., - Lafayette, California - 2006. Book.

Brackman, Barbara "Civil War Sampler" - Published by C & T Publishing, Inc., - Lafayette, California - 2012. Book.

Bradley, Michael R. and Shirley Farris Jones – "Murfressboro in the Civil War" -
Published by The History Press – Charleston, North Carolina – 2012. Book.

Brown, Joseph E – "The Mormon Trek West" – Published by Doubleday & Company, Inc. – Garden City, New York -1986. Book.

Catton, Bruce – "America" – Published by Promontory Press – New York, New York – 1979. Book.

Chiaverini, Jennifer – "The Loyal Union Sampler" – C & T Publishing – Lafayette, California – 2013. Book.

Civil War Times – "The Battle of Stones River" – Eastern Acorn Press – 1987. Special Edition Periodical.

Civil War Times – "Battle at Stones River and War in Tennessee" – Published by Historical Times – Harrisburg, Pennsylvania – June 1986. Magazine.

Clarke, Dwight L. – "Stephen Watts Kearny, Soldier of the West" – Published by The University of Oklahoma Press – Norman, Oklahoma – 1961. Book

Cooper, William J. – "We Have the War Upon Us" – Published by Alfred A. Knopf – New York, New York – 2012. Book.

Cozzens, Peter – "No Better Place To Die" – Published by University of Illinois Press – Chicago, Illinois – 1990. Book.

Dallas, Sandra – "The Quilt That Walked to Golden" – Published by Breckling Press - Elmhurst, Illinois – 2004. Book.

Earley, Gerald L. - "I Belonged to the 116th" – Published by Heritage Books –Westminster, Maryland – 2007. Book.

Fitch, John – "Army of the Cumberland"- Published by J. B. Lippincott & Co. – Philadelphia, Pennsylvania – 1864. Book.

Gallagher, Gary W. – "The Confederate War" – Published by Harvard University Press – Cambridge, Massachusetts – 1997. Book.
Goodwin, Doris Kearns – "Team of Rivals" – Published by Simon & Schuster – 2005. Book.

Goss, Warren Lee – "Recollections of a Private – Published by Thomas Y. Crowell & Co. – New York, New York – Reprinted in 1984 from the 1890 edition. Book.

Harwell, Richard B. – "The Civil War Reader" – Smithmark Publishers – New York, New York – 1994. Book.

Hascall, Mil S. – "Personal Recollections Concerning the Battle of Stone River" – Times Publishing Company – Goshen, Indiana – 1889. Paper.

Hazen, William B. – "A Narrative of Military Service" – Blue Acorn Press – Huntington, West Virginia – 1993 Reprint from 1885. Book.

Hedin, Robert - "Old Glory" - Published by Persea Books – New York, New York - 2004. Book.

Holmes, Louis A. - "Fort McPherson, Nebraska" – Published by Johnsen Publishing Company – Lincoln, Nebraska -1963. Book.

Howard, John Tanker – Historical Notes – "A Treasury of Stephen Foster" – Published by Random House – New York, New York – 1946. Book

Jenkins, Mary and Clare Claridge – "Making Welsh Quilts" – Published by KP Books – Iona, Wisconsin – 2005. Book.

Jordan, Robert Paul – "The Civil War" – Published by The National Geographic Society – 1969. Book.

Kaufman, William J. – "The Mormon Pioneer Songbook" – Published by Theodore Presser Company – Bryn Mawr, Pennsylvania - 1980. Book.

Kendall, Henry et al – "The Battle of Stone's River 1862-1863"

– Published by Lightning Source UK Ltd – New York, New York -2010. Book.

Kimberly, Robert L and Ephraim S. Holloway - "History of the 41st Ohio" - Published by W. R. Smellie – Cleveland, Ohio – 1897. Book.

Kirk, Elise K. – "Music at the White House" – University of Illinois Press – Chicago, Illinois – 1932. Book.

Kostyal, K. M. – "The Civil War Letters of Thomas J. Halsey" – Published by National Geographic Society – Washington, D.C. – 1951. Book.

Logsdon, David R. – "Eyewitnesses at the Battle of Stones River" – Compiled and edited by David Logsdon – Nashville, Tennessee – 2002. Compilation.

Lowenfels, Walter – "Walt Whitman's Civil War" – Published by Alfred A. Knopf, Inc. – New York, New York – 1960. Book.

Marcy, Randolph B. – "The Prairie Traveler" – Published by Applewood Books – Carlisle, Massachusetts – Reprint, Originally in 1889. Book.

Mastai, Bolesaw and Marie-Louise D'Otrange – "The Stars and Stripes"- Published by Alfred A. Knopf, Inc. New York, New York – 1973. Book.

Meacham, Jon and tim McGraw – "Songs of America" - Published by Random House – New York, New York - 2019. Book.

McCullough, David - "The Pioneers" - Published by Simon & Schuster – New York, New York - 2019. Book.
McDonough, James Lee – "Shiloh" – Published by The University of Tennessee Press – Knoxville, Alabama – 1977. Book.

McDonough, James Lee – "Stones River" - – Published by The University of Tennessee Press – Knoxville, Alabama – 1934. Book.

McPherson, James M. – "Battle Cry of Freedom" – Published by Oxford University Pressk Inc – New York, New York - 1988. Book.

"Nebraska History – After the Indian Wars" – Nebraska State Historical Society – Spring 2014. Periodical.

"Nebraska History" – Nebraska State Historical Society – Winter 2006. Periodical.

"Nebraska History" – Nebraska State Historical Society – Fall 2001. Periodical.

Parakilas, James – "Piano Roles" – Published by Yale University Press – New Haven, New Jersey – 1999. Book.

Richards, Jay C. – "More Bugles, Battles and Belvidere" – Printed by Flayre Printing, Inc. – Belvidere, New Jersey – 1999. Book.

Stratton, Joanna L. – "Pioneer Women" – Published by Simon & Schuster – New York, New York – 1981. Book.

Street, James Jr. and the editors of Time-Life Books – "The Struggle for Tennessee" - Published by Time-Life Books – Morristown, New Jersey – 1985. Set of Books.

Stowe, Harriet Beecher – "Uncle Tom's Cabin" – Published by Barnes & Noble – 2013 (First published in 1852) – New York, New York. Book.

Time-Life Books – "The Confederacy" – Published by Time-Life – Alexandria, Virginia – 1998. Book.

Time-Life Books – "The Union" – Published by Time-Life – Alexandria, Virginia – 1998. Book.

Time- Life Books – "The Civil War" - Published by Time-Life – Alexandria, Virginia – 1998. Book.

Tuchman, Barbara W. – "Practicing History" – Published by Alred A. Knopf – New York, New York – 1981. Book.

Wert, Jeffry D. – "A Glorious Army" – Published by Simon & Schuster – New York, New York – 2011. Book.

Woodward, C. Vann - "Mary Chesnut's Civil War" – Yale University Press – New Haven, Connecticut – 1981. Book.

Youngs, Rosemary – "The Civil War Love Letter Quilt" – Published by Krause Publications – Iola, Wisconsin -2007. Book.